VICTORIA BYLIN

fell in love with God and her husband at the same time. It started with a ride on a big red motorcycle and a date to see a *Star Trek* movie. A recent graduate of UC Berkeley, Victoria had been seeking that elusive "something more" when Michael rode into her life. Neither knew it, but they were both reading the Bible.

Five months later, they got married and the blessings began. They have two sons and have lived in California and Virginia. Michael's career allowed Victoria to be both a stay-at-home mom and a writer. She's living a dream that started when she read her first book and thought "I want to tell stories." For that gift, she will be forever grateful.

Feel free to drop Victoria an email at VictoriaBylin@aol.com or visit her website, www.victoriabylin.com.

JANET DEAN

grew up in a family that cherished the past and had a strong creative streak. Her father recounted wonderful stories, like his father before him. The tales they told instilled in Janet a love of history and the desire to write. She married her college sweetheart and taught first grade before leaving to rear two daughters. As her daughters grew, they watched *Little House on the Prairie,* reawakening Janet's love of American history and the stories of strong men and women of faith who built this country. Janet eagerly turned to inspirational historical romance, and she loves spinning stories for the Love Inspired Books Love Inspired Historical line.

PAMELA NISSEN

loves creating. Whether it's characters, cooking, scrapbooking or other artistic endeavors, she takes pleasure in putting things together for others to enjoy. Pamela lives in the woods in Iowa with her husband, daughter, two sons, a Newfoundland dog and cats. She loves watching her children pursue their dreams, and is known to yell on the sidelines at her boys' games and being moved to tears as she watches her daughter perform. Having glimpsed the dark and light of life, she is passionate about writing "real" people with "real" issues and "real" responses.

Brides of the West

VICTORIA BYLIN
JANET DEAN
PAMELA NISSEN

Love Inspired

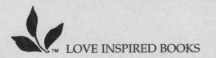 LOVE INSPIRED BOOKS

Recycling programs for this product may not exist in your area.

ISBN-13: 978-0-373-82912-5

BRIDES OF THE WEST

Copyright © 2012 by Harlequin Books S.A.

The publisher acknowledges the copyright holders of the individual works as follows:

JOSIE'S WEDDING DRESS
Copyright © 2012 by Vicki Scheibel

LAST MINUTE BRIDE
Copyright © 2012 by Janet Dean

HER IDEAL HUSBAND
Copyright © 2012 by Pamela Nissen

www.LoveInspiredBooks.com

Printed in U.S.A.

CONTENTS

JOSIE'S WEDDING DRESS

Victoria Bylin

For my daughters-in-law
Meredith Scheibel
and
Whitney Scheibel

Therefore, as God's chosen people, holy and dearly loved, clothe yourselves with compassion, kindness, humility, gentleness and patience. Bear with each other and forgive one another if any of you has a grievance against someone. Forgive as the Lord forgave you. And over all these virtues put on love, which binds them all together in perfect unity.
—*Colossians* 3:12–14

Chapter One

Rock Creek, Wyoming
May 1889

A moment with Josie Bright…that's all Ty Donner wanted as he rode into Rock Creek, Wyoming. After five years in the Wyoming Territorial Prison, he didn't deserve the privilege. He didn't deserve to breathe Josie's name, but he hoped she'd forgive him. He hadn't meant to leave her waiting at the altar. They'd planned the wedding for months. But instead of saying "I do" to the woman he loved, Ty had spent his wedding day in jail.

Today he had business to conduct before he went to the Bright ranch, and it wouldn't be easy. Keeping the gelding to a walk, he approached the church where he and Josie should have spoken their vows. What a fool he'd been… The day before the wedding, the Scudder gang stole six of his best horses. Josie pleaded with him to let the law handle it, but Ty and her brother went after the thieves. A gunfight erupted and he shot and killed Brant Scudder. Ty didn't know it, but the gang had cut the horses loose. With no evidence of their crime, he'd been convicted of manslaughter and sent to prison.

As the white church came into view, he thought of the wedding that hadn't taken place. Josie had poured her heart into making her wedding dress. It kept her busy while Ty built up his ranch. The Brights weren't wealthy, but they had enough. Ty had wanted Josie to have enough. Too late he realized what *enough* meant to her. A *wedding* would have been enough. *He* would have been enough. Instead she'd sat dry-eyed through the trial. When it was over, she'd come to his jail cell and spoken words he'd never forget.

I want to forgive you, Ty. But I can't. You love that ranch more than you love me. You love your horses more than anything.

With her eyes misty, she'd walked out of the jail. Ty wrote to her begging forgiveness, but she never replied. His only contact with Rock Creek had been monthly letters from Reverend Hall, the minister of the Rock Creek Church. Ty had opened his letters with trepidation, expecting to learn Josie had married. She hadn't, but there had been other news. Her father died four years ago of a heart ailment. Two years ago her brother perished in a hotel fire, leaving Ty to wonder how the Bright women were managing. Josie's mother had been nearly blind when he went to prison, and Josie had two young sisters with ambitions of their own. Knowing Josie, she was carrying the load for everyone.

After a year in prison, Ty stopped writing to her. With time, his feelings for her faded into memories and he'd realized something. Just as prison had changed him, sorrow had likely changed Josie. He needed her forgiveness, but he had no illusions of picking up where they'd left off. The love they once shared had most likely withered and blown away like tumbleweeds.

Ty climbed wearily off his horse, a nag he'd been given by the prison chaplain, and went to the iron gate marking the church cemetery. The last time he was here, there had been only three graves in the plot marked by a low stone wall. Now there were eight, including the resting place of Nathan Bright, Josie's brother and Ty's best friend.

The gate squeaked as Ty opened it, a reminder of the metal door of the cell he'd left a week ago. He didn't have to hunt for Nate's grave. The Bright family had bought a granite marker that stood a foot high. Behind it a rosebush held a dozen buds that would bloom in June. Ty took off his hat, approached the stone and hung his head.

"I'm sorry, friend…so sorry."

With his eyes closed, he heard the echo of Nate telling him to let the Scudders go. *Let the law handle it, Ty. You're getting married tomorrow.*

"I wish I'd listened," he said to the stone.

He opened his eyes and relived that day. He and Josie had been having supper with her parents when his hired hand rode into the yard, shouting about the Scudders stealing his breeding stock. Ty had helped himself to a Winchester in the gun cabinet and turned to Josie. *I'm getting my horses back.*

Ty, don't! You could get hurt.

She'd given him that bossy look he remembered. They'd once had that kind of fun…where she groused at him and he kissed her and they snuggled on the porch swing. That day had been different. He resented being bossed, and she'd been angry and worried that he wouldn't make it back for the wedding. He'd ridden off on Smoke, the gray stallion that could outrun anything, and he and Nate had found the Scudders. The gunfight got crazy. When it was over, Ty had killed sixteen-year-old Brant, the youngest and most innocent of the thieves. Ty made it back to Josie, but he didn't make it to the wedding. The town deputy, a man related to the Scudders, arrested him on his way to the church.

Ty stared at the stone marker. "I messed up, Nate. I don't know how to make it up to her, but I'm going to try."

It was all he could do, all he could say. With his chest tight, he bowed his head and prayed for blessings on the Brights.

The rattle of a rig reached his ears and he turned. He saw a piano buggy being pulled by a mule. The side of the hood hid his view of the driver, but he noticed a sky blue skirt flowing to the floorboard. Ty couldn't stand the thought of seeing anyone from Rock Creek, especially not a gossipy woman. He considered hopping the stone wall, but he'd left his horse by the gate. He couldn't leave without drawing attention, so he turned his back to the buggy and focused on Nate's grave.

The buggy halted, then creaked as the female climbed down. With his neck bent, he listened to the squeak of the gate as she opened it. He tried to follow her movements, but the grass muted her steps. He listened for the rustle of her skirt but heard nothing. Frozen and alert, he thought of the years he'd waited in a prison cell. He'd learned to be patient. He could be patient now. He wouldn't budge until the woman went on her way. He thought of the graves he'd seen. Was she visiting the small one that belonged to a child? A newer one with a name he didn't recognize?

A roselike fragrance drifted on the air, becoming stronger as the woman approached. Josie liked fancy soaps. She also liked roses. A soft gasp confirmed his deepest fear. This woman knew him. This woman was Josie.

"Ty? Is that you?"

He turned enough to see the hem of her skirt. It took him back to the day before the wedding and her banter about "something borrowed, something blue." She'd whispered in his ear about a blue garter, and he'd loved her more than ever. Now he looked up slowly, taking in the hard line of her mouth. Gone was the cheerful girl who'd teased him with mischievous smiles. In her place he saw a woman burdened by life. Her eyes were still turquoise and her chestnut hair gleamed under a straw bonnet, but she'd lost her sparkle.

Ty had come home for this very moment, yet he felt unprepared as he matched her gaze. Instead of the words he'd practiced, he stared into her eyes, feasting on the past until he found his tongue. "Hello, Josie," he said in a drawl. "I'm hoping we can talk."

* * *

Josie Bright had loved Ty Donner for most of her life. What she felt now, she didn't know. He'd left her standing in the wedding dress she stitched with her own hands. She'd been devastated, then the anger had set in...and the bitterness. Over the years her father and brother had died, leaving the Bar JB in her hands. She also inherited responsibility for her two sisters. Anne, the middle sister taught school and sent money home. Scarlett, the youngest, lived with an aunt in Denver and wanted to go to college.

Josie took her responsibilities seriously. The Bar JB was named for her father, Jeremiah Bright, but she shared his initials and his love for their home. She hadn't married because her family needed her. She'd also been hurt by Ty and had vowed to never be hurt again. The last two years had been particularly hard. She had a couple hired hands, but there was always too much work and not enough daylight. She'd long ago traded pretty dresses for dungarees.

Now even that sacrifice didn't help meet the family's needs. Winter had been brutal, and the Bar JB had lost ninety percent of its cattle. Josie had gone to the bank to beg for a loan to restock. Barring a loan, she needed mercy on an overdue mortgage. Not only had Lester Proffitt denied her request, he'd looked down his nose at her. *I don't do business with women, Miss Bright. Find a husband to take care of you. Have babies and be happy.* His words stung in every possible way. Of course she wanted a husband. Yes, she wanted babies of her own, but her mother and sisters needed her. If she didn't make the mortgage payment in thirty days, she and her mother would have to leave the only home Josie had known.

If Ty Donner hadn't let his pride get in the way, they'd have been running the Bright ranch together. Instead they were standing at Nate's grave, and Josie had the horrible sensation of her heart speeding up as she matched stares with the man who'd left her at the altar.

The years had been kind to Ty's looks. He was dressed in dark trousers and a tan shirt, holding his hat and standing tall. He'd been lean, almost a string bean, when they became engaged. She'd been seventeen and he'd been twenty. Now he had broad shoulders and muscles shaped by physical labor. Some men in the Wyoming Territorial Prison made brooms. She guessed Ty wasn't one of them. In addition to lean muscles, she saw creases around his blue eyes…eyes that still shimmered like sun-kissed water. Neither had his hair changed. She remembered it being brown in winter and lighter in summer. Today it was in-between, a mix of brown and gold, and it still curled over his collar.

With some difficulty, she found her voice. "This is a surprise."

"I figure it is."

"So it's been five years…" She'd known this day would come. She just hadn't expected today to be the day, nor had she imagined meeting Ty at Nate's grave. She'd noticed the horse by the wall, an old gelding laden with his gear, but it hadn't reminded her of Ty. The man she once loved had been the best judge of horseflesh in the county, maybe the state. The nag was a testament to how far he'd fallen. It also raised the question of where he was headed, or if he was staying in Rock Creek.

Her throat went dry. "What are your plans?"

"It depends."

"On what?"

"On you."

"Me?" She didn't want Ty Donner thinking about her. She didn't want him anywhere near the Bar JB. Just looking at him stirred up painful memories, especially in the shadow of the church where their wedding plans had gone to pieces. She wanted to calmly tell him to leave. She also wanted to shout and berate him. The confusion clogged her throat and threatened to turn into angry tears. She felt Ty's gaze on her face, reading her as easily as he'd read her five years ago.

He indicated the buggy. "Let's talk over there."

It felt disrespectful to argue at Nate's grave, so she let him guide her out the gate. As they approached, the mule chuffed. The Brights had come down in the world and it showed. Josie did her best with the ranch, but nothing had gone right since the death of her father and then Nate. Her sisters had problems of their own, and her mother's vision was so clouded by cataracts she couldn't read her Bible anymore. Josie read it to her, fighting every word because she'd lost her faith…fighting bitterness because she'd been so hurt. She *hated* being bitter. It tainted every breath she took, every thought she had.

Determined to put the ugliness aside, she faced Ty. He looked stronger than ever and bolder than she would have expected. Instead of cowing him, prison had made him tough. When he spoke, his eyes glinted with sincerity. "I was a fool to run after the Scudders. I'd like to think I did it for you—for us—that I was protecting our future, but the truth is plainer. I wanted my horses back, but mostly my pride got the best of me. Nothing else mattered in that moment. I've thought about that day for five years and what it cost—"

"Stop!"

"I've got to finish."

"No!" She raised her chin. "Don't say anything. It's over."

"I know that."

"Just seeing you…" She closed her eyes, but it didn't stop memories from filling her mind. Instead of seeing Ty, she saw the white dress in her wardrobe. She'd sewed every pearl button into place…all twenty-four of them. She'd worked the buttonholes for hours. Anger dried the threat of tears and she opened her eyes. "Go away, Ty. I've gotten on with my life. You should do the same."

"I will. But not until I'm sure you're all right. Nate was my best friend. I owe it to him. I owe it to *you*."

She raised her chin. "You don't owe me anything."

"I think I do," he replied calmly. "This winter was tough for everyone. How are things at the ranch?"

"I'm managing just fine."

His gaze slid to the mule and the buggy. Josie cringed, because Ty would see her poverty. The leather seat had a crack in it, and the mule lacked dignity. Next he looked at the dress she'd stitched when they'd been courting. She'd made it over a couple times, but he'd recognize it. Neither could she hide the faded color.

His jaw tensed. "You're struggling, aren't you?"

"Like I said, I'm fine."

His gaze stayed on her face. "Things don't look fine."

Just like old times, she felt as if he could see to her toes. Knowing Ty, he wouldn't back down until he got what he wanted, and today he wanted details. No way would she tell him the Bar JB had lost most of its cattle, and that Lester Proffitt refused her request for a loan. She had her pride, and she wanted Ty to leave.

But he wasn't leaving. He'd put on his hat and was reaching for her hand. Before she could step back, he clasped her by the wrist, raised her forearm and loosened her deerskin glove a finger at a time. Stunned, she thought of the day he'd dropped to one knee and proposed marriage. She'd said yes and he'd slipped an engagement ring on her finger. Her hands used to be pretty. They weren't pretty now. Why she didn't stop him from removing the glove, she didn't know. Maybe she *wanted* him to see her ruined hands, what he'd done to her by valuing his horses and his pride more than their vows.

He pulled the glove completely off, inspected her cracked nails and turned her hand palm up to show the calluses. She saw fire in his eyes and braced herself. Ty Donner wasn't going to be leaving anytime soon, and she wasn't as annoyed as she wanted to be. That softening had to be denied. He'd hurt her, and he could hurt her again. She thought of the white dress, the bouquet that had wilted, the humiliation of leaving the church alone and unwed.

She'd never forget that moment.

She'd never forgive him for what he'd done.

She simply couldn't, because looking at him made her hurt all over again. With her feelings raw, she looked into his eyes.

He let go of her hand but didn't release her from his gaze. "You need help, Josie. I'm staying until things are right."

"I don't *want* your help. Haven't you hurt me enough? Please... Just go." She waved her arm to indicate the open prairie.

Ty's jaw tensed. "Why are you working like a hired hand?"

"It's none of your concern."

He rocked back on one heel and put his hands on his hips. "You're wrong, Josie girl—"

"Don't call me that!"

He ignored her. "I was wrong to chase after the Scudders, and you're wrong to chase me off now."

She didn't know whether to cry for what she'd lost or slap his face for calling her *Josie girl*. She also yearned to accept his help. What would it be like to share the load of running the Bar JB? The grass rippled in a green wave, the sole benefit of the devastating winter. If only she could buy cattle...Ty knew everything about ranching. It was *her* needs he hadn't understood. When it came to cattle and horses, he had a gift—especially with horses, fast horses that could run like the wind. An idea formed in Josie's mind and wouldn't let go.

A month from now Rock Creek would hold the annual Founders' Day celebration. People would come from miles away for games and contests, baking competitions, and most important of all, the running of the May Day Maze. The ten-mile race tested a horse's speed and endurance. It went through canyons and across streams, over hills and ended in a straight run through a long valley. The Maze required a skilled rider and a fast horse, and Josie had both. She had Ty, and she had

Smoke, the mustang stallion Ty had owned and loved. When he'd gone to prison, the bank had repossessed his ranch. Nate had bought Smoke with the intention of giving Ty the horse when he got out.

Josie had no desire to welcome Ty into her life, but she very much wanted to win the May Day Maze. The grand prize was a thousand dollars. If he won the race on Smoke, they could split it. She could pay the mortgage and buy some cattle. But the risk… He had no place to live, which meant she'd have to offer him a spot in the bunkhouse with Obie Jones and Gordie Walker, her two hired hands. Ty would need meals and they'd cross paths a dozen times a day. The cost of asking him to ride in the race was high, but refusing his help might cost her the ranch.

Josie hadn't answered him and he was still waiting. Standing taller, she made her voice all business. "I have an offer for you."

"What is it?"

"I need someone to ride in the May Day Maze. Will you do it?"

Ty pulled his hat low, but not before she saw his eyes burn with longing. He took a breath, then another one. When he turned his gaze to the empty meadow, she knew he was remembering an old hope. He'd dreamed of winning the Maze his whole life, just as she'd dreamed of having a beautiful wedding. In their courting days, they'd often shared their hopes. It had been an exciting time. She felt that rush now and pushed it aside. This was business, she told herself. It had nothing to do with the dress hanging in the wardrobe or the veil she'd never worn. She wouldn't notice the gleam in Ty's blue eyes. She wouldn't think of anything except saving her home…she simply wouldn't.

"Say yes, Ty," she urged. "I need your help."

Chapter Two

Ty had dreamed of riding in the May Day Maze for years. Before the mess with the Scudders, he'd hoped to win and use the prize money to build a big house for Josie and the kids they'd have. He'd have entered the race in a heartbeat, but he was riding a twenty-year-old gelding he was grateful to own, and the mule pulling her buggy didn't look any better.

"The best riders in Wyoming come for that race," he said to her. "You know I want to ride in it, but on *what?*"

"I have Smoke."

"Smoke?" Ty's voice trailed to a whisper. He'd caught and gentled the mustang himself. No one else had ever ridden the crazy stallion, though a few men had tried. Josie or Nate must have bought the horse when the bank auctioned his possessions. He suddenly wanted to ride fast and free, without fences or prison bars to hold him back. He wanted that freedom almost as much as he wanted Josie's forgiveness. He could take that ride, but Josie's pardon would have to be earned. Riding in the Maze was a good start. Smoke would be five years older, maybe slower, but he was still a smart, rangy stallion.

A hush settled over the cemetery. The breeze died and the grass went still. Not even a bird chirped as Ty held her gaze. "I'll ride for you, Josie."

"We'll split the prize."

No, they wouldn't. He'd give her every cent, but they could argue about it later. Afraid she'd change her mind, he tilted his head toward the gate and said, "Let's go. I need to check out Smoke."

She headed to the buggy without a word. Ty would have handed her up, even suggested tying his gelding to the back and doing the driving, but Josie lifted the reins before he could blink.

"You know the way." She clicked her tongue at the mule, steered around the cemetery and headed for the Bar JB. Ty wanted a final word with Nate, so he walked back to the grave. Instead of taking off his hat, he pulled it lower. "This is it, friend. I'm going to make things right for Josie."

The burden Ty carried didn't ease completely, but a bit of weight lifted from his shoulders. If he could win the May Day Maze, he'd be a step closer to atoning for the worst mistake of his life. Blinking, he thought back to Reverend Gaines, the chaplain who visited the prison twice a week. Ty had been among the forty men who gathered in the dining hall for services. He'd never forget the reverend's first sermon.

Jesus calls us to walk in His shoes. Do you have the courage to love the way He did? It's the kind of love where you put your own hopes aside for the benefit of someone else.

That evening in jail, Ty had prayed with Reverend Gaines. He'd vowed to be a better man from that day forth, and he'd decided to start by making amends to Josie. The decision had come from the deep well of regret, though today he felt something along with the remorse. He couldn't stop seeing her face in his mind, and his gut stirred with the feelings they'd shared as a couple. She'd changed, but she had the same fire he'd always loved. His reaction troubled him, because he had nothing to offer except riding Smoke in the Maze.

With the sun beating on his back, he spoke to Nate. "She's prettier than ever, isn't she?"

Nate didn't answer, of course. But Ty knew what he'd have

said. He'd have teased his friend about being sweet on his little sister. Nate had heckled him mercilessly, until Ty told him to shut up because he was going to marry Josie whether Nate liked it or not.

Nate had laughed. Ty could almost hear that sound now and he answered back, "I'll do my best for her. You have my word."

Determined and unafraid, he left the graveyard, climbed on the gelding and headed for the Bright ranch. With the buggy in the distance, he looked at the hills that hadn't changed and the ruts that had. He felt more like a rut than a mountain today, but the mountains called to his blood. He was itching for wind and dust, speed, and the May Day Maze. As he took in the sky and the empty meadows, he thought of the Bible verse he'd scratched on the wall of his cell. *The earth is the Lord's, and everything in it.*

Feeling better than he had in years, he lagged behind Josie, enjoying the vast meadows and preparing himself for seeing familiar things. Mostly he recalled the porch swing where he'd proposed to her. Ty had spoken first to her father. A big man, Mr. Bright had shaken Ty's hand and told him to take good care of Josie or else. The "or else" had been a fatherly jab, but Ty felt the burden in his bones. After supper he'd sat with her on the swing. More nervous than he'd ever been, he'd dropped to one knee and asked her to be his wife. She'd said yes and they'd kissed.

Five years in prison had done nothing to dull the memory of that moment.

Five minutes in her presence made it sharper than ever. It cut through the fog of time and the effort he'd made to forget her. If he wasn't careful, he'd earn Josie's forgiveness but lose his dignity by falling in love like a calf-eyed kid.

As the Bright ranch came into view, Ty lagged behind so he could take a good look at the old two-story house. The white siding stood out against the sky, and behind it grass stretched as far as he could see. He looked to the west and saw a barn the size of a cathedral. In its day, the Bar JB had been the most prosperous ranch in Rock Creek. Approaching now, Ty saw outbuildings in need of paint, missing shingles and a falling-down fence. He looked back at the house expecting to see a garden to the left of it. He couldn't remember a spring when Mrs. Bright didn't tend to her vegetables, but today he saw weeds.

There was no doubt about it. Josie needed help. Eager to get to work—and to see Smoke—he turned the gelding toward the barn. Rounding a curve in the path, he saw Josie going toe to toe with Obie Jones. Years ago Ty had hired the man and fired him a week later. Obie was the laziest, most conniving man Ty had ever met, and the fool had a cigarette dangling from his lips…a cigarette by a barn full of hay and livestock. Ty didn't know the man behind Obie, but he recognized his type. Judging by the sneer on his face, he didn't take kindly to a woman giving him orders.

Everyone in Rock Creek knew Obie's reputation. Josie must have been desperate to hire him. Keeping a respectful distance, Ty climbed off the gelding and waited for her to finish her business.

The wait ended when Obie blew smoke in her face.

Josie hoped Ty wouldn't interfere. She'd caught Obie smoking outside the barn…again. Lazy or not, Obie was the only man in Rock Creek who'd work for the pittance she could afford to pay. The other fellow, a drifter named Gordie, had less to offer than Obie. She'd hired them out of desperation. With the bitter winter, most of the local hands had drifted south. If Obie and Gordie quit, she'd be in trouble.

Obie looked past her to Ty and smirked. "Look what the wind blew in…."

If Josie turned to look at Ty, she'd appear weak. She kept her eyes on Obie, but she heard the creak of Ty's saddle as he swung off the gelding, then the scuff of his boots on the hard dirt. His shadow stretched to meet hers, and she heard the soft exhalation of his breath.

"Hello, Obie," he said in a drawl.

Josie stole a glance at Ty's profile. He had fire in his eyes, the kind that got him in trouble. If he chased off Obie, the trouble would be hers. She didn't trust Ty to handle this situation, but she couldn't deal with Ty *and* Obie and Gordie at the same time. Caught between two bad choices, she said nothing.

Obie aimed his stubbly chin at Gordie. "This here's Ty Donner. He's been locked away in that big prison in Laramie."

Josie wanted to wipe the smirk off Obie's face. The man had no right to gloat, though why she felt protective of Ty she didn't want to know.

Next to her, Ty shrugged. "I'm out now."

"I can see that," Obie answered.

Ty indicated the man's cigarette. "Mind if I bum a smoke?"

Obie hurled his tobacco pouch with too much force. Ty snagged it with one hand. Obie smirked. "Help yourself."

"I'll do that." Ty sounded friendly, but instead of opening the pouch, he threw it as far as he could into a meadow full of tall grass. The blades waved, then went still.

Obie called Ty a foul name.

With his hands loose, Ty stepped up to the hired man, snatched the cigarette from his lips and ground it into the dirt. With his eyes narrowed, he glared at Obie. "If I *ever* catch you smoking by this barn again, you're fired."

"Oh, yeah?"

"Yeah."

Josie didn't know whether to cheer for Ty, be mad he'd presumed the power to fire anyone, or to smooth the waters with Obie. Lazy or not, she needed her hired hands. Ty was a hard worker, but he couldn't do the work of three men. At the same time, she couldn't let Obie control the situation. Like it or not, she had to trust Ty.

Obie spat on the ground. The brownish glob landed on the hem of her skirt. Gasping with disgust, she stepped back.

Ty grabbed Obie by the collar and lifted him to his toes. "A lady deserves respect. You owe Miss Bright an apology."

Obie snorted.

Ty lifted him higher. "What does that mean?"

"Mizz Bright's no lady."

Josie blanked her face, but she felt the sting of Obie's words. As the boss of the Bar JB, she'd learned to be tough. She drove hard bargains and wore trousers when she worked. She liked pretty things as much as any woman, but she'd traded lace for denim and hat pins for a Stetson. She'd also traded a wedding dress for a broken heart, and she had a ranch to run. For the sake of getting the work done, she could ignore Obie's insults.

Ty, it seemed, had no such inclination. Using both hands, he hurled Obie against the barn. Obie hit with a thud but came back swinging. Ty ducked, then landed a roundhouse punch that sent Obie to the ground. Gordie cussed, then swung at Ty. The blow landed on Ty's jaw and snapped back his head.

"Stop it!" Josie cried.

Obie lumbered to his feet. Fists flew and curses filled the air. Ty lost his hat and blood spilled from a cut on his jaw, but he didn't seem to care. Josie knew better than to get in the middle of headstrong males, either bovine or human. Furious, she paced to the water trough on the side of the barn, filled a bucket and lugged it back around the corner. Gordie was on his knees and heaving, so she hurled it at Ty and Obie. As the water fanned from the bucket, Ty landed a blow to Obie's chin. The hired hand stumbled backward, leaving Ty to take the brunt of the water.

"What the—" he stopped in midsentence and stared at her.

Josie's cheeks flamed. Dousing Ty alone had been unfair. He'd started the fight, but he'd done it to defend her honor. Judging by the marks on his face, he was destined for a black eye, maybe two. Obie was sitting on the ground, wiping blood from his nose and glaring at her as she set down the empty bucket. He lumbered to his feet and spat a mouthful of blood. "I quit."

"Me, too," Gordie added.

Josie panicked. "But—"

Ty interrupted. "Get out of here. *Now.*"

"Mizz Bright owes us wages," Obie complained.

A full month's pay... She'd gone to the bank because she couldn't meet the obligation without holding back on the bill at the mercantile. Would the juggling ever stop? She was getting ready to negotiate with Obie when Ty looked at her. "How much do you owe these fools?"

Josie knew his thinking. He intended to pay off Obie and Gordie for her. She didn't want to owe him a favor. "This isn't your problem."

"How much?" he repeated.

Gordie answered for her. "We get twenty dollars a month each."

Ty went to his horse and opened the saddlebag. He came back with a money pouch, removed a few bills and paid Gordie and Obie. Gordie took the money and stepped back. Obie snatched two sawbucks and glared at Ty. "You owe me for the smokes."

"Sure." Ty dug in the money pouch, removed some pennies and tossed them on the ground.

Obie looked at the money, spat again, then glared at Ty. "You're gonna pay for this, Donner."

"I expect so."

"I mean it," Obie insisted. "I'm going to get even with you."

Obie glared at Ty, picked up the coins, then motioned for Gordie to follow him to the bunkhouse. With Ty shadowing them, the men packed their things and saddled their horses. Josie didn't know whether to be relieved or worried. She needed help, but Obie and Gordie had given her nothing but grief. As the men led their mounts out of the barn, Ty came to stand at her side. When Obie and Gordie disappeared over a hill, Ty started to chuckle.

Josie wasn't in the mood to laugh. "What on *earth* is so funny?"

In spite of the bruises and wet shirt, Ty looked pleased with himself. "I always did like a good fight."

"That was *good?*"

"One of the best." His expression turned serious. "Obie disrespected you, Josie. I won't tolerate it."

Five years ago, *he'd* disrespected her when he'd gone after the Scudders. Before he'd taken off, they'd quarreled and it hadn't been a small argument. She'd begged him to consider her feelings, but he'd dismissed her worries and ridden off. He could apologize a hundred times, but nothing could erase the humiliation of standing in church in her wedding dress, waiting…and waiting…and waiting…until Nate delivered the news.

Josie snatched up the bucket. She wasn't sorry she'd doused Ty after all. Thanks to the scuffle, she'd lost her hired hands and she owed Ty for their wages. The debt shamed her. "I'll pay you back when I can."

"Forget it."

"I can't."

As she stepped toward the trough, Ty tugged the bucket away from her. "I'm going to need that." He bent and picked up his hat, slapped off the dust and passed her on the way to the trough. Josie wanted to leave, but his cuts needed attention, maybe even a stitch or two. He'd earned them defending her, so she followed him. When he dipped the bucket in the water, she removed a hankie from her pocket and indicated the bench next to the barn.

"Sit," she ordered.

He obeyed so suddenly she startled. The old Ty would have teased her. The new one had learned to take orders from prison guards. This subservient man wasn't the Ty Donner who'd chased after the Scudders. The change shook her up, mostly because she didn't like it. She should have been glad he'd lost his arrogance. Instead she ached for what he'd experienced behind bars.

She dipped her handkerchief in the water, cupped the back of his head and dabbed at the cut. His hair, warm from the sun, tickled her fingers. She couldn't stop her eyes from wandering to his smooth jaw. He'd once grown a mustache. When she complained that it tickled, he'd shaved it off the next day. Was Ty remembering, too? Her eyes locked on to his. As if they'd never been apart, his gaze made her melt.

Fool!

To hide a blush, she rinsed the hankie in the bucket. She had no business thinking of his clean-shaven jaw. Not only did she need someone to ride in the May Day Maze, she needed someone to muck out stalls, fix fences, mend tools, check the few remaining cattle and paint the house before it turned to splinters. She finished cleaning the cuts, decided they didn't need stitches, then said, "I hope you plan to work hard, because you just fired my only two hands."

He shrugged. "They needed firing."

"I still need help."

"I can see that." With a twinkle in his eye, he indicated his wet shirt. "Now that I've had a bath, I guess I'm hired."

She wrinkled her nose. "You needed it."

She used to enjoy sparring with Ty, and she supposed she still did. They had that way about them, where it sounded like they were bickering but they weren't. It had been a game between them, but now they had business to conduct. "About wages…I'll pay you what I paid Obie."

"Forget it."

Josie had her pride. "You can't work for free. It's just not right."

"You're paying me room and board."

"But—"

"Please don't argue."

She barely heard him, a sign he remembered their sparring as sweetly as she did. If she quarreled with him now, they'd end up recalling other spats, the ones that ended in laughter and kisses. "All right," she agreed. "Room and board it is."

"Thank you, boss."

The name annoyed her. Frowning, she emptied the bucket and set it down. Ty stood and pulled his hat low. It hid his eyes, but not the hard line of his jaw. Josie knew that look. He had something to say, but he wouldn't say it. She felt the same way. Talk would lead to remembering, and remembering would lead to trouble. She had to get away from Ty. "Smoke's in the north pasture. Go and say hello."

"I will," he answered. "But first I'll tend to my horse and your mule."

"I'll do it."

"No you won't, boss. It's my job now."

"Don't argue with me." She couldn't stand another minute of his sassy attitude. If he was going to call her *boss*, she'd act like one. "Go see Smoke. That's an order."

Ty couldn't stand another minute in Josie's presence. He could still feel her hankie against his skin, her fingertips dabbing at the cuts. The tenderness in her touch didn't erase the fact he'd taken a beating, but it made the bruises worthwhile. It would take time to win her trust, but defending her honor against Obie's insults had been a start.

Before he left, he had to square a few details. "I'll sleep in the bunkhouse. What about meals?"

"I'll bring your supper and the noon meal here. You can save some bacon and biscuits for breakfast."

So he wouldn't be sitting at the table with Josie and her mother the way he used to with Nate. "Anything else?"

She indicated the dilapidated barn. "You can see what needs to be done."

"Yes, ma'am." He could have been saying *Yes, sir* to a prison guard. It would take time to get used to being free.

Josie gave him a peculiar look, then went to put up the animals. Ty headed for the pasture. The path took him past the spot where Gordie had upchucked. He kicked dirt on the mess to save Josie the sight of it, then he rounded the corner of the barn. Flexing his knuckles, he felt the sting of broken flesh. Obie had earned his punishment, but Ty regretted making an enemy. He regretted a lot of things. Some of those regrets were best forgotten, but others could be fixed. He couldn't make up for ruining Josie's wedding day, but he could win the race for her.

As he neared the pasture, he searched the perimeter for Smoke. He hoped the horse remembered him. It had taken weeks to earn the stallion's respect, and he didn't have time to start over. The Maze was less than a month away.

At the fence he propped a boot on the bottom rail and crossed his arms over the top one. In the far corner he spotted Smoke. The stallion's coat had darkened, but he still had a silvery sheen that stood out against the sky and grass. If the mustang had the same fire inside, he could outrun any horse in Wyoming. Ty put two fingers in his mouth and whistled the signal he'd taught Smoke when he'd caught him as a yearling. The stallion raised his head, looked in his direction and froze. The first blast had wobbled a bit. Ty tried again. This time the notes were high and sharp.

Smoke broke into a run. Ty hopped the fence. The next thing he knew the horse was nosing his chest in search of carrots. With his heart brimming, Ty wrapped his arms around Smoke's neck and gave thanks. He'd felt his kind of joy just once before. The day he walked out of prison, he'd felt both free and burdened by his bad choices. He'd wanted to be baptized, so he and Reverend Gaines walked fully clothed into the Cayenne River. The reverend said a prayer, then he bent

Ty back and held him tight so he wouldn't fall. Water rushed up his nose and he'd come up sputtering and full of joy.

He felt that joy now...a good measure, pressed down like grapes giving their juice. It tasted sweeter than honey. In this precious moment, he prayed for Josie, that he could be her friend and save her home. He prayed she'd forgive him. Another prayer formed in his mind, but he didn't dare give voice to it. He had no right to think about loving her again, and if the truth be told, she'd hurt him, too. Not a single letter... Not even an angry one.

Smoke nosed him again. The force pushed Ty into the railing, and he thought of prison bars. Who said horses didn't understand jail? Smoke wanted to be free...so did Ty. He wanted to go far and fast until he lost himself in a cloud of dust. He didn't need a saddle to ride Smoke, so he swung onto the horse's back. They circled the pasture once and came back to the gate. Ty reached down, unlatched it and Smoke broke into a gallop.

Breathing in perfect rhythm with his horse, Ty felt strong and free. With God's help, he'd win the race for Josie. He'd give her back the life she'd lost. Maybe then he could make a new life for himself.

Chapter Three

Josie walked into the house, closed the door and leaned against it. She needed to clear her head before she spoke to her mother, but the older woman was coming down the hall in measured steps. Winnie Bright had no trouble navigating her home of twenty-five years. She'd lost the ability to read and see distant mountains, but she could detect patterns of light. She described her vision as looking through fogged glass. She couldn't identify faces, but she had sharp hearing and remarkable intuition.

"Josie, is that you?"

"It's me, Mama."

The older woman emerged from the hall into the front room. Red gingham curtains were tied back, giving the sun full access to the parlor. The rays caught the silver in her mother's braided coronet, a sharp contrast to the auburn that matched Josie's own hair. The women would have been the same height, but Mama had shrunk with age and had stooped shoulders. Her posture worried Josie, mostly because she knew her mother's back hurt all the time.

The older woman walked to her rocking chair and sat. "What happened with Mr. Proffitt?"

"He said no, but it might not matter."

"Why not?"

"I have a new plan." Josie sat on the divan. This was her

place, where she sewed and fretted. "I found someone to ride in the May Day Maze… Someone who can ride Smoke."

Mama tilted her head. "That horse belonged to Ty Donner."

"That's right."

"Are you telling me—"

"He's back." In a brusque tone, Josie told her mother about Mr. Proffitt denying them a loan, meeting Ty and the decision to ask him to ride in the race. She ended the story with the description of the fight with Obie and Gordie. "I'm stuck with him now," she said, sounding disgusted. "I hope he can do the work of three men."

"Working hard was never Ty's weakness," Mama replied. "As I recall, the boy worked too hard."

"He's not a boy anymore." Josie tried to sound disinterested, but she'd noticed Ty's new maturity, both physical and otherwise. She couldn't help but mourn the marriage and children she'd been denied. Biting her lip, she recalled going with Ty on a picnic and how they talked about the future. She told him that she wanted to give him a son, and he'd kissed her.

I'd like that, Josie girl. But I want a daughter, too.

She'd been surprised. *Really?*

She'll grow up to be like you, and I'll be scaring off boys like me… Someday she'll wear your wedding dress.

The dress…Josie wished she'd sold it. Instead she'd wrapped it in muslin and shoved it to the back of the top shelf of her wardrobe. She couldn't think about the gown without feeling bitter, but neither had she been able to part with it. The ruined wedding had been a fulcrum in her life, the tipping point where hope turned to loss and her faith dissolved along with it. If she got rid of the dress, would she heal or would she stay bitter forever? She didn't know.

Mama put her rocking chair in motion. "Prison changes a person. I imagine Ty's done some maturing."

"I suppose."

The bowed wood creaked against the floor. "Even so, it has to hurt to see him."

How did her mother do that? Even without clear vision, she saw past Josie's nonchalance to the pulp of her heart. Josie had been angry with Ty for chasing after the Scudders, but mostly she felt unloved. Just one day for a wedding…that was all she had asked. But it had been too much. Ty set aside her needs for his own, and they'd both lost everything.

Josie stood and went to the window. A line of trees marked the creek where she and Ty had stolen kisses. Her fingers knotted on the wide sill. "I wish he'd never come back."

Mama kept rocking. "You have to forgive him."

"I can't."

"Forgiveness is a choice, Josie. No matter what you're feeling, you can say the words and ask God to make them true."

"It would be a lie."

"Or a start," Mama countered. "Sometimes the feeling comes after the talking."

"Why should I even try?" She sounded childish, but she didn't care. "He left me waiting at the church. It was humiliating!"

"None of us is perfect. We've all made mistakes, but God loves us anyway. Ty paid dearly for what he did."

"So have I."

Mama let out a sigh. "Where is he now?"

"With Smoke."

"I hope you invited him to supper."

"I'll bring a plate to the barn. I don't want him in the house."

The older woman raised her brows. "Perhaps *I* do. He was Nate's friend, Josie. He was like a son to me. I've missed him."

If the three of them ate supper together, Josie would remember the day he went after the Scudders. She'd watch him put too much salt on his food, and she'd know that he cut his meat into tiny bites, a habit from growing up poor and wanting to make the food last. She couldn't bear the thought of being with him, so she shook her head. "I can't do it, Mama. I'll bring him a plate, but that's it."

"I won't argue, Josie. But I hope you'll think about it."

"There's nothing to think about." But there was…she could think about the dress, the embarrassment and the life she should have had. If she thought about anything else—Ty fighting for her honor, his determination to win the Maze—she'd be on the verge of caring for him again. She had too many worries to let old feelings rise to the surface. She couldn't let anything interfere with saving the Bar JB.

She took a final glance at the trees, then stepped away from the window. "I'll start supper." She went to the kitchen, but she didn't go alone. She felt her mother's prayers following her, whispering the words she couldn't abide… *Forgive him.*

Ty couldn't stay in the bunkhouse without speaking to Mrs. Bright. She'd been like a mother to him, and he'd hurt her when he'd let down Josie. He needed to apologize to her, and he wanted to offer his condolences for Nate's passing. Josie didn't want to see him, but he had to return the basket she'd used to deliver his meal. When he finished eating, he cleaned the plates and utensils, put them in the basket and walked to the house. Instead of going through the back door as he would have done five years ago, he went to the front door and knocked.

"Who is it, please?" Mrs. Bright called.

Ty cracked open the door. "Mrs. Bright? It's me, Ty Donner."

"Ty! Come in!"

He set the basket by the door and walked into the parlor. Mrs. Bright was on her feet and holding her arms wide. "Get over here, young man! I want to hug you."

For one stupid moment, he was twelve years old again, even younger, and he was following Nate into the house like he belonged. With four kids in the Bright family—Nate and the three girls—Ty had been a welcome ally to the Bright males.

He'd also been Josie's particular nemesis in games of tag and other family fun. That had changed at a church dance. He'd seen her in a rose-colored dress with her hair half up and half down, and he'd forgotten all about tag. He'd asked her to dance, and a year later he'd proposed on the porch he'd just crossed. A year after that, he'd broken her heart.

Ty had expected Mrs. Bright to be polite but distant. Instead she had tears in her eyes. A bit choked up himself, he hugged her hard, then stepped back. "I'm sorry about Mr. Bright and Nate."

"Of course, you are."

"And I'm sorry about what happened with Josie. I'd do anything to change that day."

"I know you would."

As she sat in the rocker, Ty dropped down on the divan. Judging by a nearby sewing basket, Josie still favored the spot by the window. It was here that she sewed the buttons on her wedding dress. He'd never seen it, but she'd described the pearls to him. Back then he'd felt both proud and desperate to provide for her. He felt the same way now, though the pride felt lonely and provision depended on Smoke and winning the Maze.

Mrs. Bright started to rock. "Josie's taking a walk. She does that after supper, but she'll be back soon."

Ty remembered her walks. He used to go with her. "I brought back the supper dishes, but mostly I wanted to see you. Josie told me about your money woes. I'm sorry you're struggling."

"We had a hard winter."

"The worst." Ty had experienced it in prison, hemmed in by both walls and snow. "I want to help you by winning the Maze. Whatever Smoke and I win, it all goes to you and Josie."

"Did she agree to that?"

"Not exactly." He thought of sparring with her and smiled.

"She thinks we're splitting it, but I intend to give her everything."

Her brow furrowed. "You don't need to do that, Ty."

"Yes, I do."

She reached across the space between them. He saw her intention and gripped her hand. "I forgive you," she said. "So does God."

"Josie hasn't. I ruined her life."

"Hogwash!" She released his fingers and pushed off in the rocker with surprising force. "*You* didn't ruin Josie's life anymore than being blind ruined mine. Bad things happen. We carry on or we quit. Josie's not a quitter, but she's had trouble getting over the heartache, maybe because we've had so much of it. We lost you first, then Jeremiah and Nate...sometimes it's just too much."

"I understand." He'd felt that way in prison.

"You came at the right time, Ty. If anyone can win the Maze, it's you riding Smoke."

"I hope so." For Josie's sake he had to win, but today's ride had opened his eyes to a harsh fact. Five years was a long time. Ty was older, stronger and wiser. Smoke was older and slower. It would take some effort to get ready for the race, something he would have to do in between chores.

He could have sat with Mrs. Bright for another hour, but he didn't want to irritate Josie so he stood. "I should be going."

"You're welcome to Nate's room," Mrs. Bright offered.

Nate had slept in a room on the first floor. Josie and her sisters had occupied the second floor, a space Ty hadn't seen except a few days before the wedding when he'd lugged her cedar chest down the stairs and into his wagon. The chest had belonged to her maternal grandmother, who'd hauled it all the way from St. Louis. It had been stuffed with bed linens and things for her kitchen...things Ty had never seen. When he'd been convicted, Nate had hauled the chest back to the Bright ranch. Ty could only imagine what Josie experienced when she'd opened it.

All of a sudden, he felt caged. "I appreciate the offer, Mrs. Bright. But I'd rather stay in the bunkhouse."

"Whatever you'd like, but come and see me again." Her eyes looked glassier than usual. "An old woman gets lonely, you know."

"I know. But I don't want to step on Josie's toes."

"It's my home, too. You're invited for supper any time."

"Thank you." Ty bent and kissed her cheek. "Good night, Mrs. Bright."

"Good night, Ty."

He left through the front door, closed it and glanced at the porch swing. Instead of the vacant spot he expected, he saw Josie and froze. In the grayish light, her auburn hair stood out like a flame. Her skin had the luster of pearls, and her turquoise eyes matched the twilight sky. He couldn't stop looking at her...all those years in prison, he'd tried to forget her. He thought he'd succeeded, but looking at her now, he knew the truth. This woman owned his heart lock, stock and barrel. He'd never stopped loving her and he never would.

To keep from hurting, he focused on the most ordinary of things. "Thanks for supper. You always were a good cook."

"I enjoy it, even if it's just for Mama."

She sounded lonely in the mournful way of the wind. Ty knew that sound well. In prison he'd stand in the yard behind the fifteen-foot walls, not feeling the wind but hearing the hollow sound of it. No one could understand unless they'd stood in that spot. He understood Josie because they'd both sat on that swing. They'd both grieved for what might have been, but she didn't want that kinship. Unable to help her, he walked away.

"Ty?"

He faced her. "Yes?"

"Can you really win the Maze?"

"I don't know," he said honestly. "But I'll do my best."

"That's all anyone can ask."

He waited, hoping she'd say something else, but she turned her head and stared at the pinkish horizon. There was no romance in the sunset, no hope in the fading light, so he murmured, "Good night, Josie," and walked alone to the bunkhouse.

He wouldn't be sleeping behind bars tonight, but in a way he'd entered a prison of another kind, one that could only be unlocked by Josie's forgiveness. Whether she knew it or not, she was trapped behind the same wall. The sweet girl he'd loved had turned into a hard woman. It troubled him greatly.

"Help her, Lord," Ty said out loud. "Help us both."

Josie stayed on the swing, watching Ty's long stride as he walked away from the house. When she'd asked him about winning the race, she'd expected bravado and bragging. The old Ty would have been full of talk. The new one had a humility that confused her. She couldn't trust boastfulness, but she admired honesty. As he neared the barn, he faded from her sight, changing from a man to a shadow and then to a memory. One memory led to another, until she recalled waiting for him at the church. When Nate delivered the news of the arrest, her mother had comforted her. Anne, the middle sister and Josie's maid of honor, had explained to the guests. Scarlett, a junior bridesmaid, had looked stricken.

The next day Josie had visited Ty in jail. He'd insisted the trial would blow over. He'd shown no respect for how hurt she'd been, how the delay tainted what should have been a beautiful day. Two weeks later she'd watched guards load him into the black prison wagon. He'd stared at her through the bars, apologizing with his eyes and mouthing, "I love you, Josie. I'm so sorry...."

She'd said nothing back. In that moment, her bitterness had taken root. It lived in her heart the way the dress stayed in her wardrobe—wrapped tight, sealed, unchanging. She didn't want to be resentful, but she didn't know how to stop the ugly feelings. Her mother had encouraged her to trust God through the sadness, but Josie didn't have the will. She went to church because someone had to take her mother, but she didn't listen to the sermons. Neither did she pray, though tonight she recalled the girl who'd loved God and Ty Donner with her whole heart.

Her throat ached with unspoken words…angry words that burst out with unexpected force. "God? Are You listening? I don't want to feel this way. I don't want to hate my life, and I don't want to lose the ranch. Mama says I have to forgive Ty, but I can't. It's just too hard. He hurt me! He ruined *everything*! Why did You let it happen? *Why?*" With her eyes squeezed tight, she choked out, "Amen."

The prayer brought no relief, no peace. She looked accusingly at the stars, then down to the bunkhouse. A light flared in a window, a sign Ty had arrived and lit a lamp. She thought of his honesty concerning the race, the way he took orders without quarreling. He'd changed. Josie wanted to change too, but mostly she wanted to rake him over hot coals. But she wouldn't. She'd stay behind her wall of indifference where he couldn't possibly hurt her.

Chapter Four

"I'm not feeling well," Mrs. Bright said to her daughter. "You and Ty go to church without me."

Ty had just knocked on the door and was waiting for the women on the porch. He hadn't expected to be going to Sunday services, but last night Mrs. Bright asked him to do the driving. The three of them had been having supper, another invitation from Mrs. Bright, when she'd asked the favor.

He didn't want to step on Josie's toes, so he'd looked at her for permission. She shrugged and said he could do whatever he liked. He liked going to church, so he'd accepted the invitation with a politeness that matched Josie's. He'd been at the ranch for two weeks now, and they hadn't exchanged a single sharp word. The place no longer looked neglected and Smoke had regained his fitness, but Ty was no closer to winning Josie's forgiveness. If Mrs. Bright stayed home, the ride to town would be colder than January.

He might have backed out of the trip, but he had another reason for going to town. Wayne Cooper, an old friend and the owner of the livery stable, ran the May Day Maze. Ty needed to sign up for the race, and he wanted to hear about the competition. First, though, he had to get to town. He'd always been punctual, but prison had honed that tendency into nervousness.

Being late to church made him uneasy, so he knocked again on the doorjamb. "Josie? Mrs. Bright? It's getting late."

Mrs. Bright called to him. "Josie's on her way."

Ty heard whispering, stepped back to the carriage and waited until Josie came out of the house alone. Her green dress made him wish he'd dressed up a little more. So did her prim hat and white gloves. When he offered to hand her into the carriage, she accepted as if he were a footman. He climbed up next to her and took the reins with Josie glaring at the road. "This wasn't my idea," she grumbled.

Hoping to ease the mood, he kept his voice light. "Mine neither, but I can't say I mind."

"*I* do."

"It's a pretty day."

"It's too warm."

She'd disagree with whatever he said, so he said nothing. After a mile, he glanced at her profile. Her gaze had the stone-like quality he'd seen in the eyes of inmates with the longest sentences and the least amount of hope. He'd kept his distance from Josie out of respect, but now he wondered if he'd made a mistake. All that anger was simmering. A good stew got better with a time on the fire, but coffee burned and turned bitter.

Josie needed to empty her coffeepot, so to speak. If she couldn't do it herself, Ty would do it for her. The worst thing about prison for Ty had been the helplessness. That's why the Sunday services in the dining hall had appealed to him. His renewed faith had given him a sense of purpose. Josie had the ranch to fight for, but he had the feeling she really wanted to fight with him. If she needed a sparring partner, he'd be glad to oblige. He'd been a cocky kid. He could be an equally cocky man. "Give it up, Josie. If you want to yell at me, just do it."

"Who says I want to yell?"

"I do."

"Drop it, Ty. You don't know me anymore."

But he did… If there was one thing that got Josie fired up,

it was women's rights. He agreed—women were as capable as men—but he didn't mind using politics to rile her. "Come on, Josie. Admit it. Running the ranch is too much for you."

Her gaze slid in his direction. "Considering the winter, I've done just fine."

"I guess. But it's a big job for a woman."

"It's a big job for *anyone*."

"But especially a *woman*," he insisted. "Especially a *single* woman."

Josie's jaw tensed. "I'll have you know, a *single* woman can manage as well as a man."

"Maybe, but it's not a woman's place. Women are better suited to cooking and darning socks…picking flowers… reading silly poetry. They like stuff that doesn't take a lot of thought."

Josie glared at him. "Stop it."

"Stop what?"

"You're trying to make me mad."

"Is it working?"

"Hardly."

"Why not give it a try?"

"Because I don't want to." She turned her gaze back to the road, a sign she was finished with the conversation.

He'd have preferred a tongue lashing to her silence, but silence was what she gave him. It lasted all the way to the church, until he halted the mule in front of the steps leading to the wide porch. He came around the carriage and offered his hand.

She took it as if he were a distant cousin. "You're welcome to join me, of course. I sit in the third row."

"I remember." The Bright family had occupied the third row as long as Ty had known them.

Josie turned and went up the three steps. Ty drove the carriage to the field where families left their rigs, then he walked back to the church and slipped inside. He saw Josie's green hat and a space next to her, but he didn't want to draw attention. Instead he slid into the back pew.

When the organist struck the opening chords of "A Mighty Fortress Is Our God," Ty stood with the congregation. He'd sung the hymn in prison and liked it, but today it sounded all wrong. The voices should have been deep and male. Instead he heard the birdsong of Josie's soprano and he remembered... The last time they'd been in this church had been the Wednesday before the wedding. Reverend Hall had told them what to expect during the ceremony, then he'd counseled them in God's plan for marriage. He'd talked about wives respecting their husbands and husbands loving their wives. He'd also told Ty to put his dirty socks in the laundry and to bring his wife a gift now and then. He'd told Josie to laugh at Ty's jokes, even the silly ones, and to appreciate his hard work.

Last, he'd said words Ty would never forget.

Don't let the sun go down on your anger.

Josie had been angry with him for five years. All that time, her bitterness had been festering. If she'd smiled in the past two weeks, he couldn't remember it. Bitterness did that to a person. Ty knew, because he'd felt its grip in prison. He'd been wrong to go after the Scudders, but the judge and jury had been harsh. Not until he'd forgiven everyone—the jury, himself, even God—had he found peace.

Josie needed that same surrender. With the hymn filling the church, Ty bowed his head and prayed. *Please help her, Lord. She needs to forgive me as much as I need to be forgiven.*

The ponderous hymn droned to a close. Ty usually appreciated the gravity of it, but today he felt burdened. The church felt too crowded, too full of goodness and hope, so he slipped out the door before the congregation sang the final "amen." He couldn't do anything for Josie except win the race, so he headed to the livery to see Wayne. Hungry for silence, he walked the long way instead of cutting through town. When he arrived at the livery barn, he felt steadier.

Wayne saw him first. "What can I do for you, sir?"

"Sir?" Ty laughed. "It's me—"

"Ty Donner!" Wayne crossed the barn, shook Ty's hand and clapped him on the back. The livery owner was as strong as ever, though his hair had signs of gray. "When'd you get out?"

"A few weeks ago."

"It's about time." Wayne shook his head. "You paid a terrible price for shooting a horse thief. Do you need a place to stay? How about a job? How long are you staying, anyhow?"

Ty grinned. "You always did ask a lot of questions."

"So answer 'em."

"I'm working for the Brights, and I'm staying as long as it takes to help Josie get on her feet."

Wayne's expression sobered. "The Bright women have had a hard time, first Jeremiah and then Nate. Josie's working herself to the bone."

"That's going to change," Ty answered. "I'm working for them now. If I can win the Maze, Josie can restock and hire decent help."

Wayne raised his brows. "The Maze, huh? What are you riding?"

"Smoke."

"Well, how *do* you do!" the man exclaimed. "It's going to be a glory of a horse race."

"Where do I sign up?" Ty asked.

"Follow me."

Wayne led him to the back room he used for an office, opened a ledger and wrote Ty's name and the date. The race didn't require an entry fee, which meant there would be a wide range of horses and riders. Ty craned his neck to see the list of names, but Wayne's printing looked like chicken scratches. He gave up and asked, "Who all is riding?"

Wayne went down the list, describing every horse and rider. Ty recognized most of them, but two stood out. Grant Harper, an Englishman, bred Arabians in addition to running cattle.

He'd be riding to win, and he had horses that could do it. The second name made Ty see red. Obie Jones had tossed his hat into the ring, but he hadn't listed a horse.

"What's Obie riding?" Ty asked.

"He said he was still sorting that out."

The more information Ty had, the more prepared he'd be if Obie caused trouble. "Where's he living these days?"

"Dyer's Boardinghouse."

Ty's nose wrinkled. "Is it as bad I remember?"

"Worse."

The Dyers were known for bad food, dirt and fleas. Ty would have been stuck there if he hadn't hired on with Josie.

Wayne crossed his arms. "I hear you ran Obie off the Bright place."

"That's right."

"I'm glad you did." Wayne got a faraway look. "Winnie and I go way back. If Jeremiah hadn't come back from the war, I'd have swept her off her feet."

Ty knew the feeling. He'd do anything for Josie…anything at all. "If you hear talk about Obie, let me know."

"Will do." Wayne indicated a pot on a round stove. "Got coffee if you want it."

"No, thanks."

The men shook hands and Ty left the barn. He wanted to be back for the closing hymn, so he cut through town. The route took him past the Dyer place and he thought of Obie. The fool could make all the threats he wanted, but Ty intended to win the Maze.

As the church came into view, Ty walked faster. The service hadn't let out, so he slipped through the door and into the back pew. He looked for Josie, but instead of her green hat, he saw an empty seat. It wasn't like Josie to leave in the middle of a sermon. Worried, he went to look for her.

The coughing fit that drove Josie from church hadn't been faked. She'd gotten a tickle in her throat the minute Reverend

Hall read today's scripture. *Be ye angry, and sin not: let not the sun go down upon your wrath...* She tried not to listen, but the minister had looked right at her from the start of his sermon.

We forgive because we've been forgiven.

He'd jumped all over the scriptures, and every word had hit like an arrow, especially the last one he'd quoted.

Let him whose slate is clean cast the first stone.

That's when she started to cough. It was either cough or cry, and so she'd coughed enough to justify leaving and gone to the carriage. That's where she was now...blissfully alone and angry enough to spit nails. The frustration had started when her mother forced her to ride alone with Ty. It increased when he tried to make her mad. She *had* gotten mad, but she didn't want to show it. If her anger drained away, she'd be left with the hurt. She couldn't stand the thought, but neither could she stand being angry. Determined to be done with it, she confessed to the sky. "I want to *strangle* Ty Donner!"

A male laugh—deep and satisfied—came from ten feet behind her. She'd know Ty's voice anywhere, anytime. Furious, she faced him. "What's so funny?"

"Us."

"I'm not laughing."

His eyes twinkled even brighter. "So yell instead. It'll feel good."

"No." She hesitated. "Where have you been?"

"Signing up for the Maze." He picked up a rock and offered it to her. "Want to throw it? You can pretend you're aiming at me."

"I don't care about the rock." But she did. She wanted to throw the rock as hard as she could, and Ty knew it. He knew her better than anyone, a truth that put a lump in her throat.

He touched her shoulder. "Josie—"

"Don't touch me!"

When he lowered his hand, she started to cry. The gesture showed that he understood...and he cared. She saw the blue eyes that made her shiver, the jaw that jutted when he was being stubborn, but she didn't see the man who left her to chase a bunch of horse thieves. She saw someone else... someone who'd learned to listen. She thought of all the nights the sun had gone down on her anger. Then she thought of the wedding dress and made a decision. Today she'd take the dress out of the wardrobe. She'd forgive Ty for hurting her, or she'd get rid of the dress that embodied her lost dreams.

Ty offered her a bandanna. She wiped her eyes, then said, "I want to go home."

"Sure."

He helped her into the carriage and off they rode. Josie remained silent, but her thoughts ran in circles. What would happen when she saw the dress? Would she hate Ty even more, or would she find peace? She didn't know, but she resolved to find out. Today she'd examine her heart and maybe she'd know what to do.

The spring sun warmed her face as they bounced down the rut-filled road. She stole glances at Ty, noticing how the cuts from the fight with Obie had healed, but mostly she stared at the winding road. On occasion she sensed his gaze on her cheek. The carriage wheels usually squeaked, but today they rolled in silence. Ty must have greased them, a chore she'd ignored. She wanted to ignore *him*, but she couldn't stop looking at his hands holding on to the reins, or his boots on the floorboard, slightly apart and worn from work. The silence thickened until they reached the front of the house. The instant he stopped the rig, she climbed down from the seat. Her petticoat caught on something sharp, tore but didn't come loose. The tears she'd stifled threatened to break loose.

"Hold on," Ty ordered. "Let me help."

"I can do it." She tugged on the petticoat, but it was caught on a spring. The harder she pulled, the more tightly it wedged.

Ty came to her side of the carriage, reached over the wheel and freed the cloth. Intending to politely thank him, she looked into his eyes. The courteous words melted on her tongue. Instead she finally yelled at him. "I can't stand it! Why did you come *back?* Why do you *do* this to me!"

"I don't mean to do anything." He took her gloved hand in his. "I care about you, Josie. I always have—"

"Don't say that!"

His fingers stroked hers. "This hardness between us has to stop, and it has to stop today. Check on your mom and then come to the barn."

"Why?"

"You and I need to take a ride."

"Where to?"

"Boulder Gorge…the place where I shot Brant Scudder. I want to forget it, but I can't."

Josie knew about memories that refused to be laid aside. She looked into Ty's eyes, saw a plea and thought of the wedding dress. She'd intended to open the wardrobe immediately, but Ty deserved to be heard. "All right," she said. "I'll meet you at the barn."

He climbed back into the carriage and snapped the reins. Sighing, she went into the house, told her mother she and Ty were taking a ride, then retreated to her room where she opened the wardrobe. Instead of retrieving her split skirt, she stared for a moment at the muslin package holding her wedding dress. She didn't know which frightened her more—reliving old memories or making new ones on today's ride. The dress could wait. The ride couldn't, so she put on her riding clothes and went to meet Ty.

Chapter Five

After leaving Josie at the house, Ty went to the barn to saddle Smoke and a brown mare named Maggie. Josie had always liked that name… She'd mentioned it when they'd talked about naming their children. Their first son would have been named after her father; the second would have been Ty Junior. If he hadn't gone after the Scudders, by now they'd have had two babies, maybe three. They would have—

"Stop it," he muttered to himself.

He lifted a saddle onto Maggie's back, scowling as he worked. He had no time for self-pity. Today he had just one wish. He wanted to talk to Josie…really talk…about that awful day. With its ugly memories, Boulder Gorge struck him as a fitting spot to clear the air. God had forgiven Ty's sins and he knew it. Josie was still holding a grudge, and he hoped today he could convince her to let it go.

He finished with Maggie, then saddled Smoke. As he led the horses out of the barn, he saw Josie walking up the path in a split skirt and a wide brimmed hat. Even if she called him awful names, it would be preferable to the cold civility he saw on her face now. Even better would be her forgiveness.

She came up to Maggie and scratched the horse's ears. "I'm ready."

Ty helped her mount, then climbed on Smoke. He led the

way to the trail to the gorge, commenting on the grass and water conditions to pass the time. The conversation took them all the way to the edge of a ravine that zigzagged for miles. From a distance, it looked like a knife wound. Ty reined Smoke to a stop and climbed off.

"This is it," he said to Josie.

She slid off Maggie and handed him the reins. He tied both horses to a bush blooming with Indian paintbrush, propped his hands on his hips and stared at the slash in the ground. "This is where I killed Brant Scudder."

"Nate told me about it."

"I've thought about this place every day, but it's the first time I've come back since I got out. It looks the same…feels the same."

"Some memories are burned into us. We change, but they don't."

"That's a fact." He looked at the bottom of the gorge. Today a streambed held a trickle of water, but five years ago it had been all sand and rock. Looking west, he pointed down the ravine. "Do you see those boulders?"

"I do."

"I was standing right here." He drew an X in the dirt with his toe. "The Scudders were riding straight at us. Nate yelled something and one of them fired. I hit the dirt and fired back. Everything went crazy after that."

"Nate said the shooting lasted five minutes."

"I don't know." Ty shook his head. "It felt like seconds before the Scudders ran off. Three of them were in a pack and riding fast. Brant was trailing behind and firing his pistol over his shoulder at Nate and me. Nate stopped shooting. He said to let him go, but I had to get in one last shot. I should have listened to Nate."

Josie said nothing. She just stared at the boulders.

So did Ty. "Brant fell off his horse next to those rocks. His brothers were long gone, so he crawled for cover. He was still alive when I rode up, and do you know what I did?"

"No."

"I didn't do a blessed thing. I stood there like a king, all puffed up and justified because the Scudders had stolen from me. Nate came up behind me. He saw the kid was dying and gave him water. He prayed with him, too. I wish I'd done that. Instead I told Brant he could rot for all I cared."

Josie's breath caught.

"Yeah, I know." Ty grimaced with shame. "It was an awful thing to say. Brant was younger than me. He needed comfort—even forgiveness—and I'd have spat on him if Nate hadn't been there." Heavy with guilt, he turned to Josie. "You begged me not to go that day. You were worried about the wedding, but there was more to it. I think you were afraid of what I'd do."

"I was," she admitted.

"If I'd listened to you, Brant would be alive. He deserved to go to jail, but he didn't deserve to die. I wanted to think I was justified in killing him, but I wasn't. We all mess up, just in different ways. I hurt you the same way Brant hurt me. He stole my horses…I stole your future. That's why we're here today, Josie. I want you to know that I understand what that day cost." To be sure she heard his next words, he took her hand. "I'm asking you to forgive me for everything I did wrong."

He needed her to say something, anything, but she was staring blindly into the gorge. Finally she tightened her fingers around his. Their hands made a fist of sorts, though whether it signaled unity or anger he didn't know. Nothing stirred. Not a blade of grass. She released his hand slowly, as if she didn't realize she'd been holding it, then she pressed her palm to her chest and faced him. "Do you know what that day was like for me?"

"I've imagined it."

"The whole time you were gone, I prayed you'd come back *alive*. I wasn't even *thinking* of the wedding. I was thinking of *you*." Her voice barely rose above a whisper. "Do know how long you were gone?"

"Too long." He and Nate had taken Brant's body to town. They'd talked to the law, then gone to the saloon and each downed a shot of whiskey. Ty had raised a toast to justice. The irony of that moment still stung. So did the memory of arriving at the Bright ranch in the light of a full moon and seeing Josie pacing in the yard. "I know it was late," he admitted.

"It was after midnight!"

He remembered, too. When he'd ridden into the yard, she'd hoisted her skirts and run to him. He'd slid off Smoke and into her arms.

Josie glared at him. "I was too relieved to be angry. Do you remember what you said?"

"I remember kissing you."

She blinked, but her eyes stayed hard. "You said you were sorry to scare me, but you'd do it all again."

"I wouldn't do it now."

"*Now* doesn't matter." She looked at him as if he were stupid. "We invited the whole town to watch us get married. My mother baked our cake. It was the last one she ever made because of her eyes. I spent hours making the dress, not because I love to sew but because I loved *you*. I'd never been happier in my life…then Nate came to the church. Not you…"

"I wanted to go myself, but you know what happened. The sheriff arrested me on my way there."

"It wouldn't have mattered." She stared back at the gorge. "The damage was done, and things got worse with every day that passed."

"Because of the trial."

"Yes." She clipped the word. "People offered condolences instead of congratulations. I felt like a widow without ever being a wife." Her voice quavered. "And it didn't stop… For six months people asked me about you…about us. The rude ones asked if I was going to wait for you."

He'd wondered about *that* himself. "What did you say?"

"I said *no.*" She faced him with a bit of a smirk. "That led to some very nice invitations."

For five years Ty had wondered about something. "Did that jerk Paul Whitman come calling?"

"Paul's not a jerk."

"So he did."

"Yes," she admitted. "But I didn't love him. I couldn't, and that's what hurt the most. I wanted to be *your* wife, not his! I *loved* you—" Tears welled in her eyes. "And I can't seem to love anyone else."

"Ah, Josie." He reached for her, but she turned her back, perhaps to hide her face and the threat of tears. He ached to comfort her, but he had nothing more to give. He'd done what he'd come to Rock Creek to do. He'd asked Josie for forgiveness. He wouldn't beg, but he could hope she'd find the grace to let go of the hurt. It wouldn't happen today, so he went to the horses. "I'm ready when you are."

With her chin high, she walked to Maggie. "I'm ready."

She climbed on the mare, and Ty mounted Smoke. As they turned to the trail, Josie stopped the horse in its tracks. Ty reined in Smoke. "What is it?"

"I want you to know, I heard everything you said."

"That's a start."

"Maybe." She hesitated. "I want to be done with these feelings, but I'm like a bug in a jar. I can't get out."

"It's like prison."

"Yes."

He risked a smile. "There's a sure cure for feeling trapped, and that's a hard run on a fast horse. Want to race home?"

A bit of sass flashed in her eyes, and she kicked Maggie into a run.

Ty gave her a head start, mostly because he wanted to watch her hair blowing in the wind. He loved her. He always would, but the future remained uncertain. He gave Smoke the bit and off they went. Chasing after her seemed fitting. Catching up to her was even better. Side by side, they galloped like the kids they used to be. Whether it was the end of the past or the start of the future, Ty didn't know. But he hoped it would be both.

Josie stepped into the house with her thoughts in a whirl. She'd left Ty in the barn to tend to the horses, and he'd told her not to bother with a basket for his supper. She'd never known him to skip a meal, but she hadn't argued. They both needed breathing room, and Josie would be unsettled until she looked at the wedding dress. She didn't want to speak to anyone, not even her mother, but Mama called to her as she came in. "Josie? Is that you?"

"It's me, Mama."

"How was the ride?"

"I don't know." Her voice wobbled. She stepped into the front room where she saw Mama knitting as usual. "I'm kind of tired. I thought I'd go to my room and rest."

"That's a fine idea."

Her mother no doubt wanted to hear about her talk with Ty, but Josie had nothing to say until she saw the dress. Oddly nervous, she went to her room, closed the door and approached the wardrobe that once belonged to her grandmother. Heavy and made of mahogany, it had held Josie's clothes for as long as she could remember. Slowly, as if approaching a dove instead of a piece of wood, she opened the double doors and looked at the top shelf. There she saw the muslin-wrapped wedding dress, neatly folded and tied with a piece of twine.

She remembered putting the dress on as plainly as she recalled taking it off. Both times she'd been in this room. In the morning she'd dressed with her sisters. Anne had done her hair, and her parents had driven Josie, Anne and Scarlett to the church in the freshly polished carriage. She'd felt like a princess about to become a queen, but then Nate broke the news about Ty. She'd wanted to see him immediately, but she couldn't stand the thought of walking into the jail in her wedding gown. Her father took her home, and she'd taken refuge in the room where she stood now.

Before removing the dress, she'd stared at herself in the oval mirror still standing in the corner. One by one, she'd undone the buttons, thinking of the wedding they wouldn't have. Next she'd slipped out of the sleeves. The dress had fallen at her feet in a fluttering of silk. Covered by petticoats and a chemise, she'd folded the dress and wrapped it in the muslin. She'd looked at the muslin many times, but not once had she looked at the dress.

With shaking fingers, she lifted the package and set it on her bed. She pulled on the twine and the bow unraveled. She set it aside, unwrapped the covering and lifted the dress to the light. Even wrinkled, it glowed white in the sun. She stared at the lace she'd stitched into place, the white sash she'd embroidered with roses, then she held the dress to her shoulders and looked at herself in the tall mirror.

Instead of herself as she was now, she saw the seventeen-year-old girl who'd expected life to be easy. That girl hadn't been spoiled, but she was naive. The Bright family had always had enough. The bounty showed in the wedding dress. The silk came from a San Francisco dressmaker, and the pearl buttons had cost a small fortune.

Most of Josie's friends made special dresses for their weddings, but their gowns were made to be worn again as their Sunday best. Josie's dress had been different. As a girl she'd seen a white wedding dress in the *Godey's Lady's Book*. A white gown as a symbol of purity went back to Queen Victoria, though some Americans credited the tradition to Eleanor Custis, George Washington's niece. In addition to a white dress, Eleanor had a worn a veil. The story went that her future husband first glimpsed her through a window covered with a lace curtain, and she wore the veil to capture that moment of "love at first sight."

Josie had planned to wear a veil, but she loved the dress most. Holding it against her body, she looked at the short sleeves that puffed like clouds. The front of the bodice was flat across her torso, while the back gathered to make a small train. A white sash was tied into a bow, and the tails would have fluttered as she walked.

The dress was as lovely as ever, but Josie could barely remember the girl who'd made it. She'd been so young...so naive. When Ty confessed concerns about money, she'd blithely told him not to worry. Now she knew that cattle died and mortgages came due.

"I was such a child," she said to the mirror. Ty hadn't been much older. They'd both been kids, but he'd understood money in a way she hadn't. As a boy he'd gone hungry. As a man he'd been determined to take care of her. He'd gone after the horses for a better reason than pride. He really had done it for them, though he'd also done it against her wishes.

A soft knock sounded on the door. "Josie?"

It was Mama. "Come in," Josie called.

The door opened with a creak. "Are you all right?"

"I'm fine," she said. "Just confused."

"About Ty?"

"Yes, but I'm starting to understand. Come in and sit on the bed. I want to show you something."

Mama walked five spaces to the mahogany bedstead and sat on the feather quilt. Josie approached her with the dress in hand, holding the skirt out to her. "Feel this."

Her mother ran her hands along the silk skirt, then touched a puffed sleeve and finally the row of pearl buttons. Her breath caught. "It's your wedding dress."

"I haven't looked at it in five years."

"Why now?"

"Because Ty asked me to forgive him." Josie sat next to her, hugging the dress. "I want to, but it's hard."

"I used to be angry about my eyes," Mama said in a quiet

tone. "And I was angry about your father dying. He'd been having pains in his chest for weeks. I wanted him to hire help, but he refused."

"I didn't know."

"And Nate…my only son." Her voice hitched. "Was I angry when he died? Oh, Josie. You can't begin to know. Every day I had to fight the bitterness."

"How?"

"I thanked God for the sunshine, for bread and butter, for everything good. Mostly I thanked him for *you*." Mama touched the dress. "May I pray for you?"

"Yes… Please."

"Father God, You know Josie's heart. You know the disappointment and the hurt. We pray You'll fill her heart with peace, and that she finds forgiveness for Ty. And Lord, we thank You for bringing Ty to us exactly when we needed him most. We ask You to bless him. Amen."

"Amen," Josie echoed.

As the words faded to a memory, Josie felt a sudden lightness in her body. She'd meant every word of her mother's prayer. She was *glad* Ty had come back. Tears of relief filled her eyes, and the hardness in her chest disappeared with a single deep breath. She felt like laughing—really laughing—for the first time in ages. She'd forgiven Ty at last. He deserved to hear it, but what did amends mean for the future? Forgiving him and trusting him were two different things. Falling in love again was altogether different, but she couldn't deny the thoughts crossing her mind. Nor could she deny another truth. Ty had hurt her first, but she'd hurt him back by not writing to him. Ty wasn't the only person who had amends to make. So did Josie.

"Mama?" She squeezed her mother's hand. "How would you like to help me bake some sugar cookies?"

"Aren't those Ty's favorite?"

"I believe so."

The older woman smiled. "I'd love to help."

Josie liked the idea of surprising Ty with a basket of good-ies. He'd said not to bother with supper, but she intended to bring him a basket with a meal and dessert. She'd also write him a note, one that would make them friends again. Feeling at peace, she hung the dress where she could see it. She didn't know what the future held, but for the first time in years, she wouldn't go to bed angry.

Chapter Six

Between last night and this morning, Ty had eaten eight cookies. He'd also read Josie's note a dozen times. *I forgive you. Can you forgive me?* She'd signed it with a "J," the way she used to sign notes when they were friends, and later when they were courting. He welcomed her forgiveness, but what did the cookies mean? Sugar cookies were the first things she'd baked for him, and they brought back memories. Good ones. The kind that made him want to admit to loving her, even though he had no way on earth to support her.

Standing at the pasture fence, he ate a golden cookie while Smoke nibbled grass. Josie's forgiveness tasted sweet indeed, but the second half of her note confused him. Why had she asked *him* for forgiveness? He saw no need.

"Good morning."

He turned and saw her walking up the path. When she worked in the barn, she wore coveralls. Today she had on a blue calico with tiny yellow flowers. She looked prettier than ever, while he had less than ever to give her. "Good morning." He indicated the half-eaten cookie. "I got your note. Thank you."

"I mean it." Not only did a smile appear on her pretty face, her cheeks blushed pink. "I forgive you, Ty. I hope you can forgive me."

"For what?"

"Not writing to you in jail. For going silent when we should have spoken. For holding a grudge." She looked into his eyes. "Last night I realized what I child I was. We were both so young. I still disagree with the decision you made, but I can understand it now."

"Like you said, we were kids back then."

"Yes." She stepped to his side and rested her hands on the fence. "I've put that day behind me, but what that means for the future—for us—I don't know."

He wanted to say it meant a fresh start. He wanted to take her in his arms and remind her of what they once had. But he didn't have that right. He was an ex-con with ten dollars to his name. He had a strong back and a way with horses but not much else. He certainly didn't have the means to support Josie and Mrs. Bright. Her forgiveness could mean only one thing. "So we're friends again," he said.

"Yes, but it feels strange."

It felt strange to Ty, too. When it came to Josie, he had old feelings and new ones, romantic thoughts and no money in his pocket. "A lot's happened in a short time."

She looked at him with a confusion that mirrored his own. "We both need to take things slow."

"That's smart," he agreed.

With her fingers laced on the top rail, she looked at Smoke. "I missed you as much as your horse did. Being friends again will be nice."

Ty agreed, but not fully. Friendship struck him as pale compared to the love they'd once shared. It was bread when he wanted cake. It would satisfy him, but he wanted more…he wanted to love her again. Looking out to the pasture, he had a sense of being back behind bars. Instead of steel, they were made of his inability to support her, but they were as real as the ones in prison. He wanted to break free, but he didn't see a way.

Josie still had her eyes on the horse. "The race is in two weeks. How's Smoke doing?"

"Good."

"So we have a shot at winning?"

He liked how *we* sounded, but he had to remember his place. "He's your horse and I'm a hired hand. It's your race, Josie. I'm just riding in it."

"I have two things to say." She sounded like the boss. "Smoke belongs to you. Nate bought him for a song because no one else could ride him. I'll sell him back to you for the money I owe you for paying Obie and Cordie."

The price was fair to both of them. "It's a deal."

"Good."

He hesitated, then said, "But I'm not splitting the prize money."

"Ty—"

"I don't want to argue." He turned to look at her and wished he hadn't. She seemed to look right through him. "It's not pride, Josie. I owe you."

"I thought forgiveness wiped the slate clean."

"It does."

"Then why won't you take your share?"

"You need it."

"So do you," she countered. "Don't you have plans for the future? With five-hundred dollars you could get a fresh start somewhere…even here in Rock Creek."

Had she just asked him to stick around for a while? Neither of them were ready to go past being friends, but they'd once been in love and they hadn't forgotten those feelings. If Ty owned Smoke, he could justify taking half the prize money. If he gave it to Josie after the race, he'd feel like part owner of the Bar JB. He could think about courting her. No, he corrected himself, he could do more than think about it…he could romance her like he'd done when they were kids.

"All right," he agreed. "We'll split it."

"So we're partners now."

"Business partners," he confirmed.

Smiling sweetly, she offered her hand. Ty took it, but they didn't shake on the deal and break apart. They stood with their fingers touching and their eyes asking questions of themselves and each other. Ty thought of the time he'd let her down, broke the grip and looked away.

"What's wrong?" she asked.

He frowned at the meadow. "I won't let you down, Josie."

"I know you'll do your best," she said evenly. "But winning isn't everything."

"It is to me."

"Not to me," she replied. "I'm trusting you to ride hard and fair. That's all anyone can ask. Winning and losing aren't in your hands."

"I'll show up," he assured her. "And I'll win, because it's the only way I can—" he stopped in midsentence.

"The only way you can what?"

"Never mind." He didn't dare mention courting her. Before he breathed a word of romance, he had to be able to support her. And to support her he had to win the Maze. "I better get to work," Ty said, though he could think of something he'd like a lot more…a picnic in a pretty meadow, a ride to nowhere with nothing to do but enjoy each other. Someday he hoped to have those opportunities.

They turned at the same time. When she tipped up her chin and smiled, he had to fight the urge to do what he'd wanted to do for five years. He wanted to kiss her. He wanted to marry her, and he wanted to pick up his dirty socks just like Reverend Hall had instructed. If he won the Maze, he'd do all of that and more. If he didn't…the thought didn't bear considering. He shifted his gaze from Josie's lips to her eyes. As if she knew what he'd been thinking—and she did—she gave him a sassy look. He gave her a daring one back, and she laughed. "I think I like being friends."

"Me, too."

They walked back to the barn without touching hands, trading friendly barbs as if they were kids again. But it wasn't enough…not nearly enough. For the future he wanted to give to Josie, Ty *had* to win that race. Until then, he'd be her friend, nothing more. No kissing. No hand holding. No sitting on the porch or walks in the moonlight. Friendship only and that was final.

Josie meant it when she told Ty they needed time to sort their feelings, but a week later she had her answers. She'd forgiven him and wanted to love him again. Not only did he work hard on the ranch, he'd been kind to her mother and gentle with her. Their evening suppers with Mama were the highlight of each day, with the three of them remembering Nate and Papa and the good times they'd had. Josie had expected some of her bitterness to linger, but it disappeared as completely as a caterpillar turned to a butterfly.

At night she looked at her wedding dress and imagined wearing it, but with her new hope came wariness. If Ty still had feelings for her, he was hiding them well. She also worried about his impulsive ways. He'd fired Obie without her permission, and she could see him always taking risks. The possibilities frightened her, but she could also imagine Ty kissing her, something that hadn't happened. He hadn't even come close and she didn't know what to think. That's why she was sitting in the kitchen at almost midnight with a cup of lukewarm tea. Ty had left the house two hours ago, and she hadn't shaken her disappointment in yet another polite goodbye, or her concern that he'd somehow let her down.

"Josie?" Mama appeared in the doorway "You're up late."

"I can't sleep."

Mama sat with a soft plop. "Because of Ty?"

"Always!" She chewed her lip in frustration. "The past week

has been good. I really have forgiven him, but I'm just not sure I can trust him again."

"I understand," Mama agreed. "Forgiving someone who's hurt you doesn't mean you let it happen again. It means you don't hold it against them. You start over and make new choices."

"Even that's confusing," Josie admitted. "I thought maybe we would sit on the porch like we used to, but he leaves the minute you go to bed."

"I've seen how polite he's been."

"*Too* polite."

Mama thought for a minute. "He's always had a lot of pride. Maybe he's bothered to be working for you."

"I don't think of him as a hired hand. He's more like family."

"A brother?"

Josie's cheeks flushed. "No, not at all."

"Does Ty know that?"

"I think so, but it's complicated. He's always had an impulsive streak. It's what got him into trouble, and it still worries me." She sighed. "Sometimes I think he cares about me, but he treats me like…like Nate."

Mama's voice turned conspiratorial. "Would you like some advice from an old lady?"

"You're not *that* old."

"I'm old enough," Mama replied. "Here's what you do. Invite Ty to take a walk in the moonlight. If he doesn't kiss you, then you kiss him."

"Mama!"

"I may be old, but I remember what it's like to care about a man. Men are strong and generous creatures. They'll fight and die for us, but they don't always remember that tenderness counts as much as putting a roof over our heads. I suspect that's particularly true of Ty. As for trusting him, why not take things one step at a time? Ty's turned into a man with a strong faith. If you have feelings for each other, the trust will come."

Josie curled her fingers around the teacup. "Do you really think so?"

"I do." Mama stood and smiled down at her. "Stay brave and things will work out."

"I hope so."

Mama ambled back to bed, and Josie finished her tea. By the time she took the last swallow, she'd decided that her mother had a good idea. Ty needed to know how she felt, and tomorrow night she'd show him.

Thinking of Josie as just a friend was harder than Ty ever dreamed. It had been easier to cope with her bitterness than with cookies and good times. Supper tonight had been pure pleasure and so had doing the dishes together. He washed. She dried. But they didn't tease like they used to. He dumped the water in the garden, set down the tub and was headed back to kitchen when Josie came outside.

"Let's take a walk," she said.

"Where to?"

"The stream."

The place where they'd smooched as kids...Ty shook his head. "It's late—"

"It's not *that* late." Josie took his hand and pulled him down the path. "Come with me, Ty. I'd like to talk a bit."

"All right." As long as they just talked, he'd be fine. Never mind his true feelings for her...until he won the race, he had to keep three feet away from her at all times. That meant letting go of her hand, but he didn't have the will to do it. Her palm felt warm against his. It also felt right, so he walked with her to the stream that ran a quarter-mile behind the house. As they neared the water, Ty heard crickets and water rippling over rocks. "It's pretty," he said to Josie. Suddenly aware of her, he broke his grip and hooked his thumbs in his back pockets. "What did you want to talk about?"

She crossed her arms at her waist, dropped them to her sides, then crossed them again. She did that when she was worried about something. Ty's brow furrowed. "What's wrong?

"Nothing."

"I know you, Josie. There's something wrong when you do that arm thing."

He wanted to take her hand again…to hold her and offer a strong shoulder. He settled for turning in her direction. In the same breath, she turned to him. Her hand went to his jaw, then his cheek. Common sense told him to step back. Something stronger made him step into her embrace.

Josie leaned closer, her lips slightly parted in invitation. She looked into his eyes, leaned closer still so that her mouth was an inch from his. By pure strength of will, he resisted the urge to kiss her. Her eyes clouded with indecision, then she turned bold and said, "Are you going to kiss me or not?"

"I might," he said with his old arrogance.

"Well, I just *might* let you."

He liked this kind of sass. "Oh, yeah?"

"Yeah…"

He kissed her then. It was sweet and tender, everything they'd once had and yet so much more. They'd both gotten burned, but the scars made tonight's caress all the sweeter. Ty kissed her a long time…too long but he didn't care.

Josie broke the kiss but stayed in his arms. "Why didn't you do that sooner?"

He suddenly felt like a thief. "I don't have the right, not until I win the Maze and have something to offer."

"You have something now," she murmured. "You have yourself."

"It's not enough." Or was it? He thought of leaving her to chase the Scudders, but this time there was more on the line.

She'd lose her home if he didn't win, and he couldn't give her anything to replace it, nothing at all.

Moonlight glowed on her determined face. "I don't care if you win the Maze or not. I just need to trust you. If you show up for the race, that's enough."

"That sounds like a test."

"Maybe it is."

Ty didn't like tests, but he understood her concern. "I'll be there, Josie girl. But you're wrong about showing up being enough. If I lose the race, you lose the ranch. What then? I could work for wages, but where would we live? The Dyer place with trail trash and fleas? We'd always be poor."

"I wouldn't mind."

"It's easy to say, harder to do."

She bit her lip, then lifted her chin. "There's more to life than working. If you lose the Maze, I say we sell everything and go to Denver. We'll take Mama. I could sell my wedding dress—"

"No."

"Why not?"

"Because I want to see you in it."

She hadn't exactly proposed with that mention of Denver. Neither had he proposed with the mention of seeing her in the dress, but the question hung between them. "Let's not talk about it," Ty said. "I'm going to win that race, so this is foolishness."

"I hope so," Josie answered. "Because I love you."

"Ah, Josie—"

"You don't have to say the words back." She touched his cheek. "But think about it. I don't need you to win, Ty. I just need you."

He needed her, too. But he also needed to be a man. That meant providing for her. He couldn't tell Josie that he loved her, but he had said the words in the past. She knew how he felt, but she wanted the commitment he couldn't give. Not yet.

She turned abruptly and stared at the stars. Ty did the same until his neck hurt. Finally he said, "What are you thinking?"

"I'm thinking about kissing you again."

He cocked a brow. "Oh, yeah?"

"Yeah."

They turned at the same time, looking at each other with their eyes alive with love, thinking and hoping and dreaming. Finally Josie said, "I'm done thinking." Ty kissed her just like before…just like he'd do again when he won the Maze.

Chapter Seven

The day before the race, Ty rode Smoke to Rock Creek with Josie's words ringing in his ears. They'd had breakfast together, and she'd made her position clear. *I mean it, Ty. The only thing that matters is that you keep your word to me, and that means running in the race. It doesn't mean winning.*

Ty appreciated her sacrifice, but he couldn't stand the notion of proposing marriage with just ten dollars to his name. After today, when he bought food and paid for a hotel room, he'd have even less. He wanted Smoke to be rested for the race, so he arrived midday at the livery. As he swung out of the saddle, Wayne greeted him with a handshake. "Smoke's looking strong."

"I've worked him hard," Ty acknowledged.

Wayne's brow furrowed. "You're going to have some competition, that's for sure."

"Anyone new enter the race?"

"No, but Obie Jones is riding for Susan Lee Hawkins. Do you remember her?"

"Yeah." But he wished he didn't. Susan Lee Hawkins was Brant Scudder's great-aunt. She sat in the front row during the trial, clearly wishing Ty dead.

"There's talk in town that Obie told her that you were running in the race. She's a sour thing, if you ask me. Anyhow, she's supplying Obie with a horse for the Maze. If I had to guess, I'd say Obie'll be riding a sorrel with some Arabian blood."

"Arabians are fast." They also had stamina.

Wayne gave Smoke another look. "He's in good shape, Ty. Older, of course. But more sure-footed than the sorrel."

Ty turned to Smoke. "What do you say, fella? Are you going to let Obie beat us?"

Smoke nosed Ty's chest. He probably just wanted a carrot, but Ty imagined the horse was telling him not to worry. Even so, he had a bad feeling about Obie. Ty wouldn't put anything past him—not lying, cheating or even stealing. He turned to Wayne. "Mind if I bed down in your barn?"

Wayne shrugged. "Suit yourself, but you're welcome at my place."

Ty had been hoping for an invitation, but now he couldn't accept. Leaving his horse alone was out of the question. "Thanks, Wayne. But I want to keep an eye on Smoke."

"I understand." Wayne led the way into the barn. The back stalls were full of wagon parts, so Ty put Smoke in one in the middle of the barn. Wayne indicated the stall across the aisle from Smoke. "There's a cot in the back. You can haul it up here if you want."

"I'll do that." Ty's belly growled. He needed to eat. "Are you going to be around for a while? I've got a few things to do."

"Sure," Wayne answered. "Take your time."

Ty finished tending to Smoke, then he went to the saloon, not to drink but to listen to the talk about the race. He ordered coffee and kept to himself as he listened to men placing wagers. He'd didn't recognize all the names, but those he *did* know were the finest riders around. So were the horses. They were younger than Smoke with fine bloodlines. Aside from Obie, the biggest challenger would be Grant Harper on one of his Arabians. Ty heard his own name two times, but the few men who remembered him didn't take Smoke seriously. Good, he thought. He'd enjoy surprising them.

He left the saloon as quietly as he'd come in, bought a box supper from a restaurant and went back to the livery. At dusk Wayne went home. leaving Ty with a long night ahead of him. He bedded down near Smoke, but he couldn't sleep. Instead he thought about Josie and the life he wanted to give her. He recalled the years he spent behind bars and nights like this one where sleep didn't come. When it finally *did* come, it arrived just before dawn and hit hard.

That's what happened now… After hours of tossing, he fell into an exhausted slumber, one filled with dreams of the race, then pictures of Josie in a cloud of a dress. In his dream he heard a piano playing a wedding march, then the creak of a door and finally a snort and the muted clop of hooves. It didn't make sense, not even in a dream.

Ty shot to his feet just in time to see someone leading Smoke out the barn door. "Hey!"

The thief rammed the door shut behind him. Ty charged after him barefoot, wishing he'd slept in his boots and glad he'd worn his trousers over his long johns. As he swung the door open, he saw Obie mount a waiting horse with Smoke tied behind him. Ty charged after him. He got a grip on Obie's leg, but not before Obie raised a knife. The blade flashed silver in the moonlight, then sliced into Ty's biceps. As he stumbled back, Obie kicked his horse into a run and took off with Smoke.

Ty fell to his knees. With the smell of blood filling his nose, he ripped the wet sleeve off his arm and looked at the gash. The cut was six inches long and deep enough to scare him. He used the sleeve to wrap it, then stared into the empty night. Without Smoke, he didn't have a chance at winning the race. But if he went after Obie, he risked doing the one thing that would hurt Josie. He might miss the race altogether, when all she asked was that he show up. Behind him he had a barn full of horses. He could saddle one and go after Obie, or he could do what Josie would want him to do. He could go to the law.

He went into the barn and lit a lantern. As the light flared, he breathed a prayer and he knew what he had to do. He'd go to the law, but he'd also run in the race. Wayne had a dozen horses on hand, and Ty figured he could borrow the fastest one. He wouldn't be riding Smoke and he'd be a long shot to win, but he wouldn't let Josie down. As for marrying her, he needed more than ten dollars in his pocket before he could ask the question, but she'd know she could trust him.

He put on his boots but didn't waste a shirt on his bloody arm. With the sky turning pink, he hurried three blocks to the sheriff's office. With all the activity in town, he figured a deputy would be on duty. When he pushed through the door, he saw Deputy Seth Jenkins, a man who Ty remembered as fair and having no ties to the Scudders.

Deputy Jenkins saw Ty's arm and lumbered to his feet. "I take it there's a bar fight I need to handle."

"No, sir. Obie Jones just stole my horse."

"That fool." Jenkins went to the gun cabinet and took out a rifle. "He's been flapping his jaw for three days now. Which way did he go?"

"West. Maybe to the Hawkins place." Ty told Jenkins everything he knew about Obie, including the fight at the Bar JB. "You probably remember about me and Brant Scudder."

"I sure do." Seth's jaw hardened. "The Scudders were thieves, plain and simple. They stole from my brother about a month after you got sent to Laramie. You got a bad rap, Donner."

For the first time in five years, Ty felt respected by another man. "Thanks."

"What's your horse look like?"

"A gray mustang stallion."

"I'd invite you to come along, but that arm needs attention.

Go see Doc. I'll get my partner and go after Obie. Where can I find you?"

"The livery."

Seth left and Ty went to the doctor's office. In spite of the early hour, a light was burning in the window. With all the commotion in town, Doc Rayburn had doubtlessly been busy. He greeted Ty with his customary scowl, then worked with calm efficiency as he stitched muscle to muscle, skin to skin.

Ty felt every prick of the needle, but his mind was on Josie and the race. The competition started at twelve noon. The deputies had less than five hours to catch Obie and come back with Smoke, but even if they succeeded, what kind of shape would his horse be in? Exhausted to be sure. By the time Doc Rayburn finished stitching his arm, Ty had lost all hope of winning the Maze and having the money to save the Bar JB. He thought of Josie's interest in going to Denver and winced. He didn't belong in a city. After prison he longed for open land and sky, but he longed for Josie, too.

It was a conundrum to be sure, one he couldn't solve today…unless he could win the race on a different horse.

Doc finished stitching and cut the black thread. Ty paid him and headed for the livery.

Wayne was up and feeding his stock. At the sight of Ty, his brow furrowed. "I thought you'd gone for a ride. Where's Smoke?"

Ty told him the story. "I've got to win that race. I'll give you a quarter of the prize if you'll loan me your best horse."

"They're all saddle horses," Wayne replied. "They don't like to run. You don't stand a chance without Smoke."

"Mind if I look for myself?"

"Go ahead."

Ty went from stall to stall. The selection was as bad as Wayne had said. With his arm hurting, he stared at Smoke's empty stall. To win the race, he needed Smoke. Would Josie understand if he changed his mind and caught up with the deputies? Maybe. Maybe not. He'd be with the law, but what would happen if a fight broke out? He'd be at a serious disadvantage. And what if someone got hurt, even killed, and Ty was in the middle? He couldn't stand the thought of a trial, or God spare him, even returning to prison.

"I give up," he said out loud. Whether he was talking to God or himself, he didn't know. There was still a small chance that Seth would show up with Smoke, but it seemed wise to prepare for the worst. He had promised Josie he'd ride in the race and he would. He'd pick one of Wayne's horses and do his best. He'd prove himself worthy of her trust, but they wouldn't be getting married anytime soon.

Ty inspected Wayne's horses a second time. A big gelding impressed him but not much. A mustang mare looked ornery enough to run hard, but she was too small for real speed. He chose the gelding, but he had no hope of winning, no hope of marrying Josie for a long time to come.

Josie and her mother arrived in Rock Creek about an hour before the start of the race. It promised to be a tiring day for Mama, so Josie took a small room at the hotel in spite of the inflated prices. Her mother would need a place to rest, and Josie needed a place to keep her wedding gown. Determined to be ready for anything, she had brought it with her. If Ty won the race and proposed, she saw no reason to wait to take vows. If Reverend Hall could perform the ceremony, she'd wear the dress today.

If Ty lost, Josie intended to propose to him. If he turned her down, she'd suggest the three of them go to Denver for a fresh start. Ty would fight the idea of accompanying them, but Josie would fight harder. Kissing him at the creek had been her final undoing. She loved him, and he'd assured her a hundred times that *nothing* would stop him from competing in today's race. She believed him, though she had to admit to a case of nerves. This morning when she'd folded the dress and put it in a satchel, her old bitterness had tried to come back.

She didn't want to see Ty at the livery stable before the race, so she paid extra for the hotel to see to the mule and buggy. She and Mama settled into the room, then left for the fairgrounds with Mama holding her arm. Together they navigated the crowded street to the meadow dotted with booths for games and contests. Josie described the people she saw, the dresses the women were wearing, how the younger children were playing with whirlybirds and the older boys were competing in mumblety-peg. The air rippled with excitement, much of it related to the start of the Maze. A crowd had already gathered at the starting line, but they found a spot that gave Josie a view of the riders as they took their places.

She searched for Ty and Smoke, but she didn't see them anywhere. The spring day was bright and clear, a perfect day for a race. As she looked for Ty, she saw the competition and knew Smoke would have to run his best to win.

"Have you found Ty?" Mama asked.

"Not yet."

"Shouldn't he be here?" The older woman had a keen sense of time. "It must be close to noon, and it's not like him to be late for anything."

Josie looked at the watch pinned to her dress. "The race starts in five minutes."

She couldn't walk fast with her mother, but she wanted to run to the starting line and ask if anyone had seen a man on a gray mustang. She settled for peering down the path from Wayne's stable. A minute ticked by, then another. She didn't see Ty anywhere.

"Have you spotted him?" her mother asked again.

"He's not here."

The town mayor had the honor of shooting the gun that would start the race. Josie saw him on a platform. She counted nine horses in line, all of them sleek and ready to run. Smoke should have been Horse No. 10.

The mayor shouted to the crowd. "Ladies and Gentlemen! Get ready for the May Day Maze!"

Frantic, Josie searched the meadow for Ty and Smoke. There wasn't a gray horse in sight, nor did she spot Ty even on foot. Something had happened…something bad. She saw Mr. Angle from the emporium and approached him. "Have you seen Ty Donner? He's supposed to be riding today."

"Did you say Donner?"

"Yes."

"Saw him last night in the saloon, Miss Bright. I heard talk he and Obie Jones got in a tangle."

"A *fight?*"

"I guess. The Doc's missus told my missus he was up all night stitching up rowdies. You know how it is around Founders' Day. Men drinking and brawling. It's appalling."

Josie didn't know what to think. Had Ty spent the evening at the saloon? Had he decided to get even with Obie? No matter what Obie said or did, Ty should have walked away. He knew what today meant to her…what it meant to them.

The mayor raised one arm to the sky. "Gentlemen! On your mark!"

The riders started straight ahead, so did the horses.

"Get set!"

Everyone leaned forward.

"Go!"

And so the race began… Without Ty and Smoke. Josie stared in disbelief. What had kept him away? What could have been more important than keeping his word? Had he fought with Obie for a good reason? Another thought came and it haunted her. Mr. Angle's comments suggested Ty had seen Dr. Rayburn. How badly was he hurt? Fear and anger mixed into a bitter brew of confusion. Ty had let her down. Maybe he had a good reason… Maybe he didn't.

Her mother squeezed her arm. "Give him a chance."

"I don't know, Mama."

"He could have a very good explanation."

"Or he could have gotten mad and punched Obie. It's just like before." She thought of the dress. She wouldn't be wearing it today, after all. "He promised to be here, and he's not."

She wanted to find him and give him a piece of her mind, but first she had to take her mother to the hotel. Aching inside, she tucked Mama's hand against her elbow. "I'll take you to the hotel, then I'm going to find Ty."

They were nearly across the meadow when shouts erupted near the starting line. Josie turned to the noise and saw a silver horse gallop across the starting line, ridden by a man she'd know anywhere. She didn't know why Ty arrived late, but it didn't matter. He'd kept his word.

"Mama!" she cried. "It's Ty, and he's riding Smoke."

Josie wanted to rejoice, but Ty was so far behind that she didn't see how he could win. She thought of his insistence that he win the race before proposing marriage. What were the chances Smoke could catch up? Not very good, she decided. And why had Ty been late in the first place? Josie didn't know what had gone wrong, but she saw an obvious solution to all their problems. She turned to her mother. "I need to speak with Reverend Hall."

"Why?"

"I'm going to ask Ty to marry me."

Mama smiled. "That's a fine idea."

"Whether he wins the race or loses, we can get married today."

"Ty feels strongly about providing for you. What if he says no?"

"I'll have to change his mind," Josie replied. "Come on, Mama. I need to hurry."

"Don't you want to see the end of the race?"

"I've already won," Josie said with a smile. She had arrangements to make, so she walked with Mama to the booth sponsored by the Rock Creek Church. She saw Reverend Hall and breathed a sigh of relief.

"Reverend!" she called.

"Hello, Josie." He took her hand in both of his. "It's good to see you."

"I need a favor." She spoke hurriedly, because she had to finish before the race ended. For her plan to work, she had to take Ty by surprise. "Could you meet with Ty and me at four o'clock?"

"Of course." When she told him her plan, he smiled. "You've forgiven him, then."

"I have, but he's worried about providing for us."

The reverend nodded. "I respect a man's need to provide, but bounty comes from the Lord. He'll make a way if you honor Him."

"I believe that." Josie had made her peace with God. Now she had to hope Ty would put love before pride and marry her.

She said goodbye to Reverend Hall, then walked with her mother to the hotel. On the way they passed the sheriff's office, where she saw two deputies leading a horse with Obie on its back, his hands tied and a gag in his mouth. Josie put the pieces together. Obie had stolen Smoke. Instead of chasing after him as he'd done with the Scudders, Ty had apparently gone to the law. The timing told the rest of the story. They'd come back with Smoke but not soon enough for Ty to win the Maze.

More than ever, Josie believed in her plan for this afternoon. At the hotel she borrowed paper and a pen and wrote a note asking Ty to meet her at the church at four o'clock. She gave a delivery boy two bits to hand it directly to Ty.

As the boy ran off, Josie led her mother to their room on the third floor. Even if Ty knocked, she wouldn't answer the door. As for the race, she didn't care who won. Like the reverend said, God would provide. As for Ty Donner, Josie hoped her love would be prize enough to convince him to become her husband.

Chapter Eight

Ten minutes before the start of the May Day Maze, Ty was mounted on Wayne's best horse and fifty feet from the starting line.

"Donner! Get back here!"

He turned the big gelding and saw Wayne running after him. "What is it?"

"Seth's back and he's got Smoke."

Ty wheeled the gelding around and galloped to where Wayne was puffing like a locomotive from his run. "How's he look?" Ty called to him.

"Good."

"Is he spent?"

"He's not as bad off as I am right now!" The poor man could hardly breathe.

Ty made a split-second decision. He'd rather ride Smoke than any horse in the world. He galloped to the livery, pulled up the gelding short and slid off. Never mind his aching arm. He had to get Smoke saddled even if he pulled every stitch. He started to take his saddle off the gelding, but Seth stopped him. "I'll do that."

Ty let him. If he popped the stitches, he'd bleed all over the place. But he could handle the bridle. While he worked, he noticed a second deputy waiting with Obie, who was tied up and gagged. The gag gave Ty particular satisfaction, but he didn't waste time thinking about it.

The instant Seth finished, Ty climbed on Smoke and headed back to the starting line. He had maybe three minutes before the race started, but the street was congested with people, and the meadow was even worse. He was a quarter-mile away and trapped in a crowd when he heard the gun go off. He called to people to clear the way, but it didn't do any good. Children were everywhere.

Finally the path cleared and Smoke had room to maneuver. The race was ten miles long and would take about two hours because of canyons and switchbacks. As much as Ty wanted to ride hard and catch up, it would be foolish. He crossed the starting line at an easy gallop, waving to the officials to confirm he'd arrived.

And so began the race… The first half couldn't have been more solitary. He and Smoke were in the middle of nowhere. The rough terrain suited Ty's mood, and he hoped it would give the rangy stallion some advantage.

They passed Horse No. 1 at the halfway mark. The roan had picked up a stone, and the rider was hunched over and taking it out. Ty and Smoke rode past them with Ty waving to give his respect. Horses No. 2 and 3 came into view at the top of hill. Smoke passed them with ease, and Ty started to hope. He'd ridden the route with Smoke a dozen times. He knew every turn, every hill. As he came upon a mild slope, he looked down and saw Horses No. 4, 5 and 6 in a cluster. Smoke, a competitor, broke to the outside of the trail and passed them.

Six down.

Three to go.

Smoke stopped at a shallow stream and drank. Ty climbed down for a minute and did the same. The hardest part of the race lay ahead of them. As much as he wanted to win, he wouldn't push Smoke to the point of ruin. When the horse finished sucking in water—a sound that always made Ty smile—

he climbed back on and they took off. A mile later, Ty saw Horse No. 7 and felt sick. The animal stood heaving at the side of the trail with blood in his nose. His fool of a rider looked angry, when he should have been ashamed of abusing his horse.

They had a mile to go and two horses to pass. Smoke took an uphill slope like a freight train. When they reached the crest, Horses No. 8 and 9 came into view. No. 8 was a feisty mare he'd heard about in the saloon. Horse No. 9 was Grant Harper's Arabian. Ty wanted to win more than he wanted anything, but he loved his horse. Smoke would run until his heart burst, a thought Ty couldn't abide.

"It's your choice, boy," he murmured to Smoke. "You can quit if you want to."

Smoke gathered his strength and charged into a full run. The mare put up a fight, but Smoke blew by her. No. 9 now had the lead. Smoke caught him in ten strides. Neck and neck, the animals poured on the speed, but especially Smoke who crossed the finish line by half a length.

Ty pumped his fist in the air and gave a victory yell. As Smoke slowed, Ty imagined Josie seeing the victory. He turned Smoke with the hope of seeing her, but she was nowhere in sight. Grant Harper rode up next to him.

"Congratulations, Donner!" said the Englishman. "That's quite a horse. Any interest in selling him?"

"Not a chance."

"How about breeding him to one of my mares?"

"Sure." Ty smiled. "For a price."

"Of course." The man offered his hand and they shook. "I'm Grant Harper. Where can I find you?"

"The Bright place."

Grant tipped his hat. "I'll be in touch."

Ty could hardly believe his good fortune. Not only had he won the race, Smoke had earned a reputation that would allow Ty to build up a new herd of horses. They'd have an income apart from raising cattle, but it didn't matter. With the win, he and Josie had become full partners. But where was she? He wanted her at his side when they collected the prize money. Still on Smoke, Ty spotted Wayne by the judge's booth and shouted to him. "Have you seen Josie?"

"I sure haven't."

Surely she hadn't missed the finish of the race? Ty peered at every face in the crowd, but he didn't see Josie anywhere.

Wayne called back to him. "Get over here, Ty. It's time to award the prize."

Ty rode to the judging stand, climbed off Smoke and took his place as the winner. Instead of listening to the mayor's long-winded speech, he considered Josie's absence. Had she seen the beginning of the race and assumed he'd failed her? Had she gone home? The situation rankled him. He'd kept his promise, yet she'd run off at the first sign of disappointment. He was a bit annoyed—no, he was downright mad—that she didn't trust him enough to stick around. As soon as he collected the prize money, he'd take care of Smoke then head to the Bright ranch on one of Wayne's horses.

The prize ceremony seemed to take forever, but finally Lester Proffitt handed Ty a bank draft for a thousand dollars. Ty shook his hand but glared at him. "Some of this is going back to you for the Bright's mortgage."

"That's fine by me," Proffitt replied.

Ty tucked the check in his shirt pocket, acknowledged the cheers from the crowd, then left the stage and took Smoke by the reins. Together they made a beeline for the livery. People swarmed around him, offering congratulations and wanting to see his horse up close. If Josie had been at this side, he'd have enjoyed every minute. Instead he had to grit his teeth as he accepted congratulations that couldn't replace sharing the moment with the woman he loved. The livery barn came into view. To the side he saw a buggy he recognized. Someone had put up the mule, so where was Josie? He scanned the yard, but he didn't see her anywhere.

An adolescent boy approached from the street. "Are you Mr. Donner?"

"I am."

"Here." The kid handed him a note. "Miss Bright said to read it right away."

Ty unfolded it and read words that raised more questions than they answered. *Come to the church at four o'clock.*

Why meet in the place where he'd left her waiting all those years ago? Ty had kept his word, but did Josie know it? Wouldn't she have been eager to celebrate together? Why a curt note instead of a kiss? Maybe she'd had second thoughts just because love sometimes hurt.

Ty looked at the boy. "When did she give you this?"

"About ten minutes after the race started."

So she might not know what had happened. "Where is she now?"

"At the hotel."

Ty gave the boy a quarter for his trouble, then led Smoke into the barn for a rubdown. While tending to the horse, he thought about Josie. Did she know he'd run in the race like he had promised? Or did she think he'd let her down? He considered going to the hotel and having it out with her right now. On the other hand, she'd be at the church at four o'clock, and a church was a perfect place to make a promise…a new one he'd never break. With that thought in mind, Ty made plans of his own.

The last time Josie had been this nervous, she'd been seventeen-years-old. She'd been wearing the dress she had on now, and she'd been standing in the same little room to the right of Reverend Hall's office. She'd been counting the minutes until her father walked her down the aisle. Her sisters had been with her, and her mother had been able to see her oldest daughter in her wedding gown. Her brother had been dressed up in a suit, and she'd teased him about it.

Today she had only her mother. Mama could hardly see now, but in the hotel room she'd buttoned the wedding gown by feel. Josie missed her sisters and especially her father and brother, but some of the changes were good. Her love for Ty had deepened. Tested by disappointment and made stronger by forgiveness, that love had a new strength.

No matter how the Maze ended, she hoped Ty felt the same way. Back at the hotel she'd asked the clerk if he knew who won but he didn't know. With the hotel and church on the opposite side of town from the finish line, she hadn't heard the result. When she asked Reverend Hall at the church, he'd been enigmatic. *Does it matter?* Not to Josie, though she doubted Ty would agree.

Someone knocked on the door to the little room. "Josie?" The voice belonged to Mrs. Hall. "Ty's coming down the path."

Josie hugged Mama. "Say a prayer."

"I will."

Leaving Mrs. Hall to guide Mama, Josie went to the foyer and peered out the window. Her eyes went straight to Ty, who looked nothing like a man who'd just lost the biggest race of his life. She expected to see him in dungarees and a cotton shirt, the clothing he'd been wearing when they'd met a month ago in this very place, but somehow he'd purchased a suit. It was black and formal and he had on a shirt as white as a cloud. His hair was clean and combed, but it still curled over his collar the way she loved.

Even more startling than Ty's appearance was the crowd following him. She turned to look for Reverend Hall, who was coming out of the main church.

"Why is everyone following Ty?" she asked.

"He's famous," the man said with a smile. "He won the Maze in a finish that will go down in history."

Josie pressed her hands to her cheeks in shock. "He *won?*"

"By half a length."

With tears of joy, Josie realized what Ty had in mind. He planned to propose, but she'd spent the past hour practicing what she wanted to say, and she still wanted to say it. She opened the door and went to the steps, standing on the top one as Ty approached. At the sight of her waiting for him, his eyes caught fire. He was seeing her gown for the first time, and it revealed that she, too, had come to the church with a plan. He stopped at the bottom of the three steps. Josie put her hands on her hips in the sassiest pose she could manage. In a loud voice, she said, "Ty Donner, will you marry me?"

"I might."

"You *might?*" She flashed to their conversation about kissing. She knew where this was going and wanted to enjoy every minute. She marched down the steps and lifted her chin. "Just what does *might* mean?"

"I'm thinking about it."

He took a step closer.

So did she. "You better think fast, because you don't get to kiss the bride until we take vows."

His eyes twinkled. "Is that a fact?"

"Yes, it is."

"Then I better ask the question." There was no sass in Ty's voice, only love. With his eyes bright, he dropped to one knee and took her hand. "I love you, Josie. I pledge my life and my heart to you, today and forever. Will you marry me?"

"I will."

The crowd burst into applause. Men whistled and women cheered. Ty pushed to his feet. She wanted to step into his arms then and there, but he offered his elbow to lead her into the church. Mrs. Hall escorted Mama, and the reverend stood at the door, inviting the folks to come inside.

Arm in arm, Ty and Josie walked to the front of the church. There they faced each other and held hands. Mrs. Hall settled Mama in the front pew, then went to the piano and played a joyful hymn as people filed in. Word must have spread, because Josie saw dozens of people she'd known most of her life. Many of them had been at the first wedding. It was almost as if there had been no gap at all.

With everyone finally seated, Reverend Hall took his place at the front of the church. "Ladies and gentlemen, we are gathered here today to witness the marriage of Tyler Jacob Donner and Josephine Margaret Bright. As most of you know, this day has been a long time coming. The delay brings to mind Proverbs 13:12. 'Hope deferred maketh the heart sick: but when the desire cometh, it is a tree of life.' Today Ty and Josie are planting their own tree of life. It's a tree that will grow into a common future, a tree that will sustain their family, young and old alike, for generations to come. It's a tree that will bear the finest of fruit because that fruit will be fed by love. Their love is strong now. It's been tested by heartache and strengthened by forgiveness. They know what it means to respect each other."

Ty's fingers tightened over Josie's. She stole a look at this profile and felt a rush of tears. Five years ago the reverend's words wouldn't have made sense. Today she understood every one.

The reverend focused on Ty. "Today's wedding is about more than nice clothes and rings. It's about loving each other more than you love yourselves."

"Yes, sir," Ty answered.

The man looked at Josie next. "Today is about forgiving each other when the mistakes seem unforgivable."

Josie nodded in full agreement.

The reverend scanned the entire church. "Unless anyone has an objection, we'll get to the vows."

No one moved. No one breathed. This wedding would *not* be interrupted. Ty faced Josie and gripped her hand. Satisfied, Reverend Hall began in a solemn tone. "Do you, Ty Donner, take Josie Bright to be your wedded wife. To have and to hold, from this day forward, for better, for worse, for richer, for poorer, in sickness or in health, to love and to cherish until death do you part?"

"I do."

The reverend repeated the vows for Josie. She heard every word, every nuance and promise. Tears slid down her cheeks, but they were the finest kind. When the reverend asked the last question, Josie said "I do" in her strongest voice.

Reverend Hall turned to Ty. "Do you have a ring, son?"

"Yes, sir." Ty took a gold band from his pocket. Shiny and new, she figured he'd bought it with the prize money. He held her fingertips, watching her face as the reverend led them in the final vows.

"Ty, repeat after me. 'With this ring, I thee wed.'"

Ty smiled and said, "With this ring, I thee wed…and if Reverend Hall doesn't mind, I'd like to say that there's no *might* about it. I love you, Josie." He slipped the ring onto her finger, over her knuckles to the crook at the top of her palm.

"I love you, too," she murmured.

Reverend Hall's lips curved up. "I now pronounce you man and wife. Ty, you may kiss your bride."

Ty faced Josie and leaned close. Josie lifted her face and leaned into him. Their lips came closer, closer still and then Ty stopped and grinned. "Are you going to kiss me or not?"

"You bet I am." A bride at last, wearing the dress of her dreams, Josie kissed her husband with all the joy in her heart. Forgiveness tasted sweet indeed.

* * * * *

Dear Reader,

Do you have a favorite wedding memory? Either from your own wedding or from the wedding of a son or daughter, a sibling, maybe a friend? I do. It goes back to the day after my husband and I decided to get married. Neither of us wanted a big wedding for all sorts of reasons. We liked the idea of eloping, actually. We'd been Christians for just a few weeks, and eloping struck us as romantic in a Bruce Springsteen "Born to Run" kind of way. When I told my dad, I thought he'd be pleased. After all he wouldn't have to pay for a wedding on top of paying for my college education.

When I told him Mike and I planned to elope, he looked a little dismayed, then calmly said, "I think your mother might want to see you get married."

I talked to my mom, only to discover that she thought eloping was a fantastic idea. No fuss. No muss. No losing twenty pounds and shopping for a Mother of the Bride dress. As you've probably figured out, it was my dad who wanted to see us take those sacred vows.

As things worked out, we had a very small wedding. It was just Mike and me, our parents, his youngest sister and my brother. We gathered in my parents' living room on a Tuesday morning at nine o'clock. A minister read the traditional vows, we exchanged rings and took off for a weeklong honeymoon in San Felipe, a fishing village in Baja, California. It was the start of a grand adventure that's lasted thirty-two years and is going strong, and it's why I write romance. I really do believe in Happily Ever After.

All the best,
Victoria Bylin

Questions for Discussion

1. Josie is holding a grudge against Ty. Is she at all justified in her resentment? How does the resentment affect her emotionally and spiritually?

2. How did prison change Ty? In what ways did he stay the same? What might have happened to Ty if he hadn't been convicted of shooting Brant Scudder?

3. Josie doesn't want to be bitter, but she can't change how she feels. If you were her best friend, what advice would you give her?

4. The precious wedding dress has been hidden in Josie's wardrobe for five years. What kept her from looking at it? What stopped her from giving it away or selling it? What does keeping the dress say about her bitterness?

5. On the way to church, Ty decides it's time to break through Josie's cold exterior. What do you think of his method? Did it work?

6. Ty feels strongly about being able to support Josie financially before admitting he loves her. Do you respect his choice? Was he being responsible or prideful?

7. Why are weddings important? What do they signify to both individuals and society as a whole?

8. All weddings have a few things in common. Do you have a favorite moment? Is it when the groom sees his bride?

Or maybe it's the kiss or when the bride and groom speak their vows. What are some of your best or funniest wedding memories?

LAST MINUTE BRIDE

Janet Dean

To Shirley Jump and Missy Tippens,
who generously gave their time
and savvy suggestions to improve my story.
To the Seekers, prayer partners, forever friends,
my daily dose of laughter. To Dale, my groom,
our wedding was the best day of my life. I love you.

My grace is sufficient for thee:
for strength is made perfect in weakness.
—*2 Corinthians* 12:9

Chapter One

Peaceful, Indiana, May 1901

Men. The bane of Elise Langley's life.

In her frilly bedroom papered in rose sprigs, windows draped with eyelet, her childhood retreat, Elise swooped up her eleven-month-old daughter from her crib. Chubby legs pumping, Katie grinned down at her, drool slipping off her chin.

"Be glad you're a girl, Katie Marie. Men aren't dependable."

Elise would never tell this precious child that her father, a no-good sweet talker with the morals of a mouse, had deceived her. Her heart squeezed. Not that Elise had been innocent. Far from it. Still, she'd been a fool. Once Gaston had heard about the baby, he'd vanished, leaving her to face the consequences alone.

Inhaling her daughter's fresh scent, Elise snuggled the main consequence in her arms. The months before Katie's birth had been difficult but they'd also brought Dr. David Wellman into her life. She'd believed David loved her. Loved Katie. Instead he'd tromped on her heart with his size-eleven shoes.

After months of courting, pretending to care, David had fled the town of Peaceful in the dead of night, merely tacking a note on the office door, telling his patients to seek medical help from his partner Jeremiah Lucas.

And not one word to her.

What did it matter? Hadn't Elise learned to count only on herself and God?

A lump closed off her throat and she swallowed convulsively. She may have had her heart broken—twice—but God had brought good from the mess she'd made of her life with a remarkable gift. "I loved you before you were born," she told her baby girl. But now...

Katie was her world. More than enough.

Lord, I pray Katie is never abandoned. Never hurt. That she'll have security and happiness always.

The same happiness and security her best friends Callie and Jake had found in each other. Jake had renewed Callie's old Victorian house, as he had Callie, the young widow who had opened her home and heart to unwed mothers. Callie and Jake had been her rock in the storm, supporting Elise when others whispered and shunned her.

A month ago, Jake and Callie had asked her and David to stand up with them at their wedding in Callie's parlor. An honor Elise had been thrilled to accept. Now, with David gone, abandoning her and his patients the past three weeks, maybe forever, she'd lost the joy of their wedding.

At breakfast, she'd talked to her mother about giving Callie and Jake a reception. Though Sarah Langley had cautioned Elise about taking on more responsibilities, she'd offered to pay expenses, the one obstacle Elise hadn't known how to handle. A party would give Elise something to focus on, something to take her mind off David. Twite Hall was open on Saturdays. She'd reserve the room today.

Why, if David didn't show up for the wedding, nothing would make her happier.

The sun shot rays of light into David Wellman's office, shouting the start of a new day and grating against his every nerve.

With the soft flutter of closing pages, David set aside his Bible and leaned back in his chair, scrubbing at his face. His eyes felt gritty, as if sifted with sand. He hadn't shaved. He hadn't eaten. He hadn't slept. But he was back.

Like a toddler seeking comfort from a cherished blanket, he'd returned to Peaceful, hoping that would somehow ease the pain searing his chest. Nothing could.

Even as he believed the town's name ridiculous, he clung to its claim. And to God. Yet scripture that normally brought him solace did not penetrate his grief. God felt far away. Detached. Unresponsive. Even as the lifeblood of a young, vibrant mother had flowed out of her.

An urge to rail at his Maker snaked through him, adding another brick of guilt to the staggering load he carried.

Lord, help me.

Tears stung his eyes. The time for God's help had passed.

Across the room, the medical tomes he'd studied, valued, even trusted now merely mocked him. All that knowledge, all he'd learned in medical school, hadn't saved his sister and her baby.

Swiping at his eyes, he stumbled to his feet. He should take the note off the door. See patients. Do something.

With a sigh, he dropped to his seat. Tomorrow.

He would tomorrow.

Why pretend? Sick patients were the last people he wanted to see. *Should* see. For their sakes more than his.

He glanced at the calendar on his desk, a date circled in ink leaped out at him. May 25. Callie and Jake's wedding day.

Life goes on. For others. Not for Jillian, his precious sister. David's hands fisted as anger billowed up inside him, resentment at the unfairness of it all.

Then he released a shuddering sigh. Jake and Callie deserved happiness. He'd wanted to surprise his friends with a reception, had rented the hall days before he got the wire and raced to his sister's bedside. Then he'd forgotten his plan.

With the wedding two weeks away, he should nail down particulars though the mere idea exhausted him. What did hosting a party involve? Tables and chairs. People would expect food.

Lord, I need help planning this.

Not just with planning the party, with...everything.

If only he had a few more days to get his mind around what had happened. No matter how often he thought about each detail of those nightmarish hours, he couldn't accept he'd failed.

Failed his sister. Failed her child.

Regret pierced his soul, swirling in his chest, the pain as sharp and fresh as if he were back to that first night.

The longing to give up—to stay in this chair forever—washed over him. With sheer strength of will, he lunged to his feet. He had to move forward. Do what needed doing.

As he headed out, he passed the surgery room. He paused by the cabinet, his gaze roaming bottles of medicine, scissors and scalpels glistening in the sunlight.

Once he had believed in those medicines and instruments. Believed in his ability as a doctor. But then he had sat by his sister's bedside, performed surgery and watched her die. His medicines, his instruments, his hands of no use. Those bottles and tools promised cures when David knew the truth.

Some things couldn't be cured. Some people couldn't be saved. Some people couldn't be forgiven. Like him.

He shut the door and walked away. He would sever his ties with Elise once and for all, before she fell any deeper into the trap of believing in his ability to save anyone. Even himself.

Saturday afternoon Elise and Katie greeted Flossie Twite at her desk in the cramped office of Twite Hall. Run-down shoes planted wide apart, cotton stockings sagging at the ankle, blue dress faded, Flossie looked deprived, like she belonged on the receiving end of a soup line. But she owned this building and a couple others in town and gave generously to church and nearly every cause.

With Flossie's love of gab, getting to the point could take half the day. Elise hurried to say, "My parents and I want to give Callie and Jake a reception after their wedding Saturday, May 25. I'm here to reserve the hall."

"I can't wrap my brain around Commodore Mitchell being Jake's daddy. This town hasn't seen that much drama since the natural gas boom," Flossie said. As long as she lived, Elise would never forget that horrible day when Callie's husband and Commodore's other son, Martin, died in a fall off his roof. "Why, I remember Commodore as a little tyke living next door to Sheriff Frederick's grandparents. They used to yell at Commodore for cutting through their yard, then must've felt bad 'cause they'd give him a nickel."

"About the hall…"

"Oh, yes." Flossie pulled the ledger close. "If memory serves me right, and it usually does, Doc Wellman already rented the hall for that night."

Elise's head snapped up. She gaped at Flossie. "David reserved the room? Why? When?"

"For the Mitchell reception." Flossie ran a finger down the page. "He put money down April 14."

Mere days before David left town. Well, David might be Jake's best man, but he wasn't best for handling the party. His disappearing act proved he couldn't be counted on, obviously too busy and undependable for the job.

She wouldn't let his negligence impact Callie and Jake. "I'll oversee the party in Dr. Wellman's absence."

"Can't imagine why Doc left town like he did. You know what's going on?"

Fussing with Katie's bonnet, Elise avoided the woman's probing eyes. "No."

"If a man courted me for months then vanished like dew on

a summer morning, I'd hire me a detective." Flossie wagged a finger at Elise, as if she expected her to do that very thing.

What would that prove? That David had lost interest? Had finally realized she wasn't fit to be a doctor's wife?

"Why, I heard tell of a man who had himself three wives." She snorted. "Imagine the particulars that man had to carry in his head to keep all those women and children straight. Don't believe that of David Wellman, of course. He's my doctor. Doctor to most folks in this town."

"He *was* the doctor."

Flossie flapped a hand. "I'm not crazy about the new doc. He suggested I get help running this place. As if I'm too old to manage. Ever hear anything sillier? I gave him a piece of my mind. Along with a remedy for colds my grandma swore by. Honey, chamomile and garlic, kept it in a fruit jar in the cabinet and spooned it into me at the first sniffle."

Imaging Dr. Lucas's reaction, Elise bit back a smile. "You could run this place and half the town. Dr. Lucas just doesn't know that yet."

"Exactly."

"About the hall..."

"Oh, yes, yes." She checked the book again. "If you got a hankering to decorate like most folks, the place is yours. No events scheduled the rest of the month. Party paraphernalia is in the storage room across the hall."

"Thank you."

"The last group didn't leave things clean. Expect you to do better. Know you will. Why, you're a mama. You got to be responsible." Flossie grabbed her purse. "Need to leave. I'll post a note on the door, case someone comes looking for me."

Apparently notes on doors were the favored mode of communication in this town.

As Elise headed to the storage room, she noted the dusty footprints on the floorboards. She couldn't put Katie down anywhere until she'd swept and mopped.

Inside she located a box of supplies, mostly candle stubs and silk flowers that had seen better days. Along the back wall, shelves held dozens of glass candleholders dribbled with wax, unwashed vases and jumbled piles of tablecloths and napkins—thankfully clean but needing pressing.

Katie's hand darted out, grabbing the cotton, almost pulling off a stack of linens. "No—no, Katie," Elise admonished as she pried loose her daughter's fingers. "Mama doesn't have time to wash them, too."

With a firm grip on the box and another on her squirming daughter, Elise dragged the container into the main room, and then dropped into a chair at one of the tables. As she made a list of chores, she tucked her wiggling daughter close, swaying from side to side. Katie's mouth opened in a yawn and her eyelids drifted closed.

Elise couldn't do much today. She'd pay the bride-to-be a visit. See Callie's wedding dress. Share in her friend's happiness.

Life was perfect just as it was. With David gone. Out of her and Katie's life. Elise couldn't be happier.

Sudden tears stung her eyes. Tears of…joy for Callie. Or so she told herself.

Elise.

David sucked in a breath. For a moment he thought his eyes deceived him. As if she were a mirage he'd conjured up.

But no, she was real.

The sight of her banged against his heart. As she rocked Katie, tendrils of her copper curls danced at her nape. She never looked more beautiful.

To see sweet Katie, healthy and strong, filled him with the deep throbbing pain of regret that could only be soothed by this baby and her mother. Oh, how he'd missed them.

Yet he couldn't have them. Not when his own sister and her child died under his care. The truth trampled his heart, grinding that razor-edged truth into every cell, every particle of his being.

As he stepped into the room, Elise dropped her pen and lurched to her feet. Jolted awake, Katie howled, then babbled a baby welcome and reached chubby arms to David, as if he needed no forgiveness.

With everything in him, he fought the yearning to gather mother and child into his arms. Not that Elise would allow it. The wary, distant look in her eyes shut him out, told him that he was an outsider, separated by a wall of distrust he wouldn't scale.

"You're back." She knelt beside a box, staring inside as if she found the contents fascinating.

"I, ah, planned to check on a few things for the reception, but Flossie's not at her post."

"No need to bother. After three weeks' absence, I'm sure you're busy. I'll handle everything."

Wasn't that what he'd prayed for?

The temptation to agree rose inside him. He didn't have the energy for anything, much less planning a party, especially when holding Elise at arm's length would take everything he had.

Stretching over her mother's arms, Katie almost disappeared inside the container as Elise slipped a bouquet of silk posies past her inquisitive daughter. A tiny hand darted out and grabbed a blossom, clutching it in a chubby fist.

Katie was adorable but a handful. Elise had to manage her daughter and a full-time job. Nothing required his attention. "I want to do my part."

"Your recent conduct proves you're unreliable."

That icy tone shredded the weakening grip on his control. He wanted to tell her about Jillian, should tell her, but couldn't speak the words.

Her gaze flared with something bordering on concern. "You look…awful. Apparently your getaway didn't agree with you."

A wave of nausea swept over him. He swallowed hard.

At his silence, her eyes hardened. "I'm surprised you didn't mention renting the hall. As Callie's bridesmaid, I expected to be included in any plans."

"I, ah, intended to tell you, but we were overrun with patients and I forgot."

"Always the absent-minded doctor," she said softly.

Their gazes locked. The questions he read in her eyes made him look away.

"I'd prefer handling the party without your interference. I'm sure once you have had time to think about it, you'll be relieved to have the responsibility off your hands."

He stiffened. She was getting back at him for leaving without an explanation. As if he'd had time to do more than scribble a note to his patients and grab a change of clothes.

Who was he kidding? In the weeks since Jillian's death, he could've contacted Elise, sent a telegram or letter. Some things were too horrible to talk about. Even with her.

With a shaky hand, he plowed through the hank of hair falling across his forehead. If he explained how he had failed his sister, Elise would be grieved for him, for his family. With her compassionate nature, she'd insist on comforting him. How could he stay away from her then?

Rosebud lips in a determined line, Katie jerked her entire body and parted the flower from the stem, then tossed the bloom to the floor. With a squeal, she shoved both hands into the bouquet. As the stems swayed, she clapped dimpled hands.

David retrieved the flower. When had Katie learned that trick? Gone three weeks and he'd missed so much. "Looks like you could use help." He dropped the bloom on the table. "We can work on the party together."

Elise turned to him, her dark eyes as unyielding as granite, cutting through the numbness inside, awakening his resolve. "You're stuck with me," he said.

Mother and daughter faced him. Auburn hair, pert noses,

much alike, both beautiful. "I suppose I have no choice." Elise's words as sharp as a surgeon's scalpel.

A lump wedged in his throat. As much as her poor opinion of him hurt, her anger made stepping away possible. She saw his absence as abandonment when he had wanted only to protect her. His silence now added to the wound. In time, her pain would fade, leaving no more than a faint scar, a reminder to avoid the David Wellmans of this world.

"I'm glad that's settled." Unable to remain in her presence another minute without gathering her into his arms, he glanced at the door, then back to her. "I need to…to get organized."

Elise flinched as if he'd slapped her. "Fine, I'll be here Monday after work, if you're still determined to help."

With a nod, he strode out of the room, feeling her eyes on his back, eyes no doubt shooting darts.

In his entire life, he'd never felt more like a snake. A snake Elise would no doubt like to skin.

Chapter Two

The murmur of voices and the bang of a closing door traveled the upstairs hall of Callie's Victorian house. Evidence that the unwed mothers Callie sheltered and nurtured were moving about, handling chores on a Saturday afternoon. Callie had appropriately named her ministry Refuge of Redeeming Love, exactly what she and the house had been for Elise.

Eager to see Callie's wedding gown, Elise, Katie and Mildred Uland, Callie's elderly friend and neighbor, trailed Callie into her bedroom.

Baby Ronnie cooed a greeting from his crib. "Ah, my little man's awake," Callie said.

The room, the entire house, had been dilapidated until Jake had arrived in town. In the process of making the house safe for Callie and the unwed mothers in residence, Jake won the expectant widow's heart.

Every sound, every sight, the very air she breathed reminded Elise that she had once resided here. She'd never tell Katie that when Elise had needed him most, Mark Langley had renounced his unwed pregnant daughter, insisting she give up her baby. With that ultimatum, Elise refused to stay under his roof. She'd always be grateful Callie had taken her in.

Callie had done the same for Grace, for Joanna, for other young women since, who had found themselves alone, unmarried and pregnant. At first, Callie had faced town opposition to the home, but in the end, had won over her biggest critics.

The night of Katie's birth, Elise and her father had made peace. A few weeks later, she and Katie had moved home with her parents. Still, months of Papa's aloofness had hurt.

With a glance at her baby girl, Elise's heart lost its rhythm. What would Katie think of Elise one day, when she was old enough to realize the circumstances of her birth? Old enough to realize her father had not claimed her? Old enough to realize Elise had not lived the faith she had professed? Tears stung her eyes. Katie's parents weren't good enough, didn't deserve her.

Lord, protect Katie. Always.

With a shriek, Katie lurched to all fours and crawled toward the crib where Ronnie babbled, pulling his toes to his mouth. Katie grabbed a slat, rose to her knees, and then pulled herself to her feet. "Ba-ba."

A tender expression softened Mildred's face. "Katie and Ronnie may marry one day."

Elise's breath caught. Sweet Ronnie wouldn't hurt anyone, but boys grew up, became men.

Callie opened the wardrobe and brought out her wedding gown, holding the white silk against her. The dress was trimmed in lace with a flounced skirt that glowed, almost as much as Callie.

The sight thudded inside Elise with the force of a slab of Indiana limestone. For a while she'd expected a gown, a wedding day, a ring on her finger. That was not to be.

She'd share in Callie's joy and never admit the sting of all she'd hoped for and lost. "Your gown's magnificent. You'll be a beautiful bride!"

"Thanks to Mildred, who insisted on buying the fabric, far nicer than anything I could afford."

White hair haloing her head, Mildred drew Callie close.

"Callie's like family. I can't sleep nights I'm so excited about this wedding."

Callie giggled. "That makes two of us."

Even with her dark hair knotted in a simple bun, the skirt and blouse she wore unadorned, Callie was beautiful, radiating joy, her aquamarine eyes dazzling.

"Jake is a wonderful man." Elise gave her friend a hug. "You'll have a happy life."

Callie hung her dress in the towering wardrobe. "You will too, one day. I'm sure of it."

With a plop, Katie dropped to the floor then made a beeline toward the open door and the stairway beyond. Elise plucked her daughter from potential harm. "Maybe. We'll see."

"God will bless you, Elise, as He did me." Callie scooped her son from the crib. Dark hair and aquamarine eyes, the image of his mother, Ronnie's grin revealed two tiny white teeth.

As the five of them headed downstairs, holding on to the banister, solid and smooth thanks to Jake's carpentry skills, the front door swung open and Jake strode inside.

He was a kind, hardworking, dependable man—qualities Elise had once believed David shared. How wrong she'd been. David and Gaston were made from the same loose-woven cloth.

The corners of Jake's green eyes crinkled with a smile. "You're a sight to behold. Three beautiful ladies and the cutest babies God ever made."

With a shriek, Ronnie reached for Jake. Katie did the same. Soon both children perched on his forearms, pure contentment on their faces as they leaned against him.

Jake kissed the top of each of their heads. "Soon, I'll marry the woman of my dreams and be Ronnie's daddy. Add a houseful of women and we'll have a large family. What I've always wanted."

Moist eyes filled with love, Callie gazed at her future husband. "When you showed up at my door asking for work, I was leery, but you were God-sent."

"Leery?" Jake chuckled. "You were downright suspicious."

Callie plucked Elise's sleeve. "Keep that in mind. Not everything is as it first appears."

Not that Elise accepted Callie's claim, but she gave a nod that she'd heard then took Katie from Jake.

The hall clock bonged the hour. "I've got to go," Mildred said. "I'm meeting Flossie at the café."

After seeing Mildred out the door, Jake turned to Elise. "Any sign of my absentee groomsman?"

Elise's belly flopped. Why couldn't she stop reacting to the mere mention of the man? "I saw him this morning."

Jake grinned. "I'm relieved he's back. I don't understand why he left town but I'm sure he had good reason."

If he did, wouldn't David have explained?

Apparently the commitment to Jake had prompted his return. Not the unspoken commitment she'd thought he'd made to her. An ache bloomed inside Elise, pressing against her lungs until she could barely breathe. Who knew where she stood with the man?

"Still, I'm concerned." Jake's brow furrowed. "How did he look?"

An image rose in Elise's mind of pale skin, bleak eyes, a man wrung out like a used-up dishrag. "He looked...weary."

Jake turned to Callie. "I knew he wouldn't let us down. Still, I can't help wondering if something's wrong."

David had let Elise down, his patients too, but she wouldn't say as much and trample on Callie and Jake's happiness.

"I know! I'll have a welcome home dinner for David." Callie smiled at Elise. "One last chance to get together before the wedding."

Elise frowned. "Aren't you too busy to host a dinner party?"

"It'll be fun! Bring Katie. Monday at six. Our residents can eat earlier."

With a hug and quick goodbye, Elise stepped outside. As she tucked her daughter into the wicker pram, Elise sighed. Jake had planted a seed of concern about David's well-being. He hadn't looked well. Had he been ill? No, he'd have explained if an illness had kept him away. Whatever had demanded his attention for three weeks, he was not sharing the reason with her.

She'd believed they were friends. Far more than friends, yet a friend wouldn't be closemouthed about a prolonged absence. As much as she longed to demand an explanation, to ask would make her appear needy, even desperate.

David Wellman kept secrets and couldn't be trusted.

Normally she loved spending time with Callie and Jake, but she dreaded the dinner party. How could she pretend everything was fine when David had turned her world upside down?

David's world had turned upside down. He couldn't seem to find footing, yet Sunday dawned warm and sunny, prettier than yesterday. As if nature proclaimed God was in His heavens and all was right with the world.

To David, God felt far away, as if He were indifferent to the happenings here on earth. Immediately repentant for blaming God when David knew he was the problem, he forced himself out of bed and trudged to the kitchen, ignoring the rumpled clothes on the floor. The reminder of the walk he'd taken in the wee hours.

Without a destination, he'd wound up on Serenity Avenue, stopping beneath Elise's window. Her room had been dark. Quiet. As he stood staring up at that window, he fingered the tiny gold band he carried in his pocket.

He'd recaptured the moment he'd fallen in love with Elise. She'd been trying to convince him not to court her, listing all the crazy reasons she believed made her unfit to be a doctor's wife. He'd looked into her beguiling, tear-filled eyes and seen a woman with regrets, yes, but a woman who thought of others, a woman who didn't grasp how much she gave of herself, a woman who had no idea of her worth. He'd fallen hard.

The next day he'd bought the ring, planning to ask her to marry him at Callie and Jake's reception.

On the walk home his hand had fisted around the ring, clutching it so tightly, the metal had cut into his palm. He'd never propose. He'd never give her that ring. He cared about her, valued her, but no longer had the capacity to love in him.

As he lit the stove and heated water for coffee, he glanced at the clock. By now, Elise had fed Katie, had seen to the child's needs and was probably tugging a dress over the squirming tot's head. All the while believing David didn't care.

About to dump ground coffee in the pot, David's hand slowed. Didn't he believe the same about God? That God didn't care? The similarity wasn't lost on him.

Lord, the gift of Your Son confirms the depth of Your love, but... Why didn't You save my sister and her baby—even from me?

Perhaps if he kept praying, kept going to church, kept behaving like a man of faith, he'd somehow unearth the trust in God he'd lost.

After downing two cups of strong coffee, he found the energy to shave. Unable to endure the haunted face looking back at him in the mirror, he averted his gaze, focusing on the blade as he swiped the razor along his jaw and chin, removing the stubble of another sleepless night.

Dressed, he clutched his Bible and took the short walk to Peaceful First Christian Church. Patients and friends headed his way. To avoid the inevitable questions, the *welcome back greetings*, he ducked into the sanctuary and sat in the back pew, head bowed, eyes closed, his bearing keeping folks away as effectively as a barbed-wire fence.

With his thoughts scattered like dandelion fluff in the wind, he struggled to give God his burdens, but his mind refused to work. Yet, he somehow knew the moment Elise and Katie entered the church. He heard Katie's babbling and Elise's soft shushes as they settled in a pew a few rows up.

Moments later the service began. David rose for prayer, for hymns, sat when told. Yet had no idea what Pastor Steele said.

Instead his mind sped to another service. To the cloying scent of roses. To whispered condolences. To his brother-in-law's silent weeping.

Swallowing hard against the bile shoving up his throat, David clenched his trembling hands into fists. He had to get out of here before he broke down and bawled like a baby.

Eyes averted, he slipped out and slogged home, leaving Elise with the responsibility of spreading the word about the reception. Cutting yet another notch in the belt of misdeeds she should hold against him. He couldn't stop hurting her. He couldn't get a grip on his life. He couldn't move ahead.

Lord, I'm tired.

Inside his room, drapes drawn against the sunshine, he collapsed onto his bed but didn't sleep. Not with the image of Jillian's face in repose, cradling her baby, forever burned into his mind. Tears slid under his eyelids and down his face.

How often had he encouraged patients to see the bright side? To hang on to their faith during illness and tough times? To give healing, to give their problems, time? If he ever practiced medicine again, he'd be slower to hand out advice and faster to offer a shoulder to cry on.

For now, he'd put off any decisions about the future, and leave the practice in his partner Jeremiah's hands. He'd prepare for the reception. And stay out of the dark place that filled his nights and lingered in his days.

Chapter Three

Face composed, manners impeccable as always, Lenora Lucas entered the office. Blonde, beautiful and wearing a chic pink walking suit complementing her fair skin. With nary a hair out of place beneath her hat or a misspoken word out of her mouth, Lenora oozed respectability, a proper wife for Dr. Lucas.

While Elise couldn't manage her unruly rusty curls, too frequently spoke and acted impulsively. Months of pregnancy and a baby with the tendency to spit up had eroded Elise's attempt at stylishness.

"Good afternoon, Miss Langley," Mrs. Lucas said, voice soft, cultured. "Is my husband available?"

"He's with a patient, Mrs. Lucas."

"Please, call me Lenora." She smiled. "This will give us an opportunity to get acquainted. Have you lived in Peaceful long?"

"All my life."

"I spent summers in the area. Unfortunately, my husband assumes I'm familiar with outlying roads and patients' residences, vital information when making house calls. But I haven't been back in years."

"I'd be glad to show Dr. Lucas where his patients live."

A flash of disquiet traveled Lenora's face. Heat climbed Elise's neck, flooding into her cheeks. No doubt Lenora saw a single woman with a child out of wedlock as a threat to her marriage.

"That's kind of you to offer. We plan to do that very thing this afternoon, a lovely day for a drive in the country." She tapped a gloved finger to her lower lip. "My husband tells me you're planning a party for the Mitchells."

"Yes. I have no idea how to make that cavernous room in Twite Hall festive.'

"I'd be happy to help."

"Would you? I'll be there Tuesday evening around six o'clock, if you'd like to stop by and offer suggestions."

"Sounds like fun.' Lenora took a seat, thumbing through a copy of *Godey's*.

Elise tucked a wayward tendril of hair behind her ear, regretting that her impulsive nature defeated good manners or like now, put others on guard.

Most folks knew her intentions were good. But one error couldn't be excused. Elise was tainted. Sullied by sin. She wouldn't whitewash her past. Not that she could. Everyone in town knew. An upstanding doctor like David deserved a wife free of reproach. Like Lenora, pure, genteel, a respected helpmate.

Not that Elise's past mattered now. Since David's return, he'd made his lack of interest clear. She had no idea what had triggered the change in him, but David was far better off without her.

If only his rejection didn't hurt this much.

Bald-headed nine-month-old Tommy nestled in her arms, Sally Thompson breezed in from the examining room. Brown hair sparkling with silver, hazel eyes merry, Sally exuded happiness.

"Lenora, Dr. Lucas is free now," Elise said.

"Thank you." Lenora set aside the magazine, greeted Sally then swept out of the room.

Elise handed Sally an appointment card. "Dr. Lucas would like you back in a month."

"Thanks." Sally lowered her voice and leaned in. "He's nice enough but I miss Doc Wellman. Doc always took time to listen, to ask questions, to reassure me."

What did Elise say to that? That she missed him, too?

Even back in town, David was absent, somehow changed. Though he had insisted on helping with the party, he'd built a wall that shut her out. He was avoiding her. Avoiding his patients. As if he had something to hide.

"Someone said they saw Doc in church but he left before the service ended. Do you know what's going on?"

"No, I don't." She'd change the subject. "Don't worry. Dr. Lucas will take good care of you and Tommy."

"Suppose so, but Doc Wellman delivered this boy, knows his history and knew his mother."

Tommy's mother, Grace, a victim of rape, had given him up, blessing the Thompsons with this precious boy, then left town in search of a new beginning. David had taken care of her and all the unwed mothers Callie housed, whether they could afford to pay him or not, treating them with gentleness and dignity.

He'd delivered Katie, too. During the months of Elise's pregnancy, they'd forged a connection. A connection Elise had not trusted. Yet six weeks after Katie's birth, David paid a call. Soon they took nightly strolls with David pushing the pram, wearing the wide grin of a proud dad. Elise had lowered her guard. What a fool she'd been to believe he had cared.

"Doesn't seem right someone else is taking care of Tommy and will deliver this one." Sally patted the bulge beneath her skirts. "Albert and I never dreamed we'd give Tommy a brother or sister."

Childless for years, the Thompsons discovered they were expecting a baby four months after adopting Tommy. "Thanks to God for such a wonderful miracle," Elise said.

"Amen." Sally kissed her baby's forehead. "I suppose one day you'd like to give Katie a sibling or two."

The patter of feet in her house, the echo of laughter and affectionate hugs every night—the life Elise craved. Warm. Secure. Perfect. "Someday. Yes, I would."

"I thought you and Doc might get hitched." Sally arched a brow, giving Elise a pointed look.

Elise ignored Sally's nudge to confide, instead dropped her gaze to the open appointment book. What could Elise say when she didn't understand David's withdrawal herself?

"Will you be coming to Callie and Jake's reception?"

"Wouldn't miss it," Sally said, then turned to go.

"Remember it's a secret."

Secrets could be fun, innocent, but some secrets separated and hurt people. David's refusal to confide in her since his return said plenty.

Unable to remain seated, Elise wandered the empty waiting room, unusual for a Monday morning, lining up chairs with the precision of a drill sergeant lining up recruits. If only she could put her life to rights as easily.

As she rounded her desk, David stepped inside the office. Tall, broad-shouldered, blond and blue eyed, so handsome her breath caught. She'd once believed she could lean on those wide shoulders. How wrong she'd been.

His eyes were bloodshot, shadowed. What was wrong? She chided herself for worrying about a man who didn't care one whit about her.

"I hope Dr. Lucas appreciates you. He'll soon learn you're far more than a receptionist."

Like David had? "I'm sure I'm replaceable." She arched a brow. "Are you here to see patients?"

"I…I'm not sure I'll return to medicine."

She retreated behind the desk. "Why?"

David's gaze focused on a spot above her right shoulder. "I…can't. Not now."

"I don't understand."

He lowered his gaze. In his eyes she saw evidence of some terrible sorrow. "I need time off. I'm here to discuss that with Jeremiah." He cleared his throat, shifted on his feet. "Were you able to invite the congregation to the reception?"

"Callie and Jake stayed after services so I couldn't say much, but I told Flossie and Mildred Uland to spread the word."

"Then the whole county knows by now."

"Most likely." She smiled at him and he smiled back with a glimmer in his eyes she hadn't seen since he'd returned. Then the light dimmed, the moment of levity passed.

From his behavior and appearance, something had taken him away for three weeks and impacted him still. Yet he didn't trust her or care enough to explain.

"I understand dinner's at six at Callie's place. Shall I come for you and Katie?" he asked.

He behaved as if nothing stood between them. "No."

Hurt flared in his eyes. "I understand."

She sighed. "This dinner means we'll lose an evening preparing for the party. But I couldn't refuse the invitation without explaining why."

"I'll do some chores during the day."

"You prefer to handle menial chores for the reception than return to your practice?"

"My dad always said hard work never hurt anyone." He gave her a thin smile then trudged toward Dr. Lucas's office. He'd looked downtrodden, depressed, yet hadn't explained the reason. Once they'd shared their innermost thoughts. If he wasn't talking to her, she hoped he was talking to God.

Lord, help David handle whatever is wrong.

In the months they'd spent taking walks, attending church socials, working together in his practice, she'd thought they were very close and getting closer, had a future together. Concerned she wasn't fit to be a doctor's wife, she'd gone so far as

to suggest he find someone else to spend his evenings with. He'd merely smiled. Told her she wasn't getting rid of him that easily. Now he'd stepped away, holding himself aloof. Had he met another woman?

Whatever the reason, he'd abandoned her. Just like Gaston, just like her father, just like the entire town. Her hands fisted. She had no choice but to work with David on the reception. Seeing him every day would require a price. If not for her deep affection for Callie and Jake, a price Elise would not pay. Well, she could be as polite, standoffish and indifferent as him.

She'd never let another person discard her. Or Katie. She'd protect her daughter by closing her heart to David forever. Starting tonight.

David walked down the hall toward Jeremiah's office. Thanks to the open window in the outer office, he'd overheard Elise tell Sally Thompson she wanted more children. He'd failed his sister and her baby and now…now they were gone. The same thing could happen to Elise.

He'd never marry. He'd never resume his practice. Never.

Outside Jeremiah's office door, David sucked in a steadying breath and rapped his knuckles on the frame, just as Jeremiah and Lenora strolled out, holding hands and gazing into one another's eyes like newlyweds. Come to think of it, they were.

Dark hair slicked back, a handlebar mustache under his aristocratic nose, Jeremiah looked more a gentleman of leisure than a doctor. "David, when did you get back?"

"Saturday. I don't want to interrupt."

"My wife is on her way home to prepare my lunch."

"I'll return at noon, Jeremiah. I want to make sure you're eating properly." She smiled at David. "Welcome back."

As with everyone else in town, David saw the unspoken question in her eyes. "Thank you."

After a tender goodbye with his wife, Jeremiah ushered

David inside. "I was going over the list of the patients I treated in your absence."

"Anyone in trouble?"

"Only the usual complaints." Jeremiah studied him. "I haven't known you long, but I'm concerned about the change I see in you. Something's wrong. Is it your health?"

"If it were, I'd be sitting in your examination room."

"Appreciate your confidence in me." Jeremiah dropped onto the edge of his desk. "Care to talk about it?"

"Talking won't change a thing." David looked at his hands. Hands he'd once trusted to bring healing. "I'd appreciate it if you'd continue handling things here."

"I like keeping busy."

"Then it's settled."

"You know, if you stay away, your patients may switch doctors."

"Couldn't blame them." David forced up the corners of his mouth. "When you asked to join the practice, I questioned if Peaceful needed two doctors. Now I see God's hand in your decision."

"God's hand and a shove from my wife. Lenora spent summers on her grandparents' farm outside of town. Has good memories of the area."

"Peaceful is a nice town."

David had lost the peace he'd once taken for granted. In a matter of minutes everything could change. With a heavy heart, he stepped toward the door.

"Doctor, what you don't know is your patients miss you. I'm second choice. They hope you're returning. I hope the same."

At the kindness of his tone, David's throat closed, cutting off his words. He gave a nod.

"Not that it's any of my business, but a certain young receptionist misses you, too."

"Elise is a wonderful woman."

"And an excellent assistant. I'm glad to have her help."

The reminder of how much he'd let down his patients, let down Elise, added to David's burden. Better to disappoint than risk failing them in matters of life and death.

Yet how long could he avoid what he'd once felt called to do? Now that call rang hollow. If not medicine, what would he do with his life?

It struck him then, he didn't even care.

Chapter Four

The aroma of fried chicken teasing his nostrils, David stepped into Callie's foyer Monday evening. His stomach rumbling in anticipation, he shook hands with Jake.

At Jake's side, Callie looked as fresh as the daisies David held. "For our hostess, one of the best cooks in town," he said, handing her the bouquet.

"Thank you!" She gave him a hug. "Good to have you back, David."

"Elise and Katie are here." Jake waved toward the parlor. "Keep them company while I help Callie put these in water."

"Since when do I need help putting flowers in a vase?" Callie said, beaming at her future husband with adoring eyes.

"David can talk to Elise without us breathing down their necks." Jake gave a wicked grin. "Besides, it'll give me a chance to breathe down yours."

A blush bloomed in Callie's cheeks.

"Only twelve more days and I can move out of that lean-to and into this house."

"Isn't that just like a carpenter? Why, I think you care more about this old Victorian than you do about me."

"We'll see about that, almost wife." He wagged his brows. "In the kitchen."

With Callie's giggle ringing in his ears, David stepped

into the parlor, a second bouquet clutched in the hand he held behind his back.

Copper curls shimmering in the gaslight, Elise sat on the sofa, studying photos in an album. Chewing on a rattle, Katie nestled on her lap. Elise was a picture herself. Not only beautiful, she possessed a generous nature and genuine warmth that had made David feel special, worthy. She lit up a room—and his heart—with her smile.

As he approached, she glanced up, brown eyes wary. No smile for him. A closer look revealed those eyes were bloodshot, as if she hadn't slept. Or had been crying. The possibility knotted his stomach.

"Hello." She closed the celluloid cover of the album.

With a flourish, he brought his hand around, revealing what he hoped would be a peace offering. "I got flowers for Callie, a thank-you for dinner. These made me think of you."

"Why?"

He felt the smile slip from his face. "Aren't violets your favorite flowers?"

She raised a palm, as if pushing him away. "Stop pretending! We *both* know nothing's between us."

The vehemence in her tone filled him with regret. Yet he knew she spoke the truth. The connection between them had been severed. Even if she'd let him, he wouldn't attempt to suture the wound.

Katie gazed up at him, dark eyes wide, as if baffled by the tension in the air.

"I agreed to come tonight, not because I wanted to, but to appease Callie." Elise lowered her voice. "Since I'm here, and we obviously have to talk, we can discuss the reception menu."

Until this moment, he hadn't realized the depth of Elise's anger. He dropped the flowers on a table. Obviously she'd been coerced into coming. The prospect of a congenial evening was wilting faster than the violets. Not that he blamed her.

"Jake's favorite food is ham," David said, an attempt to comply with her wishes.

"Callie's is deviled eggs."

David smiled. "I remember when she was expecting Ronnie she couldn't get her fill."

"Does potato salad, green beans with bacon and coleslaw sound good with ham and deviled eggs?"

"Perfect."

But nothing about this evening was perfect.

Without thinking, David reached for Katie, plucking the little girl from Elise's arms. Inhaling her powdery scent, he sat on the sofa. Katie rose on tiptoe in his lap, giggling as she faced him eye to eye. "She's so like you, Elise."

Tenderness filled Elise's eyes, but then the warmth faded. She reached out and pulled Katie into her arms, tucking the rattle into her hand.

With a feisty grin, Katie promptly slung the rattle to the floor. David retrieved the toy and returned it to Katie, who promptly tossed it again, giggling at the game.

As he continued picking up the rattle and giving it back to Katie, David's gaze roamed the parlor. "Where's Ronnie?"

"He's spending the night with his grandparents, kind of a rehearsal for Dorothy and Commodore. They're keeping Ronnie during Callie and Jake's…honeymoon."

Elise had stumbled over the word. Did the suggestion of romance remind her of what they'd once had as it had for him?

Unable to keep his eyes off her, those soft pink lips, David groped for words. "They've planned a…great trip. A train to Chicago, tickets to see the Cubs."

"And a play," Elise said, staring back at him.

"I believe, ah—" mesmerized by the tiny specks of gold in her chocolate eyes, David could barely string a sentence together "—Jake said *The Wizard of Oz*."

Something ugly shot through David, something akin to envy. Not of those baseball and theater tickets. He longed for the same happiness his friend had found with Callie. If only he were a fit husband and father, a man who could give his heart.

Jake popped his head in. "Dinner's served."

As Elise rose to their feet, David said, "We should make an effort to be pleasant. Long faces will dampen their happiness."

"I can act as well as anyone. But you— You look like you've lost your best friend."

The shock of her words knocked against his heart. He had not only lost his sister, he'd lost Elise—the best friend he'd ever had. The sorrow and shame of failing his sister, her baby, had destroyed what he and Elise had shared. He'd treasure each moment spent with them this evening.

Later, he and Elise sat in Callie's dining room with Katie sitting between them in Ronnie's high chair. With the aroma of food, the table aglow with candlelight and flowers, the room exuded romance. Callie and Jake sat side by side, smiling at them and at each other. David found he'd lost his appetite. Still he ate every bite and joined the conversation.

Animated, as if she were the happiest woman alive, Elise chatted away, the exact opposite of her demeanor in the parlor. Evidently not fooled, Callie studied Elise with troubled eyes.

"Your patients must be glad to see you back, almost as glad as Elise," Jake said with a wide smile, obviously not as astute as his wife.

No matter how much he and Elise pretended, the gaiety of the evening was forced. All this awkwardness could be laid at David's feet.

"I'm not back at the office, Jake."

"Why not?"

"I'm taking some time off. So if you and Callie need any help with the wedding, I'm available."

"I envy you. I'll have to keep my nose to the grindstone, if I hope to have Mildred's house remodeled into Peaceful's Historical Museum by fall."

"Mildred loves living in the carriage house out back," Callie said. "She doesn't feel as forlorn as she did living alone in the big house."

"Mildred's husband has been gone for over twenty years but she's still chastising the poor guy for leaving her." Jake chuckled.

The humor fizzled. Images of his brother-in-law and Jillian's motherless children paraded through David's mind.

Jake took Callie's hand. "Mildred knows the value of someone to share your life. Like Callie and me. You two should think about getting married."

Elise chocked on the water she was sipping.

Until now, David and Elise had made a valiant effort to hide their true feelings yet Jake's attempts at matchmaking had fallen flatter than an under-baked cake.

Elise bit back a sigh. The attempt to add levity to what had been an awkward evening knotted the food in her stomach. Callie had always been able to read her face and no doubt suspected something was amiss between her and David.

"Dinner was delicious, Callie," she said.

"Thank you. Want to help me clear the dishes?"

"I'll help." Jake bounded up, gathering dishes, no doubt attempting to give Elise and David time alone. Callie picked up the platters and bowls then led Jake from the room.

Refusing to meet David's eyes, Elise glanced at her daughter. Katie had been on her best behavior, picking up tiny pieces of potato, peas and chicken with her fingers, now, with her tummy full, she ran messy fingers through her hair.

Elise grabbed the damp cloth off the back of the high chair to wipe them just as Katie shoved the remaining food off her tray. "Oh-oh," she said, peering at the mess on the floor.

"No—no, Katie!" Elise said.

Eyes wide, filling with tears, lower lip protruding, Katie turned toward Elise. As she wiped her daughter's hands and face, Elise regretted her tone. Had she been unnecessarily harsh because of the pent-up emotions swirling inside her?

Beside her, David knelt on the floor, gathering the mess in his napkin. "No damage done," he said, rising to his feet. "Callie is wise not to have rugs in here."

He tapped Katie's nose. She grinned, grabbing his finger with both hands. The tender expression on David's face as he gazed down at her daughter melted Elise's frozen heart. No matter what stood between them, David cared about Katie.

If only Elise understood what had happened to destroy what they'd had.

Callie came in with dessert. A lopsided cake. The top layer looked ready to slide off the base.

"I thought about hiding this in the kitchen but decided I shouldn't be ashamed of it." Callie sliced a wedge of chocolate and laid it on a plate. "I figure if God can love us, imperfect as we are, then this cake's imperfections make it perfect."

As Elise thought about what Callie had said, she studied that cake. Once they all were served, she took a bite. "It's delicious."

"Which proves that what's on the inside is all that matters." Callie poured the coffee. "It took me a while to understand that striving to an impossible standard makes me miserable."

Tears sprang to Elise's eyes. She quickly dropped her gaze to her plate, moving moist crumbs around with her fork. She'd failed God. She'd failed her parents. She'd failed Katie. Her daughter would grow up without a father.

Against her will, her gaze darted to David. "I admire you, Elise," he said softly. "More than you'll ever know."

Elise's hand knotted in her lap. Why had he said such a thing? Yet hurt her time and again.

David turned to Callie. "You're right about cakes, about most things. But if a doctor doesn't live to a high standard, people die."

"That's true," Callie said, "but doctors are human. Only

God is infallible." She cocked her head at David. "What took you away from Peaceful?"

"A family emergency." David rose, laid his napkin on the table. "I need to go. Thanks for the delicious meal, Callie."

With that he strode out of the room. Each step echoed in the silence, then the soft click of the closing door.

"Wasn't that strange?" Callie said.

Elise kept her gaze on her plate. Though David's answer had been vague, he'd given Callie the reason for his absence but hadn't confided in her. The truth pressed against Elise's lungs until she could barely draw a breath. Whatever they'd once shared was over.

She glanced at Callie's and Jake's stunned faces then looked at the cake, tilting precariously. Perfection might not be the goal, but with its foundation wobbly, one more cut, one more slice, and that cake would topple. Just like her dreams.

Chapter Five

The whir of the treadle machine lured Elise to the sewing room where her mother Sarah worked to transform yards of gorgeous cream silk into a bridesmaid's dress. Dust motes danced in a beam of late afternoon sunlight streaming through the window, setting the yellow walls aglow.

Instead of fulfilling her parents' dreams, Elise had given them their worst nightmare. Thankfully they loved Katie and were Elise's staunchest supporters. *Now.* Still the reminder of her failing clung to Elise like her shadow.

A smile on her plump face, auburn hair shot with silver, Mama peered up at them over wire-rimmed glasses. "I'm almost finished with your dress. If you'll put the hem in, I can start Katie's."

"I'll hem it tonight when Katie's asleep." Elise skimmed a hand over the fabric, shimmering with the luster of pearls. "This is the most beautiful gown I've ever owned."

Mama's smile drooped. "I'd thought seeing you in this dress might prompt David to propose."

Elise stiffened. "That's not going to happen." She raised her chin. "If it did, I'd refuse."

"I can't imagine what's gotten into him."

"I suspect he finally realizes I'm not the woman for him."

"Now, Elise—"

"You need to accept the truth. David's out of my life."

With a sigh and the defeated expression of someone seeing her hopes and dreams spiraling away, her mother clipped the last thread and pulled her dress away from the machine.

"Katie and I are off to Twite Hall," Elise said.

Off to face David Wellman. This time she'd be prepared. This time she wouldn't let him hurt her.

Head down, hands in his pockets, David tramped toward Twite Hall, grappling with the pain he'd caused Elise when all he wanted to do was protect her.

Twice between his house and the hall, he'd been waylaid by those who loved her.

Elise's father had stormed out of his barbershop and warned David to stay away from Elise. "She won't find someone else as long as you're hanging around," Langley had said.

A block on down, as protective as a mother hen, Callie had stopped him outside Mitchell Mercantile. "I've got a prescription for you, doctor," she'd said. "Heal Elise's broken heart."

Callie's tone had brooked no excuses. He had no answers. His world had flipped off its axis. He couldn't get his bearings. He was a hollow man with no plan for tomorrow. Even if he had the remedy to heal all the heartache he'd caused, Elise would see the prescription as too little, too late, a bitter pill impossible to swallow. She'd never accept a man like him.

He hated how much he'd hurt her. Leaving town would be kinder than that crazy push and pull sizzling between them. Yet he dreaded the day when he'd no longer spend time with her.

Inside the hall, Elise waited. One look into those warm brown eyes David got lost in, eroded his resolve to protect Elise from himself. An intense longing for what Jake would soon have—a wife and family—rose up inside him, pounding with the tempo of a well digger's drill. Yet he'd keep his distance, lest he'd mislead Elise into believing they had a future.

Flossie popped out of her office. "Well, Doc Wellman, if you aren't a sight for sore eyes."

"Hi, Flossie."

"Knew you'd come back. You're a doc. Docs don't shirk their duty. Leastwise most don't. In '92 I heard tell of a doc in Indianapolis who refused to treat consumption. Reckon he forgot he took that there Hippocratic Oath." She shook her head, as if mystified, then peeked at Katie inside the wicker carriage. "How's that precious baby girl? Cootchie, cootchie coo," Flossie said, baby talk spilling out of her faster than an underground spring.

Wearing a proud smile, Elise picked up Katie. "Getting bigger every day. Wave bye-bye for Miss Twite, sweet girl."

Brown eyes shining, Katie flapped four tiny fingers and babbled a greeting. David memorized every tiny movement, knowing he'd soon leave and wanted to take with him the images of this precious child and her mother.

"That's a nifty trick, little lady." Flossie trailed a finger along Katie's arm, and then turned to Elise. "Loretta Frederick stopped by. All hunched over, her back in a horrible twist, probably from hiking the woods, toting that rifle. Pains bad when she's not gunning for rabbits or weeding her garden."

"Poor thing."

"Would you teach her six-year-old Sunday school class? Would only be a couple weeks at most."

David's gaze darted to Elise. Surely she wouldn't take on another thing.

"I, ah—"

"I told Loretta I would before I remembered Sunday's the Twite reunion. My niece will pitch a fit if I don't help that morning. Land's sake, don't know if I'm coming or going."

About to warn her against taking on more, David turned to Elise, but she was already nodding.

"Sure, I'll do it," she said.

"You're a lifesaver! Loretta left the supplies in the Sunday school room."

"I'll pick them up today."

"Thanks. Better get back to my tatting. Heard Callie's got a new batch of unwed mothers over at Refuge of Redeeming Love. I'm making tatted-trimmed bonnets for their babies." Flossie held out a tiny white bonnet edged with tatting.

"That's beautiful," Elise said.

"Can't have babies doing without just 'cause they don't got daddies." She patted Elise's arm. "Thanks for helping Loretta out." With a wave, Flossie disappeared inside her office.

Elise had a servant's heart, but how could she take on more?

Sometimes Elise was her own worst enemy.

Elise lowered Katie in the pram. As she turned toward the carriage handle, she bumped into David. He steadied her with a firm hand on her arm, studying her like a specimen under his microscope, bringing a flush of heat to her cheeks. "Excuse me."

All too aware of the rise and fall of his chest as he breathed, that unruly hank of blond hair falling over his forehead, the specks of gold in his gray eyes, everything within her reacted, going from wary to attraction so intense, her stomach fluttered like a love-struck schoolgirl.

She might be attracted to him, but he wasn't the man for her. Though mere inches away, he held himself aloof, kept secrets. She'd once believed David might one day become Katie's daddy. Well, no matter. She could provide all the bonnets her daughter needed.

Brow creased, eyes probing, David took a step closer. "Did I just hear you agree to teach Sunday school?"

At the bewilderment, even accusation in his tone, Elise squared her shoulders. "I couldn't turn Flossie down."

"Why? You have a child to care for, a full-time job and

a party to plan. Now you'll have to prepare a lesson before Sunday. You'll make yourself sick."

Since when did he start caring again? Why didn't he return to his medical practice and concentrate on helping his patients, the thing he'd been trained to do, instead of watching her every move? After courting for months then his sudden withdrawal, his pretense of caring had her reeling.

"What I do isn't your business. How dare you give me advice? You can't manage your own life."

The glint in his eyes dimmed, leaving a hollow, lost expression. "You're right. I'm sorry I interfered."

Without a backward glance, he walked toward the kitchen, leaving her standing there. As much as she wouldn't admit the truth to him, she'd spoken without thinking, agreeing to take on a task she had no time to handle. Why couldn't she say no and stop volunteering when she barely kept up with the demands of her child and job?

With a sigh, she peeked inside the pram, heart melting at the sight of her precious daughter sleeping sweetly. As she parked the carriage in the corner, a desire to cuddle Katie in a rocking chair rose up inside her. Yet, across the way, stacks of rumpled tablecloths and napkins waited.

One glimpse in the kitchen had turned Elise's stomach. Before she could prepare food, she'd have to scrub every surface. Flossie had understated the hall's condition.

Preparations for the reception were wearing her down. When she had decided to give a reception, she hadn't realized how much work a party involved. Instead she'd jumped in without thinking it through. Without David's help she'd never pull off the party. She had to find a way to make peace between them until after a week from Saturday.

As she walked toward David, wondering how to smooth the waters, she noted the fresh scent in the air, the sheen on the planks. "Did you mop the floors?"

"I shoved everything off to the side this afternoon. I thought you might want to put Katie down."

The hard shell around her heart softened. David had thought of Katie. "That's very considerate." She glanced back at the carriage. "She's been fighting her nap. She's worn out and has fallen asleep. For now."

A smile lifted the corners of his lips. "She's a good baby." Then as if he'd forgotten to keep things impersonal, he swept a hand. "Does this arrangement work? I can move the tables if you'd prefer another way."

Polite yet like a stranger, giving no indication they'd courted. She'd prefer anger to his studied indifference.

"I thought Callie and Jake could sit here in the front with family and members of the wedding party."

With that plan, she'd have to join David, facing the entire town, but what choice did she have with both of them in the wedding? "Before I can prepare food, I need to have an idea of the number of people who'll attend. Looks like enough seating for…"

"Over one hundred. With the congregation and others in town, I figure we'll need at least that many."

"That means a lot of food," she said with a quiver in her voice. How would she manage? Thankfully Callie's unwed mothers volunteered to bake the wedding cake and any additional sheet cakes they might need. "Perhaps the Ladies Circle will help me."

"I'll help."

"Cook?"

"No reason I can't follow a recipe. I'll buy groceries, too. I can do that while you're at work."

"My mother credits Jake for repairing Papa's and my relationship so she insists on handling expenses."

"I'll offer to give her a hand with the shopping."

Her stomach knotted. If David offered to shop, Sarah wouldn't mince words. No doubt would demand the specifics of his family emergency and the reason he'd stopped coming around. Or worse, what if Sarah played matchmaker? She'd seen David as the perfect husband for Elise and father for Katie.

"I'm sure my mother would prefer to shop alone."

Gray eyes turned to pewter, the hue of the first wave of thunderclouds. "I won't be kept from doing my part."

Biting back a sigh, her gaze roamed the stark room. "Even without shopping, there's plenty to do. I'm not sure how to decorate this room. The congratulatory banner I painted should be dry by Thursday. I could use your help hanging it."

"Great idea. I'll bring tacks and a hammer." He glanced toward the pram. "We'd better get busy before Katie wakes up. Where do we start?"

She waved a hand at the linens. "With the room mopped, once I press the tablecloths and napkins, we can cover the tables."

A cry came from the pram. David pulled out his pocket watch. "It's getting late. Let's meet tomorrow night at the same time. While you iron, I'll clean the stove and counters."

"All right. Seems like circumstances kept us from accomplishing much. But Mama should be able to keep Katie Wednesday so we can work late." Her heart skipped a beat. That meant she and David would spend the next evening in close proximity. She wouldn't refuse his help, not with David tackling a mess she'd dreaded.

But something didn't make sense. He'd claimed a family emergency kept him away but Elise knew his family. Surely he'd share the details with her. Had that been an excuse?

What mess was David hiding?

Chapter Six

Wednesday evening, Elise found David, punctual as always, waiting for her outside Twite Hall. The concern in his eyes brought tears to hers. "Sorry, I'm late. Katie didn't want me to leave."

"I can do this alone, Elise. I know leaving Katie day and night is hard for you."

"I keep telling myself it's only for ten more days." She exhaled a long breath. "She stopped crying as soon as I was out of sight."

"How did you know?"

"I stood outside the open window and listened."

David chuckled, the sound oddly comforting, as if he knew children, knew their resilience. "The separation is probably harder on you than on Katie. Katie will lead some lucky man around by his nose one day."

Forcing up the corners of her mouth, Elise's throat tightened. She hoped her precious daughter had better success with men than her mother.

Inside they gathered buckets, sadirons and the ironing board in the storage room and carried them to the kitchen. David lit the stove and pumped water into a bucket, then scrubbed the stove of debris.

While she waited for the sadiron bases to heat on the stove,

Elise dampened the linens with her fingers, and then rolled them up. Ironing all those linens would take hours. At least she wouldn't have to round up table coverings. Or buy things she couldn't afford.

She grabbed the ironing board, ready to position it between the table and a chair back. "Let me do that for you," David said, taking the padded board from her.

"Thank you." The man was closemouthed but a hard worker.

David scrubbed the stove until the monstrosity gleamed, then filled another bucket with hot sudsy water. As he washed the countertops and sink, his muscles bunched beneath his shirt. Her heart stuttered in her chest. How many times had she felt the strength of those muscles when he'd held her close? Seen them when he'd lifted Katie above his head?

Tearing her gaze away before she scorched the cotton, she focused on keeping the hot sadiron moving. As the heat met the damp fabric, wrinkles vanished with a hiss. The first section smoothed, she moved to the next. When the iron cooled, she carried it to the stove, sidestepping David as if his touch could burn her, released the handle from the base, and then attached the hot one.

As they worked, the clock ticked the minutes, then an hour, then two. The piles of pressed linens grew. If only she could get rid of the wrinkles in her life as easily. The rumples, creases and furrows created by her bad decisions or thrust upon her by others.

Often she'd resisted those imperfections, longing to walk only smooth roads. Hoping to avoid pain, consequences, hard times that kept her awake at night.

Yet, in the middle of all those difficult circumstances, she recalled blessings, too. Callie's kindness, the unwed mothers who understood and supported her, the way others in town had grown in their faith, in their love, as she had.

The biggest blessing had been David's care, his gentle heart, the respect he'd given her at a time when she'd badly needed affirmation. The affection he'd showered on her almost daily, the laughter and smiles, all the little things that had brought such joy into her life.

But above all else, she'd seen God work in her life. He'd brought good from her mistakes. Restored her friends, her family, blessed her in countless ways, one way in particular— her precious baby girl.

Why had she let David's absence, and his silence since he'd returned, crowd out what God had done for her? The mistakes she'd made were covered by God's grace. After all He'd done for her, why didn't she trust Him now, even in matters of the heart? She would not let the trouble between her and David destroy her trust in Almighty God.

Joy slid through her. She had nothing to fear. God was in control of her life, in control of her and Katie's futures.

Across from her, David cleansed the filth others had left behind. She didn't understand him, didn't know why he'd abandoned her, but his demeanor told her something was wrong. Very wrong.

Did David need to remember God loved him? Did he need to see someone cared? Did he need to see *she* cared? Her breath caught. In her anger, she'd not been a friend to David. This gentle man had treated her kindly when she had needed kindness most. How could she not do the same?

Lord, give me the words.

"David."

As if she'd startled him, he whirled toward her. "Yes."

"I'm pressing out wrinkles and you're scrubbing away filth. I can't help comparing it to what God has done in our lives."

His hand slowed then stopped. "I'm not sure what you mean."

"I'm saying that no matter how big a mess we make of our lives, God offers forgiveness and grace."

David's eyes filled, glistening in the light from the gas fixture overhead. "I, ah, I needed to hear that, Elise. I've...I've... failed."

"You're not alone. We all fail. None of us are good enough."

Turning away, he swiped at his eyes. Was he crying?

She dropped the sadiron on the trivet and rushed to his side, but he moved out of her reach. "Are you okay?" she said.

"I'm fine."

"You don't look fine."

"Elise, would you just let it go? Please?"

His chilly tone offered no opening. She wouldn't take it if he did. She'd never force herself on a man who didn't want her.

Nor would she be trampled underfoot, not by David, not by anyone. "Don't flatter yourself. What you do with your life is your business. Obviously you're miserable. But you needn't worry. I won't question you again."

His face paled but he gave a nod then moved toward the door. "I need to discard this dirty water." He let the back door slam shut behind him.

If only he could discard what was bothering him. He'd needed to hear her words, even needed a friend, but he didn't want her. Neither did she want anything from him. They were working together for one reason and one reason only—to give their friends a party.

Scripture demanded she love everyone, even her enemies. She'd treat David kindly, pray for him, but she couldn't do more. Each time she had reached out to him, he'd given her more pain. She wouldn't make that mistake again.

A man can sleep his days away. The pattern David had fallen into after weeks of sleepless nights. He dragged out of bed around ten. Drank coffee until his mind cleared, avoiding his past, his patients, his future.

Other than to get through another day, he had no plans except to hang the banner, consider how to fancy up the hall. Evenings spent with Elise, and upon occasion, Katie, were the highlights of his existence. He had no idea what he'd do after the wedding and reception. He couldn't think about that now.

For a moment last night, he'd feared he'd break down in front of Elise. All that talk about God's forgiveness and grace had all but undone him.

With a cup of coffee in his hand, his gaze roamed his kitchen. Dishes stacked in the sink, crumbs on the floor, opened cans littering the counter. Most meals he'd eaten standing up, hurrying to leave the solitude he'd once relished, but could no longer abide, eager to flee his thoughts, his failures.

Without direction, he was adrift. Shaken.

Why not offer to help Elise's mother purchase groceries and supplies?

Around two, he gathered his courage, made the walk to the Langley house then knocked on the door. As much as he dreaded talking with Sarah, he'd do what he could to ease her burden. Even as he thought it, he suspected the burden he was trying to ease was his own.

Wearing a bib apron around her middle and a smile on her face, Sarah opened the screen door and welcomed him in. Not the reception he'd expected.

One glance at the familiar rugs on the floor, the paintings on the walls, the furnishings that had become more home to him than his own sent him back to happy times he'd spent here.

"I'm glad to see you," Sarah said, "It's been a while."

He removed his hat, turning the brim in his hands. "I've been away."

"Well, you're back now. That's what matters."

With an uneasy nod, David met her gaze. "I came by to offer to shop for the reception. With Katie to look after during the day, you're busy. I'd like to save you the trouble."

"That's nice of you! Katie is a handful shopping. Still, turning a man loose in the grocery store, well…" She flashed a brilliant smile. "I'd feel better doing it. You can watch Katie."

"Oh, no, I'll go."

"Nonsense." Sarah flapped a dismissive hand. "You're wonderful with Katie. I can get the shopping done and be back before you know I'm gone."

"I doubt Elise will approve."

"That girl is burning the candle at both ends. She's worn to a frazzle with working at the office, at the hall, staying up half the night hemming her bridesmaid's dress." Sarah's eyes turned dreamy then her pointed gaze turned on him. "She looks like a bride herself in that dress."

"Elise would look beautiful in anything."

"Oh, that's sweet of you to say. You two make a handsome couple. I can't wait to see you all gussied up for the wedding." She folded her arms, staring at him, like she wanted to say more. "If your suit needs pressing, I'd be happy to do it."

David ran a finger under his collar. "No need for that."

"The shopping should wait until next Wednesday or Thursday. Want the produce, eggs and milk fresh."

"Please check to see if Elise objects to me taking care of Katie."

"Can she count on you?"

"Yes, ma'am, I won't let her down."

"You're a good man, David. Always thought you were perfect for my daughter. But you've let her down."

David met her gaze. "I'm sorry."

"You can patch things up." She gave an impish grin. "Like any good doctor." She cocked her head. "Oh, Katie's crying. Awake from her nap. Stay and play with her?"

"Well, I…"

"Who can resist that sweet baby?"

Later, as David sat on the floor, rolling the ball to Katie, he wondered what Elise would think of her mother's plan. But whatever happened between them, David adored the tot across from him.

With both hands, Katie grabbed the ball, chortling as if

she'd found a great treasure, then gave the ball an erratic swat that sent it veering off to the side.

Soon tired of the game, she crawled to him then lifted a chubby hand. "Da-da."

A shiver slid through David. He wasn't fit to be this child's father. He'd only fail her. Fail her mother.

"Oh, listen to that." Sarah's eyes misted. "She thinks you're her daddy. You're the closest thing to a daddy she's had. Well, except for Mark, of course."

"Your husband won't like to hear that."

Sarah smiled a Mona Lisa smile. "I don't plan on telling him. When it comes to Elise, Mark's on both ends of the spectrum, either too indifferent or too involved. He'll get it figured out. In time."

If Mark Langley didn't kill David first.

"I'd better go." Still he couldn't resist gathering Katie up. He gave her a kiss then handed her over to Sarah.

Only a little over a week, then he could avoid Elise and Katie. Avoid failing them. His gut twisted. His faith in himself, in God, was as wobbly as Katie's ball.

Chapter Seven

Last evening, the mood between Elise and David had gone from congenial to chillier than homemade ice cream, and gave Elise just as big a headache.

Minutes before, her parents had left for a meeting at church, meaning Katie would spend another evening at the hall. She didn't seem to mind, but Elise did. After being separated all day, Elise would like to play with Katie, read to her, give Katie her undivided attention.

As she gathered the baby, her diapers and favorite blanket and tucked them into the carriage, she glanced at the banner lying on the counter that she'd lettered and painted with care. *Congratulations Newlyweds!* Remembering all the happy times she'd spent with Jake and Callie playing dominos, sharing their pasts over meals, she forgot her fatigue, her regrets with Katie, her frustration at David. Giving her friends a party was worth it all.

With gentle hands, Elise folded the banner accordion style and draped it over the handle, then eased the pram out the door.

The three-block walk to Twite Hall took longer than usual, as Elise used her body to shield the banner from the slight breeze. Outside the hall, she heaved a sigh of relief. The banner had made the trip without damage.

As she entered the door, she met Flossie coming out. "Doc

looks as forlorn as a puppy on a chain. Reckon he's waiting for your direction." She held the door while Elise pushed the pram inside. "Place looks great. You and Doc will give Jake and Callie a fine party," Flossie said, "if you don't kill each other first."

"Is the trouble between us that obvious?"

"Transparent as that newfangled lemon Jell-O."

Flossie patted Elise's shoulder. "You and I are two peas in a pod, Elise girl. Our tongues move faster than our minds. Don't say something you'll regret."

Tears filled Elise's eyes. "I've lost the man I gave my heart to."

"When I was about your age, I sent a good man packing. Thought he'd done me wrong. I didn't give him a chance to explain. Wondered ever since if my peeve was worth the price." Flossie's voice wavered but her gaze clung to Elise's.

"I'm sorry about all that, Flossie, but I've given David more chances than I can count."

"Give it prayer. Give it time. The Good Lord knows David's heart. Not one of us has that gift."

Elise bit her lip to keep her tears at bay then gave a nod. She missed David with every particle of her being, missed the closeness they'd once shared. Something separated them.

Not one to wave a white flag, still, she'd try for a truce. But how long could she rein in her tongue?

Inside the hall, she parked the pram in the corner. Katie was sucking her thumb, eyelids drooping. The poor little thing had her days and nights mixed up.

She found David beside the ladder, a hammer and box of tacks in his hands. Ready to hang the banner, to help any way he could. Not the actions of an indifferent man.

"Hi," she said, trying for that truce.

His gray eyes lit, filling with warmth, tenderness. "Hi."

They stared into each other's eyes, both drinking one another in as hungrily as a thirsty nomad in the desert.

All those months when Elise was expecting Katie, David had been the oasis in her storm. After her birth, he'd come alongside her. Shared in the joy and wonder of new life, supported Elise, cheered her on, cared about her well-being. Cared about her. She wasn't wrong about that.

Whatever put this impasse between them, he'd once been solicitous, affectionate, she'd even thought loving. She owed him a modicum of patience.

He set aside the tools then helped her roll out the banner on a table. "You did a great job, Elise. Jake and Callie will love this. Where do you want to hang it?"

"Behind the bridal table, but first let's put the linens on the tables."

As they unfurled then positioned the tablecloths, Elise studied David. Though he made every effort to appear vibrant, he was covering something as surely as these cloths covered the scarred tabletops. If only she dared ask. But his manner had erected a wall she didn't understand and shouldn't scale.

She tamped down her rising defenses. Her past made her see everything as abandonment. She'd try to take Flossie's advice, but she'd never been good at patience.

With the tablecloths in place, they loaded a tray with candleholders. Elise counted the number of tapers to buy then followed David as he carried the tray into the kitchen.

Neither spoke as they knocked off dripped wax, a tedious chore. Once she'd found moments of silence between them comfortable. Now the tension of unspoken hurts left her shaken. If she spoke, she'd lash out at him. Better to keep silent.

Elise drew a sink of hot sudsy water then washed the candleholders. David dried. As she laid a dripping candleholder on the towel, David reached for it. The tips of their fingers touched. Barely. Yet the shock of his touch zipped through her. How could she feel such attraction to a man this distant?

A cry from the pram hurried Elise out the kitchen door, relieved for the excuse to leave David's side.

"Ma-ma!"

"Here I am, sweet girl." Katie grinned, the gaps in her tiny white teeth reminding Elise of a smiling jack-o'-lantern. "Did you have a good rest? Grandma says you're fighting your nap."

Toting her daughter on her hip, Elise placed the now sparkling candleholders on the tables.

Finished in the kitchen, David strode to them. Katie reached for him, arms wide. "Da-da!"

Katie's greeting lurched inside Elise. Did Katie believe David was her father? Or was she merely babbling?

David's face paled. He lifted his hands, as if to take Katie into his arms, and then turned away, fiddling with the tablecloth, smoothing a nonexistent wrinkle.

Once he'd taken every opportunity to hold and play with Katie. Her daughter's woebegone face tore at Elise. To hurt her was one thing but to hurt Katie, an innocent baby was inexcusable. She'd do everything in her power to give Jake and Callie a lovely reception, but couldn't abide the prospect of working with this cold man in this awkward, stilted silence.

To be fair, David worked hard, was civil, even generous— and as closed as a safe's steel door, giving no clue to what lurked inside. That aloofness, that silence told her what she already knew. No fancy words could dress up David's desertion. His behavior toward Katie left no doubt, the feelings they'd once shared were as dead as cold ashes in an unlit stove.

As David stepped onto the bottom rung of the ladder, the banner in one hand, Lenora strutted into the hall, her fashionable dress impeding her steps.

Elise glanced down at her own dark skirt, practical, but frumpy. She might've fought for David, pushed him to explain what was behind his behavior, but she wasn't doctor's wife material. Better to remember, Flossie lived in a fairy-tale world Elise put no trust in.

"Jeremiah's on a house call," Lenora said. "Thought I'd see how preparations for the party were coming." She glanced at Katie. "Oh, precious baby, are you helping mommy?" Lenora reached her arms and Katie tumbled into them, as if Lenora was a long-lost friend. Katie babbled a reply. "Is that right? Well, you have had a busy day."

A grin wide on her face, Katie clapped her hands, obviously impressed by this genteel lady.

Lenora pivoted, taking in the room. "The tables look lovely."

"Thanks. They need some color but I'm not sure what to do."

"Hmm, I see what you mean. Perhaps the day of the reception you could sprinkle rose petals down the center of the tables."

"That's a great idea. And simple, too."

Swaying Katie back and forth in her arms, Lenora studied the bridal table. "A bouquet of fresh flowers would dress this up."

"Mildred Uland offered to provide flowers from her garden."

A smile lit Lenora's face. "You know what would be pretty? I have a double wedding ring quilt, a wedding present from my cousin. The design and pastel colors would be a lovely backdrop for the bridal table."

Elise blinked. "You'd allow us to tack your wedding gift to the wall?"

"You could turn over the hem, use pins to form a pocket wide enough to slip a rod through."

With a nod of understanding, David studied the wall. "I could attach braces to hold the rod. What do you think, Elise?"

Elise glanced at the banner in David's hand. Lenora's suggestion would look far nicer than her hand-lettered sign. "The quilt would be pretty."

"I'll ask Flossie for permission to add the supports. After

the party, some plaster, a dab of paint and the wall will look good as new."

Lenora rubbed Katie's back. "Looks like several nails have been driven into that wall, with dirty hands, too."

Elise frowned. Why hadn't she noticed how shabby the wall looked? A banner wouldn't cover up those smudges and nail holes but a quilt would.

David lifted the hammer. "I'll take care of the nails."

With Katie nestled between them, he and Lenora put their heads together on how high to hang the quilt. Elise noticed a new spark in David's eyes instead of that guarded expression he wore with her. Why did Lenora's presence energize him, while she merely left him drained?

Lenora Lucas had more style in her pinky finger than Elise had in her entire body. She wasn't the stuff professional men's wives were made of. A few minutes in the company of Lenora made that abundantly clear. David knew it, too.

Elise plucked the banner from David's hands, not that he noticed then plodded to the kitchen. The banner looked amateurish, proof Elise was more Flossie Twite than Lenora Lucas. She belonged in the kitchen, behind the scenes, ironing, cooking and scrubbing, not in the public eye. With a sigh, she draped the banner over the trash.

David walked into the kitchen. "Lenora is about to leave. Don't you want to tell her goodbye?"

"Yes. And retrieve my child before Katie follows her home."

His brow furrowed. "What?"

Elise hurried out. Took Katie from Lenora then thanked her for the suggestions. Though shoving the compliment between her lips took enormous effort.

"You're welcome. I can bring the quilt by the office tomorrow. Or, I can bring it here. Whatever is easier for you."

"Why don't I meet you here at ten?" David said, coming up beside Lenora. "I'll bring brackets, a packet of pins and a rod long enough to hang a quilt."

"I'd better go. My husband will be home soon, famished." With a wave at Katie, Lenora sashayed off. "See you tomorrow, David."

No doubt David would meet the flawless Lenora with a cheery smile, instead of that guarded expression she found unnerving. She had an urge to throttle him. With a spatula or wooden spoon. Or both. Not that she would.

"What a nice woman," David said, watching her leave.

"Isn't she?"

With Katie craning her neck, eyes glued on David as he followed her, Elise strode to the kitchen.

Why didn't he just go home?

David motioned to the banner laying on top of the trash. "What's this?"

"What does it look like?"

David blinked. "If you didn't like the quilt idea, why didn't you say so?"

"Who said I didn't?"

Her eyes were hard as quartz, face beet-red, chest heaving as if pursued by a posse bent on hanging. "You look...mad."

She glanced away. "Perhaps I am. Not at Lenora. She's perfect."

"Then what's wrong?"

"If you must know, I'm mad at you. Mad you're all smiles with Lenora while your face droops to your knees with me."

"I didn't realize—"

Leaning toward him, she planted fisted hands on hips. "And I want to know why. I want to know where you were those three weeks you were gone. I'm sick of pretending I don't care."

He felt the blood drain from his face. She was asking the impossible, more than he could give. "I...I'm sorry. I can't."

"Can't or won't?"

He wanted to beg her to understand. But how could she trust him when he'd built an impenetrable wall that kept her out?

Katie reached for him. With trembling hands he took her, holding the baby against his chest. The top of her dark head fit into the hollow just below his neck. Eyes closed, he ran a palm over her silky hair, inhaling her sweet baby scent.

"David, what's wrong?"

"I have no right to ask this, Elise, but…I need you. Will you let me hold you?"

Tears welling in her eyes, Elise stepped into the circle of David's arm. He pulled her close, holding her tight, fighting for control.

"Whatever is wrong, David, we'll work it out. It'll be okay."

Nothing would ever be okay. He jerked away. "No, it's too late for that." Refusing to look her in the eyes, he handed over Katie.

The baby let out a wail. Elise patted her daughter's back. "Everything's all right, precious. Everything's all right."

But everything wasn't all right. Katie appeared as upset and baffled as Elise.

"David, can't you talk about it, at least to me?"

She'd meant to comfort him. Yet her words merely added to his guilt. His pain.

She sighed. "If you cared about me, you'd share whatever is troubling you. Obviously we have no future. You've made that abundantly clear. I hope God will help with whatever is troubling you." She rushed out of the kitchen, carrying Katie.

The finality in her face, the acceptance in her tone told him that he'd lost Elise forever. God would see Elise through. Odd how he knew that when he couldn't feel God working in his own life. "Lord, take care of Elise. Help her find someone to love her."

Chapter Eight

A knock.

David rolled over and glanced at the clock, then staggered to his feet. Nine o'clock. Friday. He donned Levi's and a shirt, fumbling with the buttons as he strode to the door.

Green eyes somber, the smile missing from his face, Jake stood on the other side. "Looks like I awakened you."

"Yeah, come on in."

"It's late. Even for someone taking time off from his calling."

David ignored the jab. "You saved me from missing an appointment. I'm grateful you're here."

"I'll fix coffee and give you another reason to thank me."

Once he'd finished his morning ritual, David shoved into his boots and let the aroma of coffee lead him to the kitchen.

He accepted a mug from Jake, then leaned against the counter and took a sip. "You make good coffee. Thanks." Though he'd need the entire pot to prepare for Jake's answer, he asked, "So what brings you by?"

"I suspect your three-week disappearance is connected to your refusal to practice medicine. But who knows. You're not talking." Jake's gaze turned stony. "That silence is hurting Elise. Callie's fretting mere days before our wedding—"

"Elise paid Callie a visit."

"She stopped by on her way to work." Jake folded his arms across his chest. "Elise is like a sister to me. I won't tolerate you worrying her. Mend your fences."

"A man can want something he has no right to have."

"You're talking gibberish. If you've got something to say, spell it out."

"I'm not good for Elise."

Jake glowered at him. "I have no idea what's come over you, but you're letting down a lot of folks in town, especially Elise. You'd better wake up before they discover they're fine without you."

"They'll be better off," David said though the prospect of life without Elise left him empty, cold.

Jake scrubbed his face with a hand. "I'd cut off my right arm for you. But, tarnation, man, I'm close to slugging you for putting the women in a tizzy." He sighed. "Not that they've explained what's got them riled."

Elise had confided in Callie, probably revealed he'd come close to crying like a baby, yet they hadn't spilled their guts to Jake.

"David, you owe Elise an explanation for your behavior."

"I know."

"Then give her one." Jake clapped David on the back. "Callie found out about the reception. We're grateful."

David released a gust, heavy with exasperation.

"No secret is safe in a small town."

"Yours will come out, too."

Jake's words ricocheted through him. Bad news traveled fast, even from a hundred miles away. He wouldn't let Elise find out about Jillian from anyone but him.

"Talk with Elise. I don't want anything to put a damper on our wedding."

"I'll talk to her." A glance at the clock had David ushering Jake to the door.

Last night he'd been a coward. He hadn't been able to bear

seeing Elise's respect turn to disdain. Though he had no idea how he'd get the words passed his lips, he'd explain tonight.

No, not tonight. Elise had another commitment. Soon. He'd tell her soon.

Elise cleaned the equipment Dr. Lucas had used stitching up a jagged cut in a patient's thumb. The man kept muttering about a fishhook and knife. The moonshine on his breath told the real story.

With the room set to rights, Elise strolled to the waiting room. No appointments the rest of the morning. Perhaps she'd take a long lunch and run home to see Katie.

Hat cocked at an attractive angle, Lenora swept through the door, skirts swishing around her booted toes. "Good morning, Elise."

Elise greeted her with a smile. Lenora had been popping into the office to chat, as if she had time on her hands. With no children, she probably did. Elise's smile slipped. Could Lenora want her job? If she did, she was the boss's wife. What chance would Elise have of keeping the position?

"David's hung the quilt." Lenora beamed. "The entwining rings of soft colors are perfect for a wedding."

"Callie will be pleased."

The door opened. David walked in, arm around Flossie, and holding a blood-soaked cloth to her forehead.

"Flossie tripped and hit her head."

Elise zipped into action. "Lenora, will you hold on to Flossie's other arm? Let's get her on back."

"Land's sake, I'm as clumsy as a toddler, falling over my own feet. Katie would do far better," Flossie said.

"Katie isn't walking yet," Elise reminded her.

"My point exactly. Now most babies walk around a year. Some earlier. Earliest I ever heard tell of was Loretta's husband, Hal Frederick. Reckon that get-up-and-go is why he's sheriff of Peaceful."

For all her bravado, inside the surgery room, Flossie plopped into a chair, as if her legs gave out from under her.

Elise eased back the cloth, revealing a deep gash bleeding profusely. "What do you think, Doctor?"

"It'll require stitches."

"If so that'll be the second time today." She replaced the soaked cloth with a clean one, then turned to David. "Will you handle it?"

He shook his head. Elise wanted to demand why not, but bit her tongue.

"Lenora, will you please tell your husband he has a patient?" he said.

A soft moan was her reply. All eyes turned toward Lenora. Pale as paper, she swayed on her feet.

In a couple steps, Elise reached Lenora and gently pushed her into a chair. "Put your head between your knees."

David grabbed the smelling salts and stuck them under Lenora's nose, keeping an eye on Flossie, who thankfully, was handling her injury far better than Lenora.

"I'll get Jeremiah." David hurried off, returning within seconds with the doctor close behind.

Dr. Lucas laid a hand on his wife's shoulder. "You don't look too good."

"I'm fine."

"I know how you get at the sight of blood." He glanced at David. "I'd appreciate it if you'd take care of Miss Twite while I get my wife to the waiting room."

"I can manage." Lenora rose then stumbled.

"Let me help." Dr. Lucas put his arm around his wife and walked her out.

Adam's apple bobbing, David's gaze darted around the surgery room, as if getting his bearings, then scrubbed his hands and prepared the needle. Elise helped Flossie lie down on the table.

seeing Elise's respect turn to disdain. Though he had no idea how he'd get the words passed his lips, he'd explain tonight.

No, not tonight. Elise had another commitment. Soon. He'd tell her soon.

Elise cleaned the equipment Dr. Lucas had used stitching up a jagged cut in a patient's thumb. The man kept muttering about a fishhook and knife. The moonshine on his breath told the real story.

With the room set to rights, Elise strolled to the waiting room. No appointments the rest of the morning. Perhaps she'd take a long lunch and run home to see Katie.

Hat cocked at an attractive angle, Lenora swept through the door, skirts swishing around her booted toes. "Good morning, Elise."

Elise greeted her with a smile. Lenora had been popping into the office to chat, as if she had time on her hands. With no children, she probably did. Elise's smile slipped. Could Lenora want her job? If she did, she was the boss's wife. What chance would Elise have of keeping the position?

"David's hung the quilt." Lenora beamed. "The entwining rings of soft colors are perfect for a wedding."

"Callie will be pleased."

The door opened. David walked in, arm around Flossie, and holding a blood-soaked cloth to her forehead.

"Flossie tripped and hit her head."

Elise zipped into action. "Lenora, will you hold on to Flossie's other arm? Let's get her on back."

"Land's sake, I'm as clumsy as a toddler, falling over my own feet. Katie would do far better," Flossie said.

"Katie isn't walking yet," Elise reminded her.

"My point exactly. Now most babies walk around a year. Some earlier. Earliest I ever heard tell of was Loretta's husband, Hal Frederick. Reckon that get-up-and-go is why he's sheriff of Peaceful."

For all her bravado, inside the surgery room, Flossie plopped into a chair, as if her legs gave out from under her.

Elise eased back the cloth, revealing a deep gash bleeding profusely. "What do you think, Doctor?"

"It'll require stitches."

"If so that'll be the second time today." She replaced the soaked cloth with a clean one, then turned to David. "Will you handle it?"

He shook his head. Elise wanted to demand why not, but bit her tongue.

"Lenora, will you please tell your husband he has a patient?" he said.

A soft moan was her reply. All eyes turned toward Lenora. Pale as paper, she swayed on her feet.

In a couple steps, Elise reached Lenora and gently pushed her into a chair. "Put your head between your knees."

David grabbed the smelling salts and stuck them under Lenora's nose, keeping an eye on Flossie, who thankfully, was handling her injury far better than Lenora.

"I'll get Jeremiah." David hurried off, returning within seconds with the doctor close behind.

Dr. Lucas laid a hand on his wife's shoulder. "You don't look too good."

"I'm fine."

"I know how you get at the sight of blood." He glanced at David. "I'd appreciate it if you'd take care of Miss Twite while I get my wife to the waiting room."

"I can manage." Lenora rose then stumbled.

"Let me help." Dr. Lucas put his arm around his wife and walked her out.

Adam's apple bobbing, David's gaze darted around the surgery room, as if getting his bearings, then scrubbed his hands and prepared the needle. Elise helped Flossie lie down on the table.

Not everything is as it appears.
Much lies below the surface. Hidden.
Her breath caught.
Like David.

Chapter Nine

Saturday morning, Katie had awakened with a fever and croupy cough. Four days caring for a sick baby had claimed Elise's every moment, bringing preparations for the reception to a halt.

Back at her desk early this Wednesday morning, Dr. Lucas, a thoughtful, generous man had insisted Elsie take off not only the rest of the day, but the remainder of the week.

Now with her hands loaded with a stack of white dinner plates, Elise trudged toward the buffet table, all but staggering under the weight. Then set them down with a soft moan and rubbed her aching back. At last, serving pieces dotted the buffet, the tables were set and the cake and gift tables decorated.

Mama would call her stubborn for handling this alone. But David and Jake were gathering folding chairs for the ceremony. Though David had insisted he'd be back to help, he hadn't arrived. Not that his presence would give her peace of mind, but she could use his brawn.

With a satisfied sigh, she surveyed the room, pleased with the result. The tables looked lovely with silverware, glasses and candles. She'd add the rose petals Saturday before the ceremony and the centerpiece of flowers Mildred would arrange. Lenora had adorned the bridal table with swags of organza.

Hanging behind the table the double wedding ring quilt's snippets of pink, blue, green, lavender, yellow—a rainbow of colors—transformed the stark space into a lovely setting for the bride.

As she pictured Callie's delighted reaction, Elise smiled. That smile faltered. This lovely quilt was a reminder of what Elise had lost. Would she ever share the joy of a wedding with a man she loved? Ever find a man who loved her and Katie? If she was to go through life alone, was she enough? Enough to be both a father and a mother to Katie?

As she made her way into the kitchen, she entered a hum of activity. Mama, Callie's mother-in-law Dorothy and Flossie prepared food, along with two unwed mothers Elise had grown to love at Refuge of Redeeming Love.

Grace, back from Boston for the wedding, tirelessly cut cabbage for slaw. Joanna peeled and diced potatoes. A gauze pad on her forehead, Flossie prepared dressings for the coleslaw and potato salad and a fragrant sauce for the ham.

Across the way, Katie banged a wooden block on the tray of her high chair. Poor baby. How long had she sat there watching proceedings?

Donned in an apron spotted with cabbage, Grace looked up and smiled. Gone was the harsh, remote woman who'd arrived at Callie's, hauling a haunting history and an unborn baby. "Your mother asked me to tell you that she'll bring seven quarts of green beans tomorrow to add to what we already have. If that's not enough, Dorothy will open the store."

"Dorothy and Commodore have generously provided the ham."

Lenora walked in, elegantly dressed, perfectly coiffed, carrying a large basket. "I made sugar cookies for the children."

Elise thanked her. "Thanks, everyone."

A chorus of "See you tomorrow" rang out as Grace and Joanna headed to Callie's and Flossie headed home, vowing to soak her aching feet.

"Ma-ma, ma-ma," Katie called, her face crumbling.

Elise whipped off her apron, raised the high chair tray over Katie's head and picked up her daughter. "How's mama's little darling?"

With Lenora at her side, Elise carried Katie into the main room. Legs kicking, squirming to be released, Katie reached for the floor. The floor had been scrubbed clean. Nothing to harm her here.

With a pat on her behind, Elise sat her down then piled blocks around her. "Be a good girl."

The picture of contentment, Katie grabbed two blocks and banged them together.

"Lenora, I want to thank you for turning a barren room into a bride's dream. God has given you a tremendous talent. You ought to think how to use that creativity to bless others."

"I already have. I've spoken to Pastor Steele to offer my help with weddings and receptions." She grinned. "I'll see where that leads."

"That's a great idea!"

"You've taught me to appreciate who I am."

"You've taught me the same. We're all different with different talents. How boring would this world be if we were all alike?"

Lenora's gaze dropped to her hands. "I'm finally feeling like I'm more than a trophy on a shelf."

Elise gasped. "Why would you feel like that?"

"My affluent parents raised me to be a debutante, a showpiece. The summers I spent on my grandparents' farm were the happiest of my life. With them, I could just be…me."

"That's why you wanted to live in Peaceful."

"Yes. I thought maybe here, I could find who I am. I've struggled to believe Jeremiah saw me as more than someone to display on his arm." She sighed. "I want to be a helpmate, but…"

"His work wasn't for you."

"Now I feel like I have a purpose, something of my own." She laid a hand on her abdomen. "I haven't told anyone but Jeremiah, but I'll have a bigger purpose in six months or so."

Elise gave Lenora a hug. "Congratulations!"

A thudding sound then Katie's screams shot terror through Elise's limbs. Grabbing her skirts, she ran toward the entrance.

At the stairway leading to the meeting rooms above, Katie sprawled at the bottom. "Oh, Katie!"

Elise dropped to her knees, hovering over her baby just as David stepped inside. Their gazes met then turned on the small form on the floor.

David knelt beside her. "What happened?"

"She must've climbed the steps," Elise said, her voice shaky. "And fell." She moaned. "I don't know how far."

"It's my fault. I distracted you," Lenora said, wringing her hands.

David ran his hand over the lump forming on Katie's head. "Lenora, run for Jeremiah." He lurched to his feet. "Never mind, I'll be faster. Get a cold cloth and put it on the lump."

"Don't leave!" Elise pleaded. "Katie needs you."

"I—I can't."

He slammed the door behind him.

Tears welling in her eyes, Elise cradled her screaming daughter in her arms, eying the terrible lump that had risen on her forehead. Within seconds, Lenora returned with a cold compress, looking as terrified as Elise felt.

"Poor baby, my poor baby," Elise crooned, holding the compress to the lump. But Katie was inconsolable, stiffening every muscle as she thrashed in Elise's arms.

Lord, please help my child.

How could David abandon them when they needed him most?

The door opened. *David.* He'd been gone only a couple minutes. Not long enough to get Doc Lucas. He'd come back to help Katie.

In his eyes, Elise saw regret but also determination. He knelt beside her, felt the pulse in Katie's neck, lifted her eyelids and checked both eyes, and then ran gentle hands over her arms and legs. "Her pulse is strong. I see no sign of a concussion. Nothing's broken. No contusions." He glanced at Elise. "We'll keep an eye on her, but I think she's more scared than anything."

"Really?"

He pulled out his pocket watch, dangled it from the fob. Tears glistening on her cheeks, spiking her lashes, Katie quieted, watching the timepiece swing back and forth. With a click of a button, David sprang the case and laid the watch against Katie's ear.

Her hiccups the only indication she'd been crying, she turned her head, trying to see where the ticking originated.

David brought the watch in front of her. This time Katie grabbed the fob, shoving it toward her open mouth.

Elise grabbed it. "Watch fobs aren't for eating, precious."

Once again David checked the lump. Lenora returned with another cold compress and David exchanged the cloths. "She looks good, Elise."

Elise released a gust of air. "Thank God."

With Elise's thanks, Lenora headed home, leaving Elise and David alone with Katie. She handed her daughter a rattle, then returned the timepiece to David. A question burned inside her yet she couldn't bring herself to ask, not with the misery and guilt in David's eyes.

"I'm sorry I ran," he said.

"Why did you? You're an excellent doctor."

David shoved to his feet and walked to the window facing the street, unable to look at Elise when he explained the unexplainable. "My sister...Jillian and her baby..." He swallowed. "...died."

Elise gasped. "What?"

The swish of skirts, then the gentle pressure of her hand at his back. Her touch brought a knot to his throat as he willed away tears. He wouldn't cry.

Then with Katie tucked between them, he was in Elise's arms, the place where he felt at peace, whole.

"Oh, David, not Jillian. From what you've told me, she was a wonderful person."

Those warm cocoa eyes brimming with sorrow, with sympathy, would be his undoing. He pulled away. "She was."

Elise cupped David's jaw with her palms. "What happened?"

No matter how often he thought about each detail of that nightmarish night, he couldn't accept his sister and her baby were gone. He'd failed them, the truth too horrible to share.

With tears sliding down her face, Elise gazed up at him, raised a palm to cup his cheek. "I'm sorry," she said, offering him comfort, an anchor in the storm.

"Yeah. Me too."

"Jillian was your favorite sibling."

"She and I took care of the younger ones." His shoulders sagged. "Now her children will grow up without her."

"Why didn't you tell me?"

"I should've sent a telegram. I thought I would after the funeral, but I couldn't find the words. That was unfair to you. I'm sorry."

"I don't understand why you couldn't tell me since you've been back."

"It's...hard to talk about it."

A blush bloomed in her cheeks. Every emotion displayed itself in her fair skin, on her expressive face. "I understand."

No doubt she did. An unwed mother had surely struggled to utter the words that would expose her pregnancy.

Elise took his hand in hers. Katie splayed her hand over theirs. Tiny trusting fingers. David couldn't bear to have Elise or Katie need his care. He couldn't bear to have someone depending on him.

"Did you get there in time to speak with her?"

His throat closed. Unable to answer, he nodded.

"I'm glad. That has to be a comfort."

He shivered. That was his nightmare.

"Your grief is the reason you haven't practiced medicine. David, your sister would want you to go on. Want you to return to your practice."

How could he? "Maybe…later."

All he knew with certainty—nothing felt better than being in Elise's arms. No matter what happened, he'd always cherish these few moments. He tugged her close and she lifted her face to his. His gaze dropped to her lips, soft, parted. Oh how he'd missed her.

"May I kiss you?"

A wistful expression, fleeting but undeniable, turned guarded. She shook her head and took a step back as if she'd sensed that he was hiding something.

What he'd told her was a lie, a lie of omission, but still a lie. If she knew, the look of horror he would see in her eyes would destroy him. The truth would ruin her happiness for Callie and Jake's wedding. She'd worked tirelessly to give them a party. He'd keep silent. For now.

Once Elise knew the truth, she'd never trust him with her child. Katie's fall hadn't been serious, but next time it could be. Next time that panic he'd experienced could impede his judgment.

After the wedding he'd tell Elise the truth.

And destroy the last remnant of her respect.

Chapter Ten

Grief was a path David strode. Yet, for the first time since losing Jillian and her baby, he'd slept for hours and awakened Thursday morning refreshed. Perhaps his decision to tell Elise the truth after the wedding had eased the guilty burden of his deceit.

As he approached Twite Hall, he spotted Elise on the bench outside. She was talking to someone. The man held Katie on his lap, cuddling her close. Swarthy and muscled, as if accustomed to working outdoors, he gazed at Katie with a possessiveness that slammed into David's gut, putting him on his guard, ready to do battle if necessary to protect Katie, protect Elise from this stranger.

Every muscle in David's body went rigid.

Could it be? Gaston Leroy. Here?

Katie's father. The man Elise had told him about. The man who'd fled the day she'd revealed her pregnancy. What kind of a man would shirk responsibility to the mother of his child?

David exhaled. What kind of a man failed those he loved?

Of all people, David had no right to judge Gaston. If Elise loved him and wanted to unite Katie with her father, how could David blame her? Far better off with Gaston than with him, a man who couldn't promise her anything.

As he watched, Gaston lifted Katie above his head. Ribbons

on her bonnet dangling, little arms and legs fluttering like a bird in flight, Katie squealed with delight.

Gazing up at her baby, Elise's face glowed with pride. And something else. Something David hadn't seen since his return.

Joy.

The three of them looked like a...family.

The family David had once pictured for himself. Pain stabbed like a knife in his chest, spreading fingers of envy that pressed against his lungs until he could barely breathe.

He wanted to shove between them, tug Elise close, but he hadn't earned the right. Gaston was God's answer for Elise and Katie. He could offer them everything Elise wanted and David could not give. Only a selfish man would want to tie them to him.

With the look of a happy man, Gaston lowered Katie into the crook of his arm, leaned close and kissed Elise's cheek.

And then David knew. He was too late. Elise gave up on him when he gave up on himself.

With the picture of that family burned into his brain, he turned and retraced his steps, working his way to the back door of Twite Hall, where he wouldn't be observed by Elise. As he'd planned, he'd check on the final arrangements for the reception.

He tramped through the kitchen and into the main room where Grace lined up forks and plates on the cake table.

David had once feared for Grace's sanity, even her very life, but she'd not only survived, she'd thrown off the chains of her past.

She smiled. "Hi, Dr. Wellman."

"You look wonderful, Grace. Like life is good."

"It is. I thought I'd failed my son by giving him away. But since I've been back, seen Tommy with the Thompsons, I know they're giving my, ah...their son love and a good home." Tears flooded her eyes. "And I realized I wasn't a failure. I gave my son and his adoptive parents a happy ending."

"I'm proud of the woman you are."

"Thanks, I guess I'm proof people can change," she said softly. "I'm still finding my way, but in the bleakest moments, I'm learning to shift my perspective from the ugliness of the past to hope for the future."

With time, could he, too, let go of the past? Let go of his failure and face tomorrow?

How could he go on without Elise and Katie?

Elise always believed people could change, but if she hadn't seen proof, hadn't seen the raw pain in his eyes, she wouldn't have believed Gaston Leroy capable of this transformation. He'd fooled her once, but the wounded man at her side was nothing like the man who'd wooed her the summer she turned seventeen.

"You were a naive girl visiting her cousin," he said.

"You were a lonely railroader away from home."

"A lonely railroader married with three kids. I'm sorry, Elise." He exhaled, the sound laden with remorse. "From the moment I saw you, I wanted you. I lured you in with sweet talk and kisses."

"You said I was pretty, that you loved me," she said softly, her mind replaying every declaration. Why had she believed him? Her eyes found her lap.

With gentle fingertips, he tilted her face to his. "You *are* pretty. That much was true." His eyes found his feet. "I didn't care that I wronged you. Wronged my wife. Wronged God. I gave no thought to the consequences. When you told me you were expecting…" He kissed Katie's dimpled hand. "I ran."

"That's when I knew you didn't love me."

"I was a user, a coward, the worst kind of man." Tears filled his eyes. "I believed in God. Or so I told myself. Yet I cheated on my wife. I lied to you. I was headed straight to eternal torment."

"What happened to change you?"

"A few months ago, I found myself lying in a ditch that had

caved in around me, certain I would die. I didn't want to meet my Maker. Not with all I'd done. I told God every bad thing I'd ever done. I pleaded for forgiveness. I promised God, if I lived, I'd be a new man."

Tears welled in Elise's eyes. Katie could've been an orphan before she'd ever known a father. "God saved you."

"He did. I felt the strangest peace. I knew God had heard and forgiven me. Thanks to my crew, who dug me out, and God, I was given a second chance." Gaston hugged Katie to him. "To find my child. To make amends." He looked at Elise, a question in his eyes. "If I can."

Hadn't Elise been given the same? "God is the God of second chances."

A smile lit his eyes. "The day I got out of the hospital, I told my wife everything. I hated to hurt her but I wanted no lies between us. In time, she forgave me and supported my decision to find you and my child."

She believed he'd changed but did he want more than her forgiveness? "Why are you here?"

He looked at her with such hope in his eyes. "Will you forgive me, Elise? Allow me to be part of Katie's life?"

"I forgive you." Her throat clogged. She cleared it before she could go on. "I need to forgive myself. You may have lied to make me trust you, but I...I knew what we did was wrong."

Elise thought of the life ahead for Katie. And knew she'd forgive her daughter anything, no matter what she did. She loved Katie the way God loved her. God loved Gaston. God loved their child.

Her gaze roamed the streets of Peaceful, the small town where Katie would grow up, would learn life's lessons. *Please, God, less painfully than I did.*

An amazing sense of peace settled over her, like a blanket warmed by the sun. She not only forgave Gaston, she released the resentment she'd harbored, even nurtured. "I'm thankful Katie will know her father. A father she can be proud of."

Gaston closed his eyes, hugging Katie close, tears sliding down his face. Elise laid a hand on his arm, a hand meant to comfort and she knew the only feelings she had for Gaston were platonic, that of a friend. She didn't love him. Probably never had. Caught up in the attention Gaston had heaped on her, she'd fallen for romance without substance, romance without God at the center.

"I want to be part of Katie's life, if you'll let me." He removed Katie's bonnet and ran a palm along the dark silky strands of her hair. Katie grabbed his hand, giving him a drooly grin. "She's perfect, Elise. Beautiful." Gaston sucked in a gulp of air. "When I left you to deal with our baby alone, I never considered how that would impact this child." His Adam's apple bobbed. "We live fifty miles west of here, but I'd like to visit when I can." He handed her an envelope, his address on the front. "I'll send money every month to help with Katie's expenses. If you need anything, you can reach me here."

Gaston's willingness to visit and support his daughter proved the change in him was more than lip service. "Thank you. Tell me about your family."

"My wife, Rebecca, and I have two boys and a girl, Toby and Aaron, five and seven, and Melissa, three." He hesitated. "Maybe when Katie's a little older, you and Katie can visit us."

Elise found the idea of Katie having a half-sister and half-brothers both intriguing and unsettling. She knew the loneliness of being an only child, but she also wondered what Rebecca felt about Katie underneath. But if Gaston built a relationship with his daughter, Elise would make sure Katie was part of her father's family. "I'd like that."

Gaston gave Katie a kiss, and then gently returned her to Elise's arms. "It's hard to leave her," he said, swiping at his eyes. "I hope you're happy, Elise."

She was a child of God. Forgiven. Ready to begin anew. To

let go of her past. "I have my precious daughter. I'm ready for the future."

Perhaps…was it possible?

A future with David?

After telling Gaston goodbye, Elise carried Katie into Twite Hall. She fiddled with a wrinkle in a table skirt, in need of another touch of the iron. She straightened a taper, picked a piece of lint off a napkin and noted a smudge on the wall.

If only she had more time, she'd—

She stopped her frantic striving and smiled. Things weren't perfect, but they were okay, better than okay.

Years of feeling not good enough had made her overreact to David's leaving. Made her feel he, too, had abandoned her. She should've trusted David. The man he was. She should have been confident in what they'd had. And known something was terribly wrong for David to hold her at arm's length.

She'd been as guilty as he was for the distance between them. She hadn't been confident in God's love. She hadn't been confident in David's love. Perhaps Jillian and her baby's deaths had made David question God's love, too. Whatever problems he faced, she wanted to share the load. Her pulse skipped a beat. She loved David with all her heart.

If David could not risk loving her, she and Katie would be okay, too. She was enough. Enough for Katie. Enough for God.

God had seen her through every day of her life. He'd never left her, even when she'd disobeyed His commandments, and never would.

But that didn't mean she wanted to rear her daughter alone. Katie deserved to grow up in a home with two parents. Love might be a risk, but love was a risk worth taking. The time had come for a certain man to know that, too.

She grinned. David Wellman was about to meet a strong independent woman worthy of love. If the man knew what was coming, he'd either run for cover.

Or into her arms.

Chapter Eleven

David relived every detail of Gaston Leroy kissing Elise. The guy had come back to do the right thing by Elise, far too late in David's estimate. But then, Elise wasn't asking for his opinion.

David fisted his hands, nails biting into his palms. How could he manage to appear excited about Jake and Callie's wedding when Gaston could, at that very moment, be proposing to Elise?

"Is moving this furniture too much for you, old man? The way your hands are shaking, I'd think you were getting married Saturday."

"Just take an end of that sofa," David ground out between his clenched jaws.

Leaning toward him, Jake thrust his hands in his pockets. "What's wrong?"

"Nothing."

"Nothing, my eye. You look like you've lost your best friend when you're supposed to be standing up with him in a couple days."

"I've lost the woman I was afraid I'd fail. Losing her hurts more than I'd ever imagined."

"What in tarnation are you talking about?"

"Elise had a visitor."

Jake flicked a piece of lint off the sofa. "Who?"

"Gaston Leroy, Katie's father."

Jake's scowl resembled a thundercloud in a stormy sky. "Well, he's almost two years late."

"Exactly. Apparently Elise doesn't share our opinion."

"Why do you say that?"

"I saw him kiss her. She looked…" He swallowed, then forced out, "overjoyed."

"I find that hard to believe. The man's a jerk."

"Jerk or not, Elise is the kind of loyal woman who'd love a man for a lifetime."

"About time you realized that," a feminine voice he'd recognize anywhere said.

Heart pounding in his chest, David whirled toward the door. *Elise.*

Hands planted on hips, eyes glowing with happiness. His heart plunged. No doubt anticipating wedded bliss with Katie's father, she was beautiful, lovelier than he'd ever seen her.

"I'll take this as my cue to leave," Jake said, slipping by Elise. "I'll be in the kitchen, if you need me, old buddy."

With a nod to Jake, David moved toward the window, staring out at the setting sun, in sharp contrast to the squall raging inside him. Every muscle tense, feet planted, breath held, he braced himself for the words he knew were coming.

Why not get it over with? He turned to face her. "When's your wedding?"

"What?" Wearing a faint frown, she tilted her head, a quizzical expression in her eyes, as if he were talking gibberish.

Why didn't anyone understand plain English? "I saw you and Katie with Gaston. I saw him kiss you. You looked happy. Like a family."

"Gaston has a family, a wife and three children."

David's jaw dropped. "He's not here to marry you?"

"Bigamy is against the law."

That no-good loser deserved a taste of the misery he'd given

Elise. David was just the man to give it to him. "Are you okay? If he's hurt you, I'll—"

"I'm fine."

She stepped toward him, stopped inches away. She looked fine. Better than fine. She took his breath away.

"Then…why's he here?"

"Gaston came to see Katie. To ask my forgiveness. He's changed." She plopped dainty hands on her hips. "Must we discuss Gaston?"

"Well, no. Of course not."

She leaned toward him then, those dark eyes of hers searching his. "Would marrying Gaston have been okay with you, if he'd been free and wanted to marry me?"

"I…ah." He wanted to shout no. To tell her how relieved he was. But she deserved more than him. "I wouldn't ruin your chance for happiness."

"Nonsense!" She released a sigh. "What happened to the David I fell in love with?"

She loved him? Still? A spark of hope lit inside him, a small ember that flickered then died, smothered by the heavy weight he carried.

His gaze settled on the fireplace hearth, a gaping black hole. Empty, cold, lifeless. Like him.

"I used to believe I wasn't good enough to be your wife."

His gaze snapped to hers. "Now who's talking nonsense?"

"I had a baby out of wedlock, David."

"That's hardly news to me. I delivered Katie."

Her eyes glistened with sudden tears. "I'm not pure. I—"

"Your past doesn't matter. Not to me! You've always been special. Always been blameless in my eyes."

"Blameless?" She gave a harsh laugh. "I believed I deserved to be abandoned. By my father. By the town. By Gaston. When you left and returned without an explanation, that hurt, but underneath, I believed I deserved that, too." She released a breath. "I believed I wasn't good enough for anyone to stay. The fear of abandonment made me leery of giving my heart. Yet to fear love is a living death."

"Oh, Elise, you are worthy. To me, you're perfect. The kindest, most hardworking, most caring woman I know."

"I'm hardly perfect. None of us are. But I'm a child of God. That means I'm worthy. It's taken me a while but I'm learning that what we feel is not always what's true."

He frowned. "What do you mean?"

"Why won't you open up to me? Since you've returned, you're distant. That's merely another kind of desertion."

He let out a short, bitter laugh. "You said you didn't think you were worthy of me. That's ironic."

"Why?"

"Because…"

His eyelids closed, shutting out the pretty lavender and pinks of the evening sky, going back in his mind to that dark moonless night. That night when everything turned ugly.

"Because what?" she probed with soft words, a gentle touch on his arm.

Undeserving of her concern, dreading her reaction, he pulled away. His gaze returned to the fireplace. Useless without a log for fuel. He had no fuel, no reserves. "Because…I'm not worthy to be anyone's anything!"

"Why? Why on earth would you say that? You are the smartest, most compassionate man I—"

"I'm not!" He turned away, pressed his forehead to the glass. "I'm the man who killed my own sister and her baby."

With a firm grip on his arm, she turned him to her. Eyes wide, fierce, determined, she shook her head. "You could never kill anyone."

"Oh, but I did."

"What happened, David? Tell me."

Like a dam breaking under the pressure of flooded waters, words burst from his mouth, spilling out what he'd held inside. "Jillian's labor went on too long. I wanted to do a cesarean.

She wouldn't hear of it. Insisted she'd had three children naturally. She said, 'This one's stubborn, that's all.' I looked at her husband Ned, holding her hand as she rode another wave of contractions. Then…"

He swiped at the tears filling his eyes. "I couldn't find the baby's heartbeat. Suddenly, there was blood. Lots of blood. I'd waited too long. As I lowered the ether-soaked cloth to her face, Jillian said, 'Save my baby.' Those were her…last words."

Her gaze gentle, sad but not condemning, Elise drew him into the circle of her arms. "I'm sorry."

"I opened her abdomen, her womb. The cord was wrapped around the baby's neck three times. I held that tiny baby boy in my hands, I fought to save him, but…he was gone." A sob. "I lost them. I lost both of them. I didn't save her baby. I didn't save her! I waited too long."

"Oh, David." Elise wept against his chest, still circling him in her arms.

He jerked away. He couldn't accept compassion he didn't deserve. "I can hardly stand to look at myself in the mirror. Don't you see? I failed my sister and her baby. Because of me they're dead."

"She'd had three children without a problem. No one had a reason to believe anything would go wrong. You did all you could."

"If my own family dies under my care, what kind of a doctor am I? What kind of a man?"

With gentle fingers, she wiped away the tears on his face then tenderly kissed his damp cheeks. "Don't quit medicine because you're afraid to fail. Your patients need you." She cradled his jaw in her palms, a balm of comfort. "Don't quit me because you're afraid to fail."

With his whole being, he wanted to hug her, yet his hands remained at his side. "Don't you see? I'm not good enough for you. I could fail you and Katie in a hundred different ways!"

"I know you'd never deliberately harm Katie or me. God

only asks us to do the best we can. We're not infallible. Only God is."

"What if—"

"What if what?" She laid a palm over his heart, surely felt the thundering beat through his shirt. "David, life is a risk. Either we take that risk or we lose out on the gift God has given us." She stepped back and looked up at him. He gazed into eyes he knew as well as his own. "The question is—are you brave enough to take that risk?"

Holding her breath, Elise waited, staring into those haunted gray eyes, praying with all her heart and soul that David could forgive himself. Could accept her love. Could love her in return.

"I'm tired," he said, voice shaky and weak as if he'd gone to the ends of the earth and back. "Tired from carrying that weight. Of hiding from you. Even from God."

"Rest, David. Allow God to heal your heart. In time He will." She took his hand in hers. "You know Jillian and her baby are okay."

"I couldn't bear it otherwise." Tears continued flowing down his face. She hoped cleansing tears. "I'm heartsick for Ned, for the kids."

"Of course. You love them. God does, too. He's watching over them. Just as He watches over you and me."

David met her gaze. "I'm mad at God."

"I understand that. But faith doesn't mean the absence of trials. Faith means we walk through those trials with God beside us."

"I've seen that faith in Ned. And in you." He let out a shaky sigh.

"Can you do it, David? Can you forgive yourself? Forgive God?"

A sob. "I know no other way to survive." The remorse she'd seen in his eyes faded, then vanished, replaced with pure dazzling joy. "God loves me." David opened his arms. Elise stepped into them, rested her head against his chest. He hugged her close. "I'll do the best I can to never fail you and Katie. I'll do my best to trust God with whatever life tosses our way."

"That's all we can do."

"I love you, Elise," he said, his voice husky with emotion.

"I love you, David. Your arms are the place where I feel cherished, at home."

He cradled her face in his hands. "I want to be your husband. Will you do me the honor of becoming my wife?"

Heart pounding, she threw her arms around him, leaning back to smile up at the man she loved with all her heart. A good man. A caring man who would be a wonderful husband and father to Katie. "Yes!"

His gray eyes grew solemn, as if making a pledge. "With God's help, I will be the best husband and father that I can be."

"You know, I'm learning perfection isn't what God demands. Or even what we can do. I'll make mistakes."

"I'll make them too," David said, stroking her hair.

"Let's talk about them, not let them fester."

"I have an even better suggestion for mending hurts."

With gentle hands, he lifted her face to his and lowered his head. The soft, insistent pressure of his lips on hers soothed, promised she'd never feel abandoned again.

Her eyes drifted close as she swayed to him. She circled his neck with her arms, slipping her fingers through the hair at his nape, pulling him to her. The kiss deepened, sending a shiver clear to her toes, stealing her breath, sealing her heart forever.

They pulled apart, staring into one another's eyes, lost in the wonder of their love. In David's arms Elise felt whole, safe, valued. "I love you," she said, smiling through her tears. This time tears of joy. "I'll spend the rest of my life showing you how much."

A throat cleared. "Looks like a double wedding may be in order."

Elise and David jerked toward Jake. The grin on his face surely matched their own.

"What do you say?" Jake asked. "You're standing up for us. We'd be happy to return the favor."

David studied her beneath raised brows. "Would you prefer your own day, Elise?"

Elise put an arm around David and turned to Jake. "If it's all right with Callie, we'd love to share your wedding day." She laughed. "Besides, I don't think I could stand another two weeks of wedding preparations."

David chuckled. "None of us could. Well, it looks like you and I will be making a trip to Bloomington tomorrow for the license."

"Oh, what about the food for the reception?" Elise said.

"If I know Sarah, she'll gladly oversee preparing the food, if it means seeing us married."

Elise giggled. "Mama will be in a tizzy and love every minute of it."

"Just two more days, my love. On Saturday I'll make you my wife."

He brushed her lips with his and she knew it would be the two longest days of her life.

Chapter Twelve

Elise inhaled the fragrance of spring drifting from the white peonies and gladiolas bedecking Callie's parlor where close friends and family had gathered to witness the nuptials.

Across the way, Mildred and Flossie mopped happy tears with handkerchiefs edged with Flossie's tatting. Elise carried one tucked in her bouquet of roses. Down the row Lenora and Jeremiah sat beside two former residents of Refuge of Redeeming Love—Joanna and Grace, faces glowing with joy and hope.

And why not? Hadn't Elise been where they were, unwed and wounded? Yet God had given Elise the desires of her heart.

On the front row, Ronnie slept on his grandmother Dorothy's lap while Mama held Katie, a miniature bridesmaid in a pink chiffon dress and white slippers. Elise hoped her daughter would act the part during the ceremony. With a baby, who knew what she'd do?

Thanking God for her blessings, Elise waited in the foyer, gripping her father's arm, about to marry the man of her dreams.

"You're a beautiful bride," Papa said. "Never been prouder of you, except for the day you brought Katie into the world."

"Thank you, Papa."

"I regret I wasn't the father I should've been—"

Elise placed a finger to her father's lips. "That's behind us. You're a wonderful father and grandpa."

"And David will be a good husband to you and father to Katie."

Elise's gaze moved up ahead to Callie, holding Commodore's arm. Elise wasn't the only one God had blessed. A few minutes earlier in Callie's bedroom, she and Callie had made final touches to their hair, too excited to string together coherent words, but aware they would soon marry wonderful men.

Pastor Steele and their grooms entered the parlor from a door off the porch. As Pastor Steele nodded his head, the signal to begin, Commodore escorted Callie into the parlor. Elise and Papa followed in their footsteps.

Two handsome bridegrooms waited, hands clasped behind their backs, feet wide as if fighting for balance on a pitching deck. Elise admired Pastor Steele and loved Jake as a brother, but she had eyes for only one man.

David.

A huge smile on his lips and tears glittering in his gentle gray eyes, she'd never seen David look more handsome, nor loved him more. He still grieved Jillian and her baby, but those wounds had molded him into a more compassionate human being and doctor. A man she loved now and forever.

As the two couples stood side by side before the preacher, they met Pastor Steele's kind eyes.

"This is a first for me," he said. "Not only my first time to officiate at a double wedding, but also my first time to see two precious babies blessed with daddies." Momentarily overcome, he cleared his throat. "Jacob and David, when you fell in love with Callie and Elise and proposed, you took on the responsibilities, not only for a wife, but for a family. A family not by blood but by adoption, as Christ adopted us into His family. Not a privilege to be taken lightly."

David and Jake nodded, each glancing at the baby he would

raise as his own. God had blessed their children with good men, good fathers.

Smiling, her heart overflowing with joy for her friend, Elise listened as Callie and Jake spoke their vows and exchanged rings.

Then Pastor Steele turned toward Elise. "Elise Louise Langley, in the presence of God and these witnesses, will you have Joseph David Wellman to be your husband, to live together in holy matrimony? Will you love him, honor and keep him in sickness and in health, and forsaking all others, be faithful to him as long as you both shall live?

Lost in David's loving eyes and with a steadiness she didn't expect, Elise promised, "I will."

David promised the same to her then slipped a slender gold band on her finger, repeating after Pastor Steele, "I give you this ring as a symbol of our vows, and with all that I am, and all that I have, I honor you. In the name of the Father, and of the Son and of the Holy Spirit, with this ring I thee wed."

Tears welling in her eyes, she smiled at David then glanced at the ring. The ring David had bought weeks earlier, knowing he'd fallen in love with her, planning to propose at the reception.

Pastor Steele cleared his throat. "Inasmuch as you have pledged to the other your lifelong commitment, love and devotion, I now pronounce you husband and wife, in the name of the Father, the Son and the Holy Spirit." He glanced at the witnesses. "Those who God has joined together let no one put asunder." Then Pastor Steele rocked back on his heels. "Gentlemen, you may kiss your brides."

With a gleam in his eyes, David leaned down and kissed Elise, his lips gentle, lingering, a promise of forever love.

Outside Twite Hall, the banner David had rescued from the trash and hung over the entrance, Elise's congratulations to the newlyweds, flapped in the breeze. When he'd hung it, David never dreamed the message would include him and Elise.

Outside the hall door, he and Jake stood beside their wives. The new fathers held their baby in their arms as they waited for an introduction Flossie had insisted on giving.

David couldn't take his eyes off his bride. She was breathtaking in a dress that shimmered like a starry night and hugged her curves like a kid glove. The glow of her copper curls, the joy in her eyes, the smile echoing his. Oh, how he loved her.

Flossie clanked a knife against a pitcher of water.

"Doesn't Flossie look great?" Elise said.

David chuckled. "When I invited her to the wedding, she said, 'Reckon I could wear that fancy dress I've been saving to be buried in.'"

Elise stifled a nervous giggle. No one was quite like Flossie.

As the crowd quieted, Flossie motioned to the quilt hanging behind her. "When that went up, I thought Lenora Lucas's suggestion to use a double wedding ring quilt would add a touch of class this old place could use. Had no idea that the quilt was prophetic. Double wedding, double joy, just what we got." She waved a beckoning hand. "I promised myself I'd get to the point. So let's welcome newlyweds Mr. and Mrs. Jacob Mitchell and son Ronnie."

Callie and Jake strolled in to cheers and applause. To everyone's delight, Jake raised Ronnie above his head, like a prize he'd won.

When the room quieted, Flossie smiled at David and Elise. "Some of us call the groom David. Some Doc. Whatever you call him, after the honeymoon, he'll be returning to his practice with his bride sitting at the front desk. Let's welcome Dr. and Mrs. Joseph David Wellman and daughter Katie."

Heart swelling with gratitude for the patience of the good people he doctored, David ushered Elise into the main room to stamping feet and applause. Grinning, Katie clapped dimpled hands, not one bit afraid of the hullabaloo.

The room he and Elise had bedecked in bridal white and pastels now had the aroma of ham drifting in the air. David's gaze settled on a cake, three layers iced in white with pink frosting roses, slightly off-center yet absolutely perfect.

With candlelight giving off a soft, ethereal glow, David stood with Elise at his side, greeting friends and family. Inside his pocket, his hand sought the telegram from his family, conveying their congratulations and desire to host the newlyweds at Christmas. They were with them in spirit as surely as Jillian was smiling in heaven.

While the well-wishers had gone on to find seats, Lenora led both couples to the buffet table. He and Elise had planned and prepared for what they thought would be Jake and Callie's reception. Now they were sharing the celebration. With Elise as his wife, who knew what other adventures lay ahead?

Once they'd eaten and with Katie sleeping in her grandfather Mark's arms, David found a rare moment alone with his bride.

He tugged her close. "You've made me a very happy man, Elise Wellman," he said. "I love you."

"I love you, David Wellman."

Jake and Callie strolled by, moving among their guests. "I've never seen Callie look more beautiful," Elise said. "She and Jake are glowing with happiness."

"We gave the Mitchells a lovely reception."

"We did, didn't we? Who knew we'd share the limelight."

"Dear wife, I have eyes for no one but you."

Elise slipped her arms around David's neck. "You've made me the happiest woman alive. I've always loved spring's promise of new beginnings. But now, spring is my favorite season. The season I married my hero, the man I love."

"And I married the woman I've carried in my heart since the day I met her."

With a kiss, they sealed their bond and their commitment—caring for one another, for Katie and for David's patients here in town. "You know, Elise," David said. "Peaceful has more than lived up to its name."

She shot him a mischievous smile. "Don't get too relaxed, Doctor. Your wife has a way of finding trouble wherever she is."

"I'm just the man to tame her."

With a sassy laugh, she tugged him back into her arms, the place that felt like home. "I look forward to a lifetime of taming," she said, "with the man of my dreams."

* * * * *

Dear Reader,

Thank you for choosing *Last Minute Bride* in the "Brides of the West" anthology. I found writing a story that takes place in two short weeks a challenging adventure. I love weddings! I recall fondly my own wedding, our daughters' weddings, those of family and friends. As I watch a man and woman commit to one another and begin a new life together, I make a fresh renewal of my vows.

I hope you enjoyed Elise and David's story. They strived to be good enough and berated themselves for failing. At times I fall into that trap. When I do, I remember I can only do my best then learn the valuable lessons failure teaches.

If you would like to know more about Jake and Callie, you can read their story in *Wanted: A Family*.

I love to hear from readers. Contact me through my web site www.janetdean.net or write me at Love Inspired Books, 233 Broadway, Suite 1001, New York, New York 10279.

May God give you the peace that comes from His amazing love.

Blessings always,
Janet Dean

Questions for Discussion

1. Elise wanted to give Callie and Jake a wedding reception. What motivated her? What made preparations difficult?

2. Elise had issues with abandonment. Why? How did David magnify those feelings?

3. Elise struggled with guilt and feelings of inadequacy, of not being good enough. Why?

4. David shows signs of depression, guilt and anger as he grieved for his sister and her baby. Did his silence about what happened intensify his feelings? Why did he keep silent?

5. Elise was impulsive, outgoing and good-hearted. How did those characteristics both bless others and get her into trouble?

6. In many ways, Flossie shared characteristics of Elise. What has Flossie learned that she tries to teach Elise?

7. David was methodical, thorough and closemouthed, in many ways Elise's opposite. Why were these two very different people good for each other?

8. David blames himself for Jillian and her baby's death. Do you agree with his assessment? Do you think guilt impacted that opinion?

9. Why was David afraid to tell Elise the truth about his sister and baby's deaths? What did he fail to consider?

10. Elise wanted siblings for Katie so she would not grow up to be an only child like Elise. What else might have motivated her?

HER IDEAL HUSBAND

Pamela Nissen

For Elias: A young man who dreams big
and works hard to realize those dreams.
You are a *constant* source of delight in my life.
Thank you for helping me to brainstorm this story.

Sincere thanks goes to Jacquie, Diane and Roxanne:
for being such amazing and giving critique partners.
To Tina: for pursuing me when I was still "breathing."
To my friends and family: for enduring my harried
days of doubt. To MaryAnna, Noel and Elias:
for being such beautiful sources of inspiration
and encouragement. And to Bill: for revealing
what it means to persevere in hardship.
Thank you for being my ideal husband.

May the God of hope fill you with all joy and peace in believing, so that by the power of the Holy Spirit you may abound in hope.
—*Romans* 15:13

Chapter One

Copper Creek, Colorado, 1893

"Mister, you have exactly *five seconds*," the deep male voice rumbled, stealing Lydia Townsend's next breath, "to tell me what you're doing on Gentry land."

Her heart shot up to her throat. She froze where she stood on the single step of the run-down cabin, its door hanging by a whispered prayer. Every nerve ending hummed at the sound of that voice. His voice. Deeper maybe—but as distinct as the mountains were strong.

Jebediah Gentry.

Jeb....

She'd never, in a thousand long years, forget the crushing humiliation she'd endured when last she saw him five years ago. The way she'd thrown her heart on the line with a bold declaration of love.

Squaring her shoulders, she prepared to face him when something inside her snapped like the thunder crackling the moist air hanging in the overgrown meadow. The urge to bolt straight for the thick tree line where her chestnut gelding had wandered was nearly overpowering. She could almost feel her legs and arms pumping.

Yet pride nailed her boots to the crumbling steps.

"Your time's up." His footsteps, thundering over the Colorado soil, shattered her wilting confidence.

On a faltering yawn she stepped back, off the rotting step, the long duster coat she wore sagging almost as much as her resolve. Tears threatened to well up and she reached into her coat to fish her handkerchief out and scrub them away.

Strong arms wrapped her tight. Took her down with unyielding force.

The air whooshed from her lungs as she hit the rain-soaked earth. Her head spun and chest burned. She labored for a breath. Fought to wriggle free from his unrelenting grip.

Turning her face from the mud, she grappled for a lungful of air.

His big hands pinned her down. "I'm going to say this once. I don't need a problem like you on this ranch," Jeb ground out, unaware of how his words cut to the most tender place in her heart. Or that she was a woman. Or that she didn't even own a gun, let alone have one holstered to her side.

Or that she was Lydia.

She couldn't fault him for mistaking her for a man—given the long coat she wore, the way she'd tucked her waist-length hair into her Stetson, and the way she'd jammed her work dress into her boots.

"I better not catch you on my property again." Irritation was loaded into each word.

She'd disappear right now. *Poof!* Just like that—if only she could. And he'd be left with his pride dangling by a prayer, just like the old cabin door.

When her lungs finally filled with a welcome breath, she grunted, fighting to free herself.

With effortless ease, he seized her upper arms and flipped her over as though she was a mountain trout to be filleted. Hovering over her, he pinned her shoulders to the ground and stared at her.

Lydia blinked away raindrops, or was it a sting of tears as

she lay there, humiliated by her current predicament? "I was reaching for my handkerchief," she finally croaked out, watching as recollection dawned in his face.

"For the love of—" He bolted up to standing as though he'd just been jerked back by a bullwhip. His perfectly squared jaw dropped. His rich chocolate brown eyes grew wide as he peered down at her for a lingering moment.

He pulled a quivering hand over his face, where masculine angles appeared far more pronounced than last she'd seen him. And where his nose cocked off to one side, unlike before.

No matter, he was decidedly more handsome than ever. And the fact that she noticed, aggravated her to no end.

"Lydia?" The tender way he said her name as he reached down and helped her up to standing did nothing to calm her racing heart.

She averted her gaze to anywhere but Jeb, keenly aware of the way he still grasped her arm and barely aware of the loud crack of thunder shaking the ground. "Who did you think I was?"

"There's been a thief around the area. From the back, considering the way you're dressed I thought—" His jaw ticked as he slid his gaze, slow and steady, from her toes to her head. "Why didn't you *say* something?"

"I couldn't. You knocked the air out of me." Shrugging from his touch, she made a half-hearted stab at squaring her shoulders.

"Well, are you hurt?" Jeb dipped his head to catch her gaze.

"I'm fine," she placated, struggling to ignore the dull pain at her side. She'd rather go headlong off a three-hundred-foot cliff than to let him believe otherwise.

His apologetic expression was wholly unsettling. As was the gentle way he set his hand to her back, nudging her to stand beneath the leaking porch roof. "I've never, *ever* tackled a girl—I mean, a *woman*, like that. I am *so* sorry."

"There's no need to worry. Really." When she lifted her hat

from her head, her dark wet hair collapsed down to her mud-coated duster. "You know me…I'm as rough and tumble as any boy."

"You're far from a boy, Lydia." The hint of a grin tipping one side of his mouth sent her focus shooting to the rotted porch boards as unwelcome memories inched through her mind.

When she was younger, Lydia would tag along with Jeb, six years her senior, when he'd do his chores. She'd follow on his heels to school and back, and when she was older, she'd sit right behind him in church, watching his every move and listening for his deep and manly voice. She'd memorized everything there was to know about him. Prayed that God would see fit to unite her with Jeb in holy matrimony. She'd secretly adored him for as long as she could remember.

Jeb had always been so tenderhearted—that is until that very last crushing, humiliating encounter. From the darkest corner of her memory came a vision of herself, sixteen and vulnerable, running toward him, declaring her undying love. In her idealistic and completely naive thinking, she'd actually expected him to take her into his arms and never let her go.

She couldn't have been more foolish.

His harsh words and actions had flattened her innocent hopes, singed her growing faith, and entombed her young love.

The memory exploded in her mind.

Her stomach convulsed with a familiar shame and humiliation.

"Are you sure you're all right? You look a little peaked beneath all the mud." Pulling a handkerchief from his pocket, he wiped a patch from her face, his gentleness threatening her faltering composure. "I may as well have been tying a two-hundred-pound calf for the rough way I was handling you. How can I—"

"I'm fine. Now, if you don't mind…" Intent on getting away from this man's unnerving touch, she turned to leave.

"Hey, wait a minute." Jeb sidled over to stand in front of her. "So, what are you doing here, anyway? I thought you lived in Chicago with your aunt."

She had, until she'd left with an escort and just enough money to make it out to Colorado.

"I came by for a few things." Lydia glanced up at him long enough to notice the faintest bruise beneath his eye. She also couldn't help but notice the angry scar slicing across his forehead…it hadn't been there when last she saw him. "Your housekeeper wrote to me a while back."

"Sass did? About what?"

"She said that she'd found a saddlebag of my father's things in the root cellar of the foreman's house."

"I suppose the bag was overlooked when you moved away after your father died." When he folded his arms over his chest, Lydia couldn't help but notice how much of a man he'd become. Where before he was lean, now his thick shoulders stretched wide, and even his neck was roped with muscle. "You sure didn't need to make the trip just to save us the trouble of sending it to you."

On an inevitable yawn, she tugged her coat tight against the nagging chill of the lingering April thunderstorm. "I didn't."

"You're here, aren't you?"

"I mean that I didn't come out here *just* for my father's things. I attained a position at the hotel restaurant," she explained as though the significant geographic shift was perfectly reasonable. It'd been the *only* reasonable option Lydia had had in front of he, seeing as how she had no relatives residing elsewhere. Copper Creek had been her home—far more than Chicago *ever* had.

Besides, she'd been left with no choice. The constant barrage of eligible men calling every few days—her aunt's ploy to get Lydia married off—had finally worn Lydia thin. When her aunt had taken it upon herself to arrange a marriage with one of them, Lydia had vehemently stood her ground.

She didn't want to get married. Ever!

And especially not to some man she barely even liked!

"Are you talking about the new hotel in Copper Creek?" Jeb asked, one dark brow arching in surprise.

"That's the one." It was the one place she could work and know that she hadn't been hired because of pity or obligation.

Mrs. Gussman's Boardinghouse would have no openings for another week. And although Lydia had no solid solutions to this dilemma, she refused to tell Jeb she was temporarily homeless.

She glanced at the pitiful, run-down cabin, its one small window gaping open in a silent cry for attention, and she half considered sneaking out here to sleep. Her gaze darted to the sagging door for a moment as she remembered how, as a young girl, she'd christened this little hovel *home*, tending to the place every week or so, cleaning and primping as though it was her very own. In her naive and innocent dream world, she'd spent an entire lifetime there. She'd married there. Given birth there. Grown old right there in that little piece of perfection—and with the man of her foolish and childish dreams.

Jeb.

An unwanted quiver sneaked up her spine. With the dilapidated roof, the cold that was seeping through to her bones and Jeb being so near…

"I'm going to be starting work soon, so I thought I'd stop out today to get the saddlebag."

"But *this* isn't your old place," he said, gesturing with his head to the cabin.

But this *was* the place where she'd hidden a very critical part of her heart—letters to Jeb. Throughout her youthful years she'd penned him love letters he'd thankfully never, ever read. She'd kept them hidden in her mama's etched, silver handkerchief box.

Above all else, Lydia was intent on getting the letters and box back. She could only hope that someone hadn't discovered her wistful and ardent and ridiculous thoughts she'd poured out onto pages and pages. From the looks of the structure, she may well have been the last person to set foot in the little dwelling.

"No. But I've always loved this place. I only wanted to take a peek." She struggled to keep the bitter edge from her voice. How could Mr. Gentry and Jeb allow the cabin to fall into such disrepair? "It's sure seen its better days."

Jeb paused for a lingering moment, his jaw ticking. "We've all seen better days."

The faint shadow crossing his stoic expression pricked her compassion. There was something decidedly different about Jeb, but she couldn't allow herself to look too deep. That kind of concern might grow into something more and she couldn't afford to be vulnerable. Not now. Not with Jeb.

"So, you were just going to get what you came for and leave?" The dismay etched in his furrowed brow sent shame snaking through her. "No, 'Hi there, Jeb, it's great to see you.'"

The heat of embarrassment crept up her neck to her face. She drew her lips into a tight line, sending sandy granules of mud slipping into her mouth. Grimacing, she resisted the sudden urge to—

"Go ahead…spit," he said, as though he'd read her mind. She wasn't sure if a shiver shimmied down her spine because of being cold or because of the unnerving effects of his half grin. "You used to be an expert, remember? You could hit a target from fifteen yards if my memory serves me right."

"It would be unladylike." Not that she looked anything like a lady at this moment—except for the warm blush beneath her mud-covered neck and cheeks. "I do have a little pride, you know."

"Oh, I know. I haven't forgotten." The fleeting arch of his eyebrows irked her good. "I have to know for sure…you *were* planning on saying hello, right?"

She hugged her arms to her chest, feeling strangely undone by his inquiry. After all, she'd lived the first sixteen years of her life on this ranch. He used to call her his young shadow. "I hadn't planned on it."

He paused for a long moment, his mouth drawn into a firm line and his gaze unreadable. "Well, I can guarantee you that I'll never hear the end of it from Sass if you don't stay for supper. Unless, of course, you have big plans."

A wave of sentimentality washed over her thinking about the Gentry's housekeeper. When Lydia was growing up, Sass had stepped in at times when Lydia's father, a widower since Lydia was five years old, was hard-pressed to speak a little womanly advice to his daughter. Lydia didn't remember much of her mama, except her warm smile, and the brave way she'd passed on after being ill for a long time.

"Not exactly, but…I should be going, regardless." She shoved a lock of hair from her face, knowing she must look a sight, but not really caring. "I'm sorry if I've kept you from something."

"I'm not sorry."

She narrowed a skeptical gaze on him.

"Do I look sorry?" He tipped his head her direction.

Lydia bit back a languid yawn, trying to drum up some kind of excuse why she shouldn't stay—but her daddy had raised her better than that. Besides, she was exhausted and the achy chill that had seeped all the way to her bones, begged for a little relief.

"Listen, you've got to be soaked through. And it'll be getting dark before you know it." His brows creased in concern over those deep brown eyes she'd dreamt about more times than she could count. "Please just come back to the house and stay for supper. It's the least I can offer after throwing you down into the mud. And hurting you," he added with a sympathetic wince.

He might be able to make up for hurting her just moments ago, but she'd never allow him close enough to the deep wound he'd inflicted five years ago. "I don't know.…"

Jeb took one step closer. "You'll catch your death of a cold if you don't get out of those wet clothes. And we need to see about your side in case something is broken."

"Nothing's broken." She pulled her shoulders back even when they begged to droop in fatigue. "Honestly, I feel just fine."

When he hooked a finger beneath her chin and tipped up her head to look at him, eye-to-eye, her knees went alarmingly weak. "Humor me. Please, Lydia. I feel horrible about this. At least let me make up for my rude manners."

She was really too exhausted to fight him. On a defeated sigh, she said, "Very well—but I'll be on my way after dinner."

She'd have to make do until a room at the boardinghouse opened up. And she'd have to make the best of things in Copper Creek because Aunt Tillie had proclaimed that if Lydia left Chicago, there would be no coming back.

Lydia didn't need help, though…she had her pride.

"I'm glad you've decided to stay for dinner, anyway." Jeb felt enormous relief, knowing that Sass would take good care of Lydia.

He could barely take his eyes off Lydia as she clutched her coat so tight a raindrop couldn't find its way in. He sure hadn't recognized her from the back, but in spite of the mud caking her face, he'd know those wonder-filled, crystal blue eyes anywhere. He'd pictured those beautiful eyes of Lydia's countless times over the past five years. And now, here she was.

Embarrassed. Alone. Vulnerable. And hurt.

She appeared as nervous as a rabbit that had wandered into a coyote den. There was just something about her that held him hostage. Was it her obvious attempt to look indifferent? The adorable way she tried to ward off embarrassment with that stubborn tilt of her chin? Or was it the way she seemed set on protecting herself?

"So, you have somewhere to stay all lined up, right? Or were you planning on staying in this place?"

His playful wink managed to send her gaze crashing to the ground.

"Had I known you were coming, I would've fixed the place up," he half joked, attempting to lighten her somber mood. He'd wanted to do some repairs around here after his father passed away a year ago, but there were only so many hours in the day. And if he wasn't working his hands raw, he was catching a few blessed hours of sleep.

He really couldn't even afford to take the time to have dinner with Lydia tonight, but he felt just awful for hurting her the way he had.

Lydia....

Growing up she'd worn britches more often than not around the ranch. He could count the times he'd seen her in a feminine, fitted dress, on exactly one finger. He suddenly remembered her last day on the ranch—the day she'd turned sixteen. She'd come sprinting toward the corral, where he'd been training a very spirited and unbroken stallion. He could see her now...her dark hair swishing around her shoulders like strands of rich satin, and that dress, as blue as the sky in springtime, gently hugging feminine curves he hadn't even known existed. Even from a distance he could see the frantic, almost longing-filled look in her eyes.

As she had approached, he was caught completely off guard by her striking beauty. Bowled over by the gorgeous woman Lydia had become.

And disgusted with himself for thinking of her in such a manner.

His heart had come to a sudden stop. He'd forgotten to breathe. And an undeniable sense of *knowing* had surged through his entire being.

He'd never thought of her as anything other than the foreman's daughter, six years younger than him and as innocent as a newborn kitten. Not *once* in all the time she'd tagged along with him around the ranch, had he felt that kind of attraction. It was all he could do to gather his thoughts enough to hold on to the stallion's lead rope. He remembered forcing all of his attention to the anxious stallion, bent on rearing back and throwing its massive head around.

Lydia had spoken, but her words were lost as the stallion reared, pawing at the air with furious energy. Jeb had dodged the massive hooves. Labored to keep hold of the lead rope. Frantic, he'd motioned her away, yelling for her to go before she was clobbered by the enormous beast.

He didn't remember a thing after that. Only that the stallion's massive hoof had come down, grazing his head, knocking him out and leaving a long cut slicing across his forehead.

And now, Lydia was back again. And he couldn't deny the instant longing he felt for her in his heart.

But failure loomed like an ominous storm. He'd certainly heard enough about his failures from his father, even though he'd always done his best and worked from dawn to well beyond dusk. It was all he could do not to fall prey to its wicked upheaval when everything around seemed cursed by his father's legacy.

The ranch was a shadow of what it'd been. The bank was breathing down his neck, far worse than any opponent Jeb had fought in boxing matches over the past few months. Even if he paid back every last cent of gambling debt incurred by his father, Lydia couldn't possibly want him, a man who couldn't seem to lead this withering ranch out of the red and into the black. A man who struggled to hold on to some kind of belief in himself.

So much had changed in five years.

Life had all but hardened him. He didn't know that he believed in much of anything anymore—except that he was a fighter and sometimes fighters came out on top.

He longed for the day when he could truly rest again. When

he could find joy in life again, and when he could really believe in God's goodness again. And His love.

Because right now it seemed all but impossible to have faith for anything more than just making it through the next few days.

Chapter Two

Without a doubt life had just gotten a whole lot more complicated now that a certain little lady, chin height, slender and with a stubborn thread woven into the fabric of her personality, had shown up on his property. But for some reason Jeb felt no urge to herd her out of here anytime soon.

Since her arrival last night Jeb had gotten little sleep, between getting all of his chores done and checking in on her every hour or so. She'd had good intentions of leaving, but the poor thing had barely been able to keep her eyes open enough to make it back to the main house. Peering at her now from the front parlor doorway, and seeing the way her brow creased in discomfort as she shifted on the sofa, he was glad she'd stayed. Very glad.

He'd get her on her feet again and then she'd walk out of his life. And that would be for the best.

He had nothing to offer a woman like Lydia.

When he spotted her rousing, he moved a little closer. The midmorning sun streamed in through the window and bathed her fair face in a wash of light. Her eyes fluttered open as soft as a butterfly's wings. She blinked several times, then turned her head and focused on him, her gaze clouded with sleep.

For a moment, he could almost imagine himself waking up beside this beautiful woman—every day for the rest of his life.

"Good morning, sleepyhead," he said, offering her a half grin.

A look of horror flitted across her face as she shifted her focus to the window. *"Morning?"*

"Yes, ma'am." Jeb hunkered down and sat on the table in front of the sofa. "You've been sleeping for almost sixteen hours straight."

"That *can't* be true." Her disbelieving sigh tugged a slight grin to the corner of his mouth.

"You're saying I lie?"

"Well, no, but how did I—when did I—" She gave a small groan. "I don't even remember—"

To see the tenacious way she seemed determined to protect herself from him nearly broke his heart. He couldn't, for the life of him, figure out why she felt so wary, but he had a niggling feeling that something had happened in their last interchange that maybe he just plain didn't remember.

"I am *so* sorry to intrude like this." Her full mouth compressed into a hard line.

"It's not an intrusion."

"Why in the world didn't you wake me?" she half accused, rubbing her eyes as though to focus better.

"I didn't have the heart." Peering down at where his hands were clasped between his knees, he tried to guess just how many times he'd looked in on her, and lost count somewhere around nine. It had felt so good to have something to focus on, other than the piles of problems surrounding him. "Sass didn't have the heart, either, for that matter. She gathered extra pillows from her bedroom and we fixed up this nest for you. Is it comfortable?" He patted the fluff of pillows surrounding her.

Her cautious gaze landed on his. "It is. Very much so."

"Sass has tended to enough injuries through the years that she figured you were better off right here on the sofa."

"That was very considerate. But unnecessary," she said, covering her mouth when a wide yawn commanded her full attention. "Thank you for your trouble, Jeb, but I'll be leaving within the hour."

"You may as well stay here where you're comfortable," he reasoned. "Sass will take good care of you—probably mother you till you wish you were a little girl again."

"I don't need anyone fussing over me. Really. I'm fine." The weariness weighting her eyes said otherwise. "Besides...last night I said I was going to leave right after supper."

"I remember. You were firm about that, too," he said, watching her brace her hands beside her as though she was preparing to get up only to slump into the nest of pillows.

The way she was clearly struggling to put on a good front, pricked his compassion. "Are you all right?"

"Perfect," she said, a little too fast to be convincing.

He eyed her with a single shake of his head. "I remember you being stubborn, but not this stubborn."

"I don't know *what* you're talking about." She brushed wisps of hair from her forehead.

"Oh, really? It seems like you'd rather go to your grave than to stay here another minute."

"Don't be silly." She nervously fingered the quilt. "You know...I barely even remember making it back to the house."

He didn't know if he'd ever forget the heartbreaking way she'd nearly fallen asleep on the quarter-mile ride to the main ranch house. In spite of her obvious exhaustion, she'd insisted she was just fine. "You were pretty tired, I can tell you that."

Closing her eyes, she gave the smallest sigh. "*Please* tell me I didn't complain."

His mouth flinched in a restrained grin. "Not so that I heard."

"Good." She nodded once, apparently satisfied with his answer. "I vaguely remember Sass helping me with a bath."

"Can't say that I was privy to that part of the evening," he measured out, dropping his gaze to where he clutched his hands tight. "But yes, she did."

Lydia gave a defeated sigh. "For that, I am grateful."

Standing, he crossed to the window where the haunting sight of rundown buildings met his gaze. "I'm responsible for all of this. And believe me, I feel terrible about the whole thing. I'm going to make sure you're taken care of until you're feeling like yourself again. Are we clear?" He turned to face her.

"You are no more responsible than I am." Wincing, she sat up a little straighter. "I shouldn't have reached for that handkerchief. I don't know *what* I was thinking."

"Well, you sure had me believing you were pulling out a gun out. And with the thefts that have gone on recently…"

Swinging her focus out the window, her brow furrowed in concern. "Where's my gelding?"

"I stabled, fed and brushed him down." Leaning a shoulder against the wide pine trim, Jeb glanced toward the run-down barn that had once been a stamp of pride on this ranch—at least when Lydia's father was foreman. It still got to Jeb, thinking about some of the fine stock he'd had to sell off just to make ends meet. "It was good to see that big boy again."

"I thought he looked familiar, but I couldn't imagine you selling such a fine horse," she said, her brow furrowed in confusion.

"I sold him a few months back." And doing so had been like ripping out a chunk of his heart. "I'll go in town and return him for you today."

"Jeb…no. *No*," she stated, a little more firmly. "I can manage just fine. I've got a job to start, you know." When she folded back the quilt, she glanced down at the pristine white nightdress Sass had wrangled for her. Lydia slammed her eyes shut as though she'd just been caught wearing nothing more than her undergarments. *"Where are my clothes?"*

Jeb nodded toward the hallway. "You'll probably want to talk to Sass about that."

"That's evasive. And not very nice, Jeb Gentry."

"Hungry?" he said, amused by her feistiness.

"Not really." When the faintest blush colored her fair cheeks, he felt strangely satisfied. "I mean…no, thank you."

He knew she'd be hurting this morning after the way he'd taken her down in the mud. But for some reason he wasn't a bit surprised that she was being feisty.

"Now, *where's* my dress?"

"I burned it, dear," Sass proclaimed, entering the room with a brand new dress draped over her arm, her quick stride belying her five-foot frame, as well as the fact that she'd not had one minute of rest all night long.

When Lydia's tired gaze widened in shock, Sass quickly added, "I *did* save the coat, though. And I tell you what…it cleaned up just fine. But that dress of yours was a different story." Sass adjusted Lydia's quilt. Because of dwindling finances there'd been several times when Jeb had seriously considered dismissing Sass from her position, just like he had the two ranch hands. But when it came right down to it, he couldn't do that to the woman. She'd been on the ranch longer than Jeb was old.

Lydia fingered the ruffle-edged sleeve of her nightdress.

"I tried to scrub it clean." Sass's petite round face pinched in remorse. "But I'm afraid that had I done it justice the dress would've fallen apart. Don't worry though, dear." She smoothed back whispery strands of hair from Lydia's face. "I sent Jeb in town last night for some fabric from the mercantile."

Sass held up the dress she'd made, sliding Jeb a pleased-with-herself kind of smile.

"You made that?" Lydia leaned forward to touch the fabric. *"Last night?"*

"I sure did. And let me tell you…it was a sheer *joy* to sew on such nice fabric, too. I delighted in *every single stitch*."

"It's beautiful," Lydia whispered. When her crystal blue gaze misted over, Jeb could've wrapped his arms around her and given her a hug right then and there.

But that would be a big mistake. One he'd regret.

And one his heart would forever mourn.

"It sure is." The dress wasn't fancy by city standards, with a lot of flounce and flourish, but he was convinced it would be perfect on Lydia. "You did a fine job, Sass."

"You did *yourself* proud, too, picking out such lovely fabric," Sass said, nervously brushing at her skirt.

The look of shy appreciation in Lydia's expression made his heart stutter a beat or two.

He really had to get a handle on his emotions and keep a rein on his heart, because he was finding himself drawn to her far too easily. He had more work than one man could do and a mountain of debt that hung like some dark omen over his life. The fact was…his heart couldn't run free when it was chained to the sordid legacy left by his father.

But the breath of hope her presence had added to this place in just sixteen hours…*that* he couldn't overlook.

"Tell Lydia how you dragged the mercantile owner out of bed just to open the store for you," Sass prompted, laying the dress in Lydia's lap.

Lydia smoothed her hand featherlight over the garment. "In the middle of the *night*?"

Jeb cleared his throat. "It wasn't that late. He didn't mind all that much."

Mr. Lippman had been none too pleased with having to traipse back over to the store at a quarter past nine last night, but compared to what his mood would've been had it been two o'clock in the morning in the dead of winter, he'd been agreeable. Jeb had made quick work of his quest because the minute he'd spotted the fabric, as rich and blue as the spring sky this morning, he'd known it would be perfect for Lydia. The costly fabric was worth every penny he had left in his pocket.

The stunning hue reminded him of that beautiful dress she'd

worn, the last time he'd seen her five years ago. The day his life had taken a sharp turn down a long and dreary path. The day he'd begun to find out just what Jeb Gentry was made of.

Chapter Three

Fingering the six buttons trailing up the front of her dress, Lydia blinked back an errant and unwanted tear as she made her way to the henhouse to collect eggs. The cornflower blue dress was just lovely. There was nothing overly fancy about the garment, no expensive lace or delicate ruching, which was just fine by Lydia. The dress fit her to perfection.

She'd struggled to hold her desperate shock in check when she'd learned, just minutes ago, that her tattered dress had been burned. Even though it'd hung on her like an old wash-cloth draped over a clothesline, it was all she had. She'd have fished it out of the ashes if she'd thought it'd do any good, but deep down she knew Sass was right.

Ducking into the rickety henhouse door, Lydia turned and watched as six fat and happy hens meandered in behind her. "Hello, ladies," she said, giving the plump hens a smile as she gathered two eggs from a nest. "Don't mind me. I'm just here for your eggs."

When one of them fluffed her feathers as though showing off an extravagant ball gown, Lydia's thoughts wandered to the elaborate dress selection she'd worn and left in Chicago.

Aunt Tillie had promised that if Lydia moved back to the west, all of the dresses and fancy things would stay in Chicago, *where they belonged.* Her aunt had probably expected Lydia to stop in her tracks at that, but Lydia wasn't motivated by fancy gowns, social gatherings and instruction on how to best use her womanly wiles. And she could care less about how to steal a man's heart right out from underneath him—she'd decided that the day she'd left Gentry land.

When she reached toward a nest in the far corner, she was startled to find a gray cat sprawled over the straw.

"You are the most peculiar looking chicken I've ever seen," she said, chuckling as she stroked the feline's very pregnant belly. "Aww…you're getting ready to have your babies, aren't you?"

Gently reaching under the purring cat, she slid two eggs from the nest and added them to the basket on her left arm.

"Do the hens know you're planning on using this nest?" she asked, glancing back at where the birds looked at her as if it was perfectly normal for a cat to be draped over a chicken nest.

Sweet as could be, the mama cat squeezed her eyes tight, only to open them and then peer up at Lydia. "Sweet girl…you take it easy and rest, do you hear?" she said, giving the cat a parting scratch under the chin.

Lydia ducked out of the small building, wishing she'd get the chance to see the new kittens. But she'd be starting her job in less than a week. And she *had* to get back into town, seeing as how Jeb's very presence did the *worst* things to her resolve.

She'd thought that seeing Jeb again would taste like a sour draught on her tongue. So why, after being here for no more than a day, did she feel herself thirsting just to be near the man?

While she started back to the house, the disturbing image of Jeb's faraway and solemn look drifted into her mind. What had transpired over the past five years? The strange distance, deep and fixed in his expression, had haunted her from the moment she'd caught sight of him. Even the few grins she'd seen tipping the corner of his mouth never quite reached his brown eyes as she'd remembered. And Lydia had spent enough nights and days dreaming about him to know the difference.

Her thoughts shifted to the bruising beneath Jeb's eye, his nose that had obviously been broken and the rough and jagged scar on his face. She'd caught him absently fingering the angry scar, tracing its shape as though replaying some secluded dark memory.

Had he gotten into some kind of trouble? If so, could she help him without making herself vulnerable? Above *all else*, she had to jealously guard her heart from Jeb.

And from her own foolishness.

When she rounded the side of the barn, she came to an abrupt stop, troubled by what she saw. The structure's south side was missing several boards and the loft door hung from one hinge like an old trapper with one sagging tooth. The ranch was nowhere near the glory it had once been. Even the Double G Ranch sign hanging at the property entrance looked exhausted and all dog-eared.

Didn't Jeb and his father realize the condition of the place?

Then she remembered what Jeb had said yesterday...that *we've all seen our better days*...and her harsh thoughts were brought up short.

Just then Jeb emerged from the other side of the barn, a saddlebag draped over his arm, his expression solemn as his long legs ate up the distance to the house.

"You're certainly focused," she called.

"There you..." his words died on his lips as he pivoted and spotted her. He came to a sudden stop at the porch steps, his gaze making a slow and steady sweep from her toes to her head, as though something was horribly wrong.

"Are you all right?" She slowed as she neared him, self-conscious all of the sudden. "Jeb?"

His intense gaze settled on hers. His jaw muscles tensed.

"Jeb?" Grasping a handful of her skirt, she willed her emotions to stay firmly grounded as she eyed her father's old saddlebag draped over his arm. "Is—is that for me?"

Blinking hard, he shoved his focus to the bag. On a slow sigh, he stepped toward her. "I was just bringing this in for you."

Unfurling her hand, she willed her pulse to stop pounding all the way up to her ears. The way he'd looked at her just then had sent a quiver of odd and yet warm awareness down her spine.

Eager to shake off the last few spine-tingling seconds, she moved her focus to the bag, the distant memory of her father carrying it to the house after a long hard day's work, wafting through her mind.

"It's hard to believe that has been in the root cellar all these years." She longed to bury her face in the leather if only to catch the lingering scent of her daddy. "Who's living in the foreman's house now, anyway?"

Edging toward the steps, he gently laid out the bag. "The place has been vacant since you left."

She searched his shadowed gaze and sat down on the steps. "So, who's foreman, now?"

"You're looking at him—I run the place now." Hunkering down to sit across from her, Jeb clasped his hands, work worn and rough and scarred, between his knees. "My father never hired anyone to take Hank's place—your father would've been impossible to replace."

"He did love his job." Fingering the saddlebag's soft leather, she remembered how she used to tuck little surprises for her daddy in the satchel—drawings, little posies of flowers, a handful of fresh baked cookies wrapped in cheesecloth..."You know, he prayed often for this ranch. And your family."

"God knows we needed it."

Hugging her arms to her chest, she studied his solemn expression. "I can recall times when my father would sit beside the fire and stare into the flames—I always knew he was praying then." She never felt more secure than when he'd pray.

"He was a man of faith—you could see that in the way he treated others."

Lydia nodded her hearty agreement. Her father had trusted God. And had taught Lydia to do the same.

Guilt's swift and insolent wind suddenly whipped through her soul. She'd shied from God in the last few years, and felt as if she was letting her father down because of that. But so much had happened, starting with her father's untimely death. Somehow, she had to find a kind of peace for her soul.

"Hank taught me a lot about ranching—he taught me a lot about life, too, for that matter," Jeb said, his voice low and tight, and his heartfelt words nearly triggering a small trickle of tears.

"He always did spend a lot of time with you, didn't he?" Swallowing hard, she dragged in a deep breath.

"Like I said…it was impossible to replace him." His jaw muscles tensed. "I'm sure you must miss him."

"I do." Tugging the satchel into her lap, she found some comfort in holding this remnant of her father. "It's really wonderful that you're foreman now, Jeb. Your father must think a lot of you."

"I'm not so sure about that," he retorted, slicing in a breath. "But being six feet under, he doesn't have much to say about it."

His words hit her like a bucket of icy, mountain stream water. "Are you saying that he died?" Her stomach clenched tight as he gave a single nod. *"When?"*

He set his jaw. "A year ago."

"Oh, Jeb…. I am so sorry." Ignoring all sense of self-protection, she reached out and touched his forearm, thick and roped with tense muscles. "I had no idea."

The distant pain in his gaze gripped her soul. "It's all right."

"How terrible for you." She gave his arm a brief and tender squeeze, wanting for him to know she cared.

Maybe she could reside in Copper Creek and enjoy a friendship with Jeb without detesting the ground he walked on. Or fearing that she might worship the ground he walked on, as she once had.

Jeb dragged his fingers through his dark, slightly waved hair. "It's been hard, but not in the way you might think."

"What happened?" she asked, still stunned and even ashamed that, just a few minutes ago, she'd been blaming Jeb's father for the ranch's declining condition.

"I better let you go through Hank's things, Lydia." He shoved himself up to standing and jammed his hands into his pockets. "Can I get you anything? A glass of water or tea?"

"No. I'm fine." She fingered the worn leather straps, oddly missing Jeb's presence already, even when he was standing right in front of her. "Don't feel like you have to go, though, Jeb. Please, join me," she offered, feeling strangely desperate, and yet scared to death to keep this connection with him.

Was there some kind of bond with him that had never been broken? In spite of the years of convincing herself that she felt nothing for him?

Her thoughts drifted to the box of love letters she'd written to him, and she felt instant unease. Once she had those remnants of her heart in her possession again, then she could breathe a little easier.

Tensing his jaw, his gaze shifted to the range as though he longed to pry himself from this moment. "Sorry, but I've got too much to do. I can't afford to get sidetracked right now."

Lydia's heart slammed against her chest. He may as well have kicked her in the ribs for the piercing pain those words caused. Didn't he remember what had happened five years ago?

Well, *she* could recall the scene with perfect and excruciating clarity. It had been a week after her daddy had passed away from his injuries suffered in a tragic wagon accident…the day she'd turned sixteen. Intent on claiming Jeb's full attention, she'd bee-lined for the corral where Jeb had been breaking a new stallion.

She'd only wanted Jeb to understand how much she loved him, how much she'd always loved him and how they were meant to be together. Surely then he'd ask for her hand in marriage. She'd even dressed for the occasion, hoping he'd notice the way she'd let her hair fall free, and the beautiful dress her aunt had brought for her—especially when she usually only wore rough-and-tumble britches or simple sacklike dresses. Her heart and future had been at stake.

Bold as the sun in spring, she'd proclaimed her undying love for him in carefully chosen words she'd rehearsed from the time she was a young girl.

His response? He'd yelled at her. Scowled and motioned her back, saying that she was a *distraction*.

She'd run away as fast as her feet, clad in shiny new boots, would carry her. Never *once* looking back.

That day, Lydia had learned one very important lesson… never *ever* let your true feelings be known.

With the distinctly feminine way Lydia had looked this morning in that blue dress, reminiscent of the one she'd worn the day he'd realized Lydia had grown into a stunningly gorgeous woman, Jeb couldn't get away from her fast enough.

He couldn't seem to get back to her fast enough, either.

He spurred his stallion faster over the road to home, just to make sure she was still there. He half expected that she'd hightailed it out of there as soon as she'd had the chance.

But she had no place to go. He'd found that out from Mrs. Gussman when he'd been in town just now. Where Lydia expected to stay, he could only guess, but her accommodations wouldn't be ready for at least a week.

Jeb dragged in a ragged breath as he rounded a bend in the

road. He'd been at the bank, all but begging for another extension on the mortgage, but time had run out and unless he had a huge chunk of the debt paid off within a week, he'd lose the ranch. The brutal truth of what he faced hovered over him like a pitch black cloud, raining down the coldest and cruelest reality. Even if he won the two boxing matches he was scheduled to fight this week, thereby making some hard-won cash, it probably wouldn't be enough.

No matter, he'd go down fighting. He had to.

Facts were facts. His father had mortgaged the ranch to the hilt. There was a legacy of other debts, too, and each person wanted their money yesterday.

Turning onto the beaten-down road leading to the homestead, Jeb sent a silent prayer heavenward for God's help. Knowing that Lydia's father had often prayed for the Gentry ranch gave him a small but definable sense of peace. Hank had been a friend and a father figure when Jeb's own father had failed.

Jeb never could seem to please his father, and once Hank had passed on, the displeasure had mounted to overbearing levels. He had the deep dark scars in his soul to prove it, but he'd never let anyone see them.

Shrugging off the heavy weight of his past, Jeb rode by the tree-crowded meadow, where he'd found Lydia only yesterday. She'd said she had a fondness for the little cabin.

He did recall once, when she was probably eleven-years-old, he'd discovered her out there, all alone. He'd heard singing, the sweet voice carried through the peaceful meadow on a gentle breeze. When he'd discovered the charming voice to be Lydia's, he'd stopped, captured by the delightful sound. His young shadow had emerged from the dwelling, engrossed in sweeping the small porch, completely oblivious to the fact that he was close by listening to her lilting melody.

Jeb stared at the cabin, remembering that endearing scene when life was far simpler. He was reminded, once again, just how in-need-of-repair the ranch had become. Being the sole man left on the ranch, he had little time for maintenance. Some things required a total overhaul and the money needed was no-where to be found.

There were areas in his soul in need of a total overhaul, too. And though he'd been finding himself praying some, he had to wonder where all his prayers would lead. Would he ever find the peace and acceptance he longed for?

The overwhelming feelings of failure and loss that had plagued him the past months were there again, staring him down, demanding concession.

The hair on the back of Jeb's neck quivered to alert. His heartbeat quickened inside his chest as he maintained his ground.

He'd spent enough time in his life, taking hits from his father and walking away with nothing but regret and pain. He had to keep fighting for himself. It was his only chance.

Chapter Four

How could Lydia have been so foolish?

She'd always had a soft spot for the hurting, but this time she'd let her compassion get the best of her. She had to remember that Jeb was lethal to her mind, her soul and her heart.

Under the cover of darkness, she tiptoed down the stairs, making her way through the house to leave out the back door. She'd tack a note in the barn, thanking Jeb and Sass for their trouble, and then she'd be on her way into town—*after* she stopped by the cabin and retrieved her box of letters from its hiding place.

Shifting her daddy's saddlebag to her other arm, she ignored the dull pain at her side, longing for the day when she could ignore the wound deep in her heart. This afternoon hadn't helped matters. The hurried way he'd left her sitting on the front porch, his stinging words searing her heart, had left her speechless, dazed and hurt. She'd forgotten all about the saddlebag until just moments ago, when she'd grabbed it on her way out of the house.

Edging around a thick Ponderosa pine, standing like a steadfast guardian in the backyard, she peered again at the house to see Sass's lantern burning bright in her bedroom. She started toward the barn, when the sound of voices stopped her in her tracks.

She paused, her breath catching.

"Please, don't do this, Jeb." Sass's familiar voice came from just inside the barn, seizing Lydia's immediate concern.

She spotted a lantern's dim glow emerging from the barn's broad doorway. She could make out Sass's short frame standing there, and Jeb mounted on his sleek black stallion—the same stallion he'd been breaking that day she'd left five years ago.

"I'll be fine." He reined the horse to face Sass. "I always am. You worry too much, Sass."

Sass gave her head a severe shake, holding up the lantern and illuminating Jeb's face. "You're going to lose more than you bargained for. You need to think about that."

"Everything is going to be all right."

The worry etched in Sass's expression was tangible even from the thirty or so feet away. "I know your father wouldn't want you doing this."

What was Jeb doing that was so bad? Was he spending time at the local saloons, gambling? Or patronizing the brothels?

A sick feeling hollowed out Lydia's stomach. Her pulse slammed through her veins as she recalled the conversation about Jeb's father's passing, and the almost unaffected way Jeb had dismissed the subject. Usually she was very perceptive to a person's emotions. Had she misread the look of pain in his gaze?

"Why wouldn't he want me doing this?" Impatience tainted Jeb's deep voice. "Because *he did*?"

What had Mr. Gentry done that had been so bad? Except for the occasional meals she and her daddy would share with Mr. Gentry and Jeb at the main house, she hadn't spent much time around the man. She could recall nothing overtly bad about him, though.

Lydia's heart was pounding. She edged back toward the house, the seconds passing like hours. As much as she wished to saddle up and ride out of this place, something was holding her right there on the ranch. Some unseen force urging her to stay long enough to discover the truth of things.

She owed her father that much. He'd given his life for the success of this ranch. Had Jeb's decisions or lack thereof, wasted all her father had worked for?

The thought sickened her even more.

"Please, Jeb," Sass pleaded, the broken sound in her voice piercing Lydia's heart.

"I'll see you tomorrow." Reining his stallion around, he galloped away into the darkness.

"Just pray. Trust God and pray," Sass called after him as Lydia hurried to the house, her rapid pulse rivaling the sound of Jeb's galloping stall on.

In spite of the suspicion surrounding his departure, Lydia sent a whispered prayer heavenward for Jeb. And even as she did, she felt a gentle tugging at her own heart to trust God once again.

The feeling gave her a small amount of hope for the future—hope she hadn't had for a long time. She had to believe that there was a reason for her being back here, far bigger than escaping from her aunt's controlling clutches.

With all his might, Jeb swung the ax yet again, slicing through another log as though it was a chunk of warm butter. He'd been at it for the past half hour, chopping enough wood to replenish Sass's supply. Stopping just long enough to get his breath, he leaned his ax against the big stump. He swiped at the sweat beading his forehead, willing his focus from the throbbing pain in his hands and face and his torso.

Last night's boxing challenger had been a beast of a man from the Golden area. The opponent had been one of Jeb's toughest yet. In the end Jeb had won the match, and every last bruise and cut had been worth the cash purse. It wouldn't come close to paying off the bank, but maybe, if God had heard his prayers, the sum along with what he'd make from a win two nights from now, might just buy him a little more time.

Swinging his fists for money had been his *last* resort. One that had kept the ranch afloat. One he'd gladly lay down if only he could save the ranch. But the crowds it drew had grown considerably since he'd started a few months ago.

He'd lost his very first match. Within the first two minutes, he'd been knocked out cold. After that, he'd been told he needed to drum up some real *rage* if he had the hope of winning.

The second attempt in the ring, he'd tapped into a deep well of anger he'd buried in his soul. He'd pictured the way his father, drunk and mad as a cornered badger, would strike him with balled fists, screaming about how life hadn't been fair, and about how he's lost at the gambling tables again and how Jeb's mama would still be there had Jeb not been born. Jeb had won that second match, all right. But the dark, haunting rage that had stayed with him for several days following wasn't worth the money.

Finally, he'd used the ranch as his motivation. He'd think about this place and how the fabric of his heart and life had been woven into the land and livestock. That had proved to be all the motivation he needed. Since then he'd not gone down for the count even once.

"What happened?" Lydia said, startling him. She peered up at his face, her expression pinched with concern and something else he couldn't quite read.

Jeb swiped his forehead again in a futile effort to keep the salty sweat from burning into the cuts over his swollen left eye. "What do you mean?"

She jammed her hands on her slender waist, the willful action sparking his amusement. "You know *exactly* what I'm talking about. Your eyes and mouth and your hands." She inched closer as though to get a better look. "What happened to you, Jeb?"

Reaching down, he grabbed the chunk of wood he'd just split, tossing it over to the growing pile. "It's nothing."

"That is not *nothing*, Jeb Gentry." She pointed to his face. "Look at you!"

Jeb gave a weary sigh. He'd heard all of this from Sass dozens of times. "It's nothing that a couple days can't fix."

"What were you *doing*?" She was inches from him now, standing on her tiptoes and peering up at his face as though she'd never seen a black eye before. He was sorely tempted to take her in his arms and hold her tight, if only to ease her distress.

"This doesn't concern you." Grasping her shoulders, he gently set her aside then reached for his ax again. "Now, what is it that you came out here for? I have things that need to get done."

Lydia grabbed the ax from him, holding it in her quivering hands. "Do you think I can be put off that easily?"

The concern creasing her expression brought up short his protest. He really didn't deserve her worry. He'd done this by choice.

"At least let me take a look at those cuts." Crossing to the short, wide stump he'd used for cutting wood, she lifted her skirts and climbed on top, gesturing for him to come closer.

He stood right where he was. "I already told Sass I didn't need her fussing over me. The same goes for you."

"Please. Let me help." Dropping back down to the ground, she marched over to stand in front of him again. She took his hands in hers and looked them over, her gentle touch like a warm and soothing balm seeping way down to the deepest part of his soul. "I know you've got to be hurting. *Please*," she pleaded, her eyes glistening in the early morning sun.

He swallowed hard, shaken by her tender consideration. He knew he should pull away from her now, before his heart sprinted ahead of his common sense, but her touch undermined every argument regarding *why* he could never have her.

"Consider it paying you back for tending to me," she added, her gaze, hopeful.

He swallowed hard. "You forget that I'm the one who tackled you."

"That's beside the point. Come on, now." With his hands still in hers, she walked backward, tugging him up to the porch, stretching across the front of the house. She patted the top step. "Sit here…I'll be right out."

The minute she scurried inside, he felt oddly vacant and strangely lacking, as though a piece of him was missing. Jeb cared for Lydia—of that he had no doubt. He'd thought about her nearly every minute since she'd arrived almost two days ago. But she deserved a man who could provide a good living. When the sun went down on her time here, he had to know that he'd done right by her. And the right thing was to deny his heart, so that she could have her heart's dream—whatever that may be.

There was only one small problem. He couldn't ignore the palpable sense of divine providence he'd felt just moments ago when she'd held his hands in hers.

When the door creaked open, his pulse sped up a notch as Lydia came to kneel beside him. She set down the bowl of water then fished some medical supplies and rags from her apron pocket.

She dipped one of the rags in the water and raised it to his face, her serious and sympathetic expression making him uncomfortable.

"You can do this on one condition," he measured out, angling his head back, far from her reach.

"What's that?"

"No questions."

"But—"

"None." He held an index finger inches from her full lips.

She peered down her nose at his finger as though it was a bee ready to sting. When her innocent gaze slid up to his, he couldn't seem to keep a grin from cocking one side of his mouth.

"All right." Her breath whispered over his finger as he pulled his hand away. "No questions. But you can be sure that they'll keep me awake tonight."

"That's up to you," he said, shoving off a wince as she gently wiped his swollen and cut brow with her wet cloth.

Her forehead creased in sympathy. "This looks just awful, Jeb."

"It's not that bad."

She paused for a moment and looked at him, her beautiful face so close, the faintest scent of lilies wafting to his senses. "I'm serious. Your eye is almost swollen shut, and the bruising is as purple as a ripe plum." She set back on her haunches, softly touching his hands. "And your hands—they look like they were trampled by a herd of cattle."

"They're just a little red, that's all," he argued, well aware that his knuckles looked ugly and raw.

"Your lip looks terrible." She touched her fingertips against his lower lip, clearly unaware of the knee-weakening effect her touch had on him. "But I *won't* ask what happened."

"Good," he said once he finally found his voice.

"Is there something wrong that you want to tell me about, Jeb?"

He grasped her hand, angling a friendly kind of warning glance at her. "Only that you keep asking questions when you promised otherwise."

"How can I leave this place when you're getting yourself into trouble like this?" she argued, a little defensively.

"So you're staying longer?"

"Maybe just another night—that is, as long as it's—"

"Fine by me." Unexplainable relief flooded him at that news. She really did complicate matters for him, but he welcomed the complication. "I know Sass would like for you to stay, too. She probably loves having some female company out here," he said, watching as she opened a small brown jar of salve. "I thought you might want to know, I'm thinking about cleaning up that cabin you like so well."

Her wide-eyed gaze shot out to the road then shifted to him. "When?"

"As soon as I can." His labors might be for not if he lost the ranch, but if it'd make her happy to see the cabin fixed up, then it'd all be worth the effort. "Maybe tomorrow if I can squeeze it in."

Lydia blinked several times, as though dust had just flown into her eyes, but the day was perfectly still. "Some of my fondest memories come from that cabin," she whispered, giving him the smallest peek into what made her tick.

But before he could make his way into that small opening, she continued with, "I do hope your eye doesn't get infected, Jeb. Did you make sure you cleaned it after you..." she prompted, as though waiting for him to finish her thought.

"Cute trick, but I'm not falling for it." When he shot her a wry grin, the cuts inside his mouth burned.

"Do you blame me for trying?" Lydia raised her brows as she gently dabbed some salve on the cut above his eye.

He couldn't seem to stop staring at her features. She was so beautiful. And yet so natural. His gaze slipped down to the blue dress she wore and he felt his throat go desert dry. He would never forget that moment when he'd realized she wasn't just Lydia, his young and curious shadow, but that she was a woman. Sixteen and *very much* a woman. The understanding had shaken his world off its axis.

How had she gone from a young girl traipsing around in britches to the young woman she'd become at sixteen? The woman she was today—caring and loving and able to hold her own?

"I can hardly blame you for trying, but we made a deal," he said, forcing his thoughts back to the conversation. "And the

Lydia I knew from five years ago was not one to go against her word."

"I won't go against my word," she defended, squaring her shoulders in the most adorable and stubborn way. "And by the way…the Lydia you knew five years ago is *not* the woman you see now."

He met her challenging gaze. "I realized that the minute I saw you—I mean, after I discovered it *was* you." He would never forget the overwhelming feeling of relief at seeing her again. And the cruel sense of irony that she was completely out of his reach.

"So, what happened over the past five years, Lydia?" he braved, determined to find some kind of opening into her heart.

"That's just not something I'm going to discuss with you, Jeb. Sorry." Her brow furrowed in focus as she carefully spread salve on the cut below his right eye.

He grasped her hand, stilling her nurturing touch. "Well… if ever you feel like talking, I want you to know that I'm here for you."

A lengthy silence hung between them. Several minutes ticked by as Lydia set her undivided attention on cleansing and tending his battered hands.

Over the years he'd dreamed off and on of Lydia. And each time he'd wake wishing he could see her again.

Here she was now…her tender ministrations reaching into the depths of his soul. There was a tangible, almost divine connection with this woman. And he knew she felt its power, too. He could see it in her eyes, sense it in the tender way she responded to his touch, and feel it in that certain caring way she had with him.

"Does that hurt?" She smoothed salve over his raw knuckles, her soft touch reaching clear down into his heart.

"I'm used to it," he finally said.

He'd been fighting every couple weeks for the past six

months. He'd fight again tomorrow night, too, although he wasn't sure how wise that was so close on the heels of last night's fight. Going the full rounds wouldn't be an option—he'd have to knock his opponent out early on. With the windfall of promised earnings, the bank might just reconsider giving him a little more time.

"You get tough skin when you do the same thing long enough," he added, knowing how callused and thick his hands and areas on his face had gotten from scarring.

How callused he'd become toward his father.

And how callused he'd become toward God. He'd been struggling to find God in the midst of the turmoil, remembering how Lydia's father had often talked of faith, but he just couldn't seem to find his way. It was as if he couldn't go beyond the thick wall protecting his heart—just like Lydia.

"There's one problem with that, Jeb." She wiped her hands on her apron.

"What's that?"

After slipping the medicinal supplies into her apron pocket, she looked at him. The intent way she peered deep into his gaze, as if searching for some kind of well-kept secret, as if maybe there was something about his character that provoked suspicion, made him slightly uncomfortable.

And oddly defensive.

Lydia hugged her arms to her chest. "Tough skin makes it almost impossible to feel anything—at all."

Chapter Five

On a long yawn Lydia glanced at the small clock on her night-stand, bathed in the moon's pearly light filtering through the window. It was well after one o'clock in morning, and if she didn't go out to the cabin now, like she'd been planning for the past several hours, she might fall asleep and her chance would be gone with day's light.

She secured the thick white robe Sass had given her over her white cotton nightdress. Holding up a barely lit lantern, she tiptoed through the house, careful to avoid certain creaking floorboards on her way to the front door.

Honestly, she was tired of all of this sneaking around, but tonight she had *no choice*. If Jeb was serious about cleaning that cabin tomorrow, then she was determined to get the box of letters out of there before he happened upon them. She simply would not risk those pieces of her heart landing in his hands.

Nearing the front door, her thoughts drifted to last night, when Jeb had ridden off in spite of Sass's pleas to stay. The scene had swallowed her attention and since then, she'd been doing what she could around the house just to keep her mind from running to some dramatic and far-fetched conclusion.

She'd tried broaching the subject of Jeb with Sass, but each time the housekeeper would expertly shift the conversation elsewhere. Lydia didn't know what to think of the tactic except that the woman must be fiercely loyal.

Lydia didn't *need* to know what was going on with Jeb. Except that she had an emotional investment in this ranch—after all, her daddy had died on this land.

With stealthy precision, she opened the front door, turned around and carefully latched it without so much as a faint click. Relieved, she gave a huge sigh.

"Going somewhere?" Jeb startled her.

"No," she spurted out as she whipped around to face him. She pressed a hand to her chest. Gathered in a deep breath. "I mean…maybe. I was just stepping outside to—to go for a walk."

He sat on the porch swing, his arm draped in a lazy way over the back while the moon showcased him in filtered white light. And he had the audacity to smile at her, the devastatingly handsome grin tipping one corner of his still swollen mouth, doing nothing to ease her erratic heartbeat.

"Dressed in that?" He quirked one eyebrow.

His moonlit face, battered and bruised and swollen, tugged at her compassion.

"I didn't feel like changing." She clutched the lantern handle with both hands and stood ramrod straight. When a wave of self-consciousness crowded in on her, she counted her blessings that the nightdress and robe covered her from her neck clear to her toes. "I certainly didn't imagine that *you'd* be out here."

"So…why were you sneaking?"

"I wasn't *sneaking*," she nearly snorted, feeling strangely like she'd been caught red-handed.

"Inching the door shut and tiptoeing isn't sneaking?" As casual as you please, he folded his hands in his lap, that grin of his still there on his face.

"I didn't want to wake anybody." Lydia swallowed past

the thick lump in her throat. "What are you doing up so late, anyway?"

He rested his booted feet on the porch floor, easing the swing to a stop. "Funny...I was going to ask you the same thing."

"You weren't here for dinner," she half accused, telling herself that his comings and goings weren't any business of hers. "Sass was worried about you."

His easy grin faded some. "I had chores to catch up on and a fence to repair so the cattle didn't get loose."

For a moment she felt bad for pressing him. But how could she *not* with the way he'd returned home looking like he'd been drug beneath a wagon?

Sweeping her hair to one side, she fingered the strands, wondering if he was hurting more than he let on. "You couldn't sleep?"

"Sometimes when I'm done with a busy day I like to sit out here in the peace and quiet." Prying the lantern from her hands, he turned the knob and set it down. "I just haven't made my way to bed yet, that's all."

She stared at the lantern, watching as the flame faded to black, wishing she had something to hold again that would be some kind of barrier between her and Jeb. She felt ridiculous for succumbing to this kind of timidity. After all...she'd grown up with Jeb. She'd been his *shadow* for as long as she could remember.

Shoving her wayward focus to the night's skyline, she admired how the moon's soft and gentle light bathed the rugged landscape in a certain mysterious and raw kind of beauty.

"It is beautiful out here," she whispered.

"It sure is."

The still and quiet that hung between them suddenly felt so...so comfortable, so warm and so real. She stepped over to the railing, fingering the worn wood as she indulged herself in the awesome sight. "I forgot how brilliant the stars are. Chicago is full of lights—they're everywhere. It's a city that never sleeps."

"Did you enjoy that?" The porch swing creaked as he shifted. "Living in Chicago, I mean?"

"It was so different." The moment she turned to face him, she knew she'd be better off going back inside. But she longed to stay, wishing to capture this moment in time. The brilliant night sky. The quiet. And Jeb.

She peered at him, committing to memory every little thing about him…his attentiveness despite the heartbreaking way his swollen eyelids hung weighted over his dark eyes. The perfect way the moon highlighted every firm and manly angle of his face. The significant way his shoulders, broad enough to bear the biggest of burdens, filled the porch, giving her a tangible sense of protection.

"Lydia…" he prodded, as though he somehow sensed she was lost in thought. "Chicago…did you like it there?"

She gave her head a shake, hoping the small response would rattle her good sense back into place. "It took just two months for the newness of it all to wear off. Then I was missing home—or at least the only home I'd ever known."

"Care to join me?"

She stared at the porch swing, noting how compact the seat was and how broad-shouldered Jeb was. But even so, she moved over and sat down without so much as one protesting word.

"Comfortable?" he asked.

She nodded, lifting her chin a notch, and trying desperately not to notice the instant warmth spreading through her at his nearness.

"So what made you leave Chicago, anyway? Other than missing the west? There must be something more than just getting a job at the hotel that would make you travel all the way out here."

"I wanted something more for my life," she responded, praying her vague answer would suffice.

"And what was that?" He gave the porch swing a gentle push off. "It's not as if you were in the streets every night causing a ruckus, right?"

She scowled at him. "Of course not. It was the fancy parties and the fancy dresses." She pictured the countless social galas she'd attended. "Every woman desperate for a man to swoon over and marry."

His right eye, which hadn't swollen shut, grew wide as he peered at her. "But everyone enjoys a party. Surely all of that couldn't have been that bad."

She sighed. "Every so often was fine, but at least once every few weeks there was some big to-do. The social gatherings were so very overrated. They may as well have been weddings for the fuss my aunt made over going."

"I can see your point there," he conceded, resting his hand a breath away from her shoulder, sending a quiver inching through her entire body. "But what about the fancy dresses? All women love a fancy dress."

"I'm not *all* women." She was nearing dangerous territory— *very dangerous territory*—with the heady warmth she was experiencing at his nearness. "I do enjoy getting dressed up from time to time, but I also treasure my comfort."

"That's for sure." Jeb's low chuckle settled around her like a warm embrace. "You ran the ranch in britches and shirttails."

She couldn't help but smile remembering how carefree she'd felt as a young girl. Life had changed so very much.

"Speaking of dresses..." He cleared his throat. His hand, big and work worn and bandaged, rested on her shoulder, sending a tremor shooting straight through her. "You looked beautiful in the dress Sass made for you. As beautiful as you did the day you left this ranch."

His sweet words sent her pulse ricocheting through her veins. She grappled for her emotions, but they churned in her soul like pieces of straw whipped about in a violent wind storm.

She would *not* allow herself to lose herself over this man. *Not now. Not ever.*

So *why* was she plagued with that heady, I'm-falling-in-love feeling?

"Was there ever a man that made you swoon, Lydia?" he had boldness enough to ask.

"What?" she choked out, sure he must've just heard her thoughts. Had she been talking aloud and didn't even realize it?

Her whole body shuddered, and not because she was cold. The shameful truth was that sitting next to Jeb the way she was, hearing his sweet words and feeling his mind-numbing touch, she felt as if she'd been baking in the sun for the past hour.

She chided herself for not being able to exhibit a little more decorum. To make matters worse…Jeb, in that gentlemanly and kind way of his, tenderly pulled her to his side as if to lend her his warmth.

"Better?"

No, it wasn't *better*. It was *worse*. *Far worse*. But how could she tell him that? The last thing she wanted to do was to let Jeb know how much of her heart was still pining for him. He'd rejected her once, all those years ago. She would *not* put her heart on the line again.

"So about the swooning…" he probed again, his tenacity like a maul-ax to her resolve. "I'm sure there's been some man you've swooned over—and could've married?"

How could he ask such a question?

Didn't he remember the heartfelt sentiments she'd poured out to him five years ago? That she loved him? Had always loved him? And that they were meant to be together? She'd nearly begged him to make her his wife, any pride and dignity a sixteen-year-old young woman could possess, carelessly thrown aside.

Her stomach flipped and churned with the putrid memory of his rejection. She felt sick. Disgusted. Saddened.

How could he have been so hurtful? And yet, so kind and considerate as he was now? What was it about this man that could send her falling from aversion to love within seconds?

The lazy way he brushed his thumb over her shoulder did even more devastating things to her insides. And to her resolve.

She dragged in a slow, long breath and willed her out-of-control emotions to calm. Edging away enough to think, she tried to remember why she hadn't wanted to see him again. And why she shouldn't trust him. And how things on the ranch just didn't add up—the run-down condition, the lack of help and Jeb's late-night jaunt into town despite Sass's pleas otherwise.

Was there a reason to be suspicious? She'd never known Jeb to be of a shady character. In fact, she'd always admired him for his steadfast integrity and work ethic. Her father had said as much, too.

Maybe she was just looking for something to hate him for. Something she could pin on him in order to permanently douse the feelings she had for him.

"There was a man I'd swooned over…at one time," she finally answered, fearing he'd ask again. She wasn't about to lie to him, but there was no way on the face of this beautiful earth that he'd ever know that that certain someone had been him.

"He must not have been worthy of you," was all Jeb could manage to say.

How could any man look past Lydia? She was beautiful both inside and out. Surely, she'd had dozens of men clamoring for her attention and her hand in marriage.

Jealousy lassoed him and bound him tight in no time flat.

He pulled his head to the side, his collar suddenly feeling constricted in spite of the fact that he'd loosed the top two buttons.

"I really should be going to bed," she breathed, threading her hands together in her lap.

"I thought you were going for a walk."

Her long and forced and unladylike yawn, tipped his mouth in a grin. "I suppose my walk will have to take place some other time." She fingered the soft fabric of her white robe, made almost iridescent by the moon's pearly light. "Although…I'll be heading back into town tomorrow."

"Where will you be staying?" Jeb bit back the truth—she had no place to go.

She snapped up her attention to him as he turned toward her. "What do you mean? I told you, I'm staying at the boardinghouse."

"Lydia…" He set a finger beneath her chin and urged her to look at him.

"What?" When her sweet, warm breath fanned his cheek, every nerve ending in his body came to life.

"I know that Mrs. Gussman doesn't have room until next week," he uttered, his gaze moving slowly over her perfect features.

Her face was no more than a foot from his, and the urge to plant a soft kiss on those full lips of hers was almost more than he could bear. The space between them sizzled with attraction, and he knew—he knew—she had to feel it, too. Her eyelids draped heavy over her eyes and her breathing came all soft and short. And he was almost certain he could hear her heart's rapid beat.

But then her eyelids shot open as if he'd just slapped her across the face. She pulled back. "How would you know? Have you been checking on my—"

"If you're thinking that I was doing some kind of investigation into your situation, Lydia, no."

She raised her chin a notch. "I don't want to be beholden to anyone, Jeb."

Even though he had a sick feeling that that *anyone* was him, he shrugged it off. "I'm sure you don't. I trust that you have your reasons. And I trust you, Lydia. We've always trusted each other. Right?"

She fell silent.

Did she trust him? They had years of history together, so surely she had to trust him, deep down. His father may have considered him a failure, but he'd always prided himself on being trustworthy.

"I just happened to see Mrs. Gussman when I was in town yesterday," he explained on a sigh. "One thing in conversation led to another and I found out about your living situation. Why didn't you say something?" What had happened between them that she didn't feel like she could come to him for help? "Wait. Don't answer that. I forgot…you weren't even going to stay long enough for dinner that day you showed up. If I hadn't found you out by the cabin, I'd probably still have no idea you were back in Colorado."

She hugged her arms to her chest. "I'm sorry. I just—"

"Listen, even if this place isn't your first choice, I would feel a lot better knowing you're staying here, and not homeless— at least until your job starts and Mrs. Gussman has room for you."

"I wouldn't be homeless."

"Where were you planning on staying then?"

Her gleaming gaze, filled with blatant struggle, connected with his. For a split second he thought he saw her waver.

"I don't know…."

"I don't make a habit of telling you what to do, Lydia." As soon as her brow furrowed in protest he added, "All right, so maybe I did years ago, that time when you were foolish enough to think you could sleep out in the bull's stall just because you thought he had the sniffles."

"And..." she prodded, angling a scorn-filled gaze at him.

"There were probably several times." He gave his head a shake. "But you have to know it was because I was looking out for you."

She snapped her mouth shut. The way her guilty gaze darted to the side was nothing short of charming.

Lydia.... In spite of all her willful ways and stoic attitudes, he was drawn to her like a bear to honey. Almost every single thought that passed through his mind since she'd arrived was of her. Was he falling in love with her?

Try as he might, he couldn't seem to stop thinking about living out the rest of his days with her by his side. They'd look on each new day with hope and excitement. Find great adventures in the ordinary. And they'd endure trials simply because they had each other.

If only things had turned out differently for him.

No matter what could never be, tomorrow he was going to start fixing up that little cabin she liked so well. For Lydia.

The way she looked up at him, as if she'd heard his thoughts, sent a profound chill coursing down his spine.

"Please stay here, Lydia. At least for now." He tried to sound gentle enough not to get under her skin yet firm enough for her to understand that he meant business.

Her studying gaze moved slowly over every last inch of his face. His heart skipped one beat. Two, as he gripped the edge of his seat.

"Jeb..."

"What, Lydia?" He swallowed hard, the space between them humming with untapped energy.

When she touched his hand, his breath hitched. "I know you wouldn't tell me what happened last night to make you look so horrible, but..."

He grinned at the sweetly innocent and tenacious way Lydia had about her. And in that moment he realized that since her return, he'd found himself smiling more than he had in the past few years. It was as if she'd breezed into his life, shining right through the clouds and scattering his gloom.

Had God really heard his prayers? Had He brought Lydia back for him?

She rested her hand over one of his. "I didn't mean to sound uncaring. What I was trying to say was—"

"Don't worry. I know I must look a sight." He threaded his callused fingers through hers, loving her beautiful and sensitive heart.

And sorely tempted again to kiss her right then and there.

"What about that big scar?" Reaching up to his forehead, she traced her finger, featherlight over the jagged scar slicing across his forehead.

"I got that a long time ago." His pulse thrummed at her quivering touch.

"You didn't have it before I left." She peered up at the scar, worry and sadness etching her brow as she brushed a lock of hair from his forehead. "I would've remembered."

"You're right, I didn't."

"Well then, what happened?"

Jeb reached for her hand and held it, wishing she would stop digging for answers. Half wishing she would stop touching him simply because her touch weakened his resolve to such a degree that he wondered if he'd had any to start with.

There was no way he'd tell her the whole of the story. She'd blame herself. "I was doing some work with one of the horses and got distracted. The fella reared back and when he came down I took a hoof to the face."

She gasped, holding a slender hand to her mouth. "That is horrible! You could've been killed, Jeb."

"You wouldn't have even known I was gone. Showing up here and not even planning on letting me know about it.... How could you not tell me—the guy you trailed around this ranch for most of your first sixteen years?" he teased, trying to pull a strand of lightheartedness into the conversation. But from the shocked expression on her face, he was pretty sure he'd failed.

She tugged her hand from his, her mouth drawing into a tight line. And that small opening he was sure he'd seen into her heart was gone. Just like that.

"I couldn't," she whispered as she stood and crossed to the door. "I promised myself."

Chapter Six

Grabbing the scrub brush, Lydia willed herself to stay awake as she dipped it in the water to finish cleaning the porch floor. It wasn't even midday, but she'd pried her eyes open at six-thirty this morning after a sleepless night spent rehashing the interchange she'd had with Jeb in the wee hours of the morning.

His tender ways made her ache to really *feel* again. But the instant way he'd closed himself off, as though he was hiding something, she just couldn't ignore. Although it went against her better judgment, she'd get some answers.

Swiping her brow with her sleeve, she sat back and surveyed her hard work. She'd needed something to occupy her time because there was just something about Jeb that had possessed her almost completely. Divesting herself of him was like trying to remove a huge chunk of her soul. It was elusive, something unseen and yet so very, very real. And the attraction between them—that was so real, too. She could hear it in his voice, see it in his gaze, and feel it in his warm and tender touch.

Even now, thinking about the endearing way he'd held his finger beneath her chin, sent a shiver straight down her spine and back again.

Dipping the brush in the water, she wondered if maybe she needed to let the past go. Maybe she needed to seize what was right in front of her and enjoy the moment for what it would bring. Maybe she needed to learn to love again.

It was altogether possible that she'd never stopped loving Jeb, no matter how hard she'd tried to scrape every last feeling for him from her heart and soul. Had she been fooling herself into thinking that she could be completely unaffected by his deep and soothing voice, his commanding presence and the great gentleness in his soul?

Did he have even the inkling of a feeling for her? Could she hope for that much?

Pushing herself up to standing, she wiped her hands on her apron as she tried not to dwell on the fact that he had no recollection of what had happened five years ago. How could he *not* realize what he'd done to her?

And what of his scar? She had a horrible, horrible feeling that somehow she was responsible for that angry mark streaking across his forehead. He'd been so vague in the story he'd relayed—too vague. But she remembered the way he'd struggled with the young stallion that day, five years ago. She'd nearly flown over the gate, so desperate to run to the altar with him that she'd thrown all common ranch-sense aside. She could see nothing but her goal.

Jeb.

It hadn't been until weeks later that she could even think about that life-altering situation without being reduced to a pitiful and sickening puddle of tears. But once she was finally able to allow the whole situation to play out in her mind, she had to admit…she hadn't used the *best* judgment in her approach that day. Desperation, good or bad, sometimes drove her toward the extreme.

Lifting the bucket of dirty water, she strode over to the side of the house and dumped it out. The idea that she might be responsible for Jeb nearly getting killed by his stallion was horribly unsettling. He'd never come right out and admit such a thing—Jeb wasn't the kind of man to do that.

Could it be that she'd spent all these years believing she'd been the only one hurt, when he'd been wounded, too? Had she left while he was wounded? The thought, even now, made her stomach churn.

Had she been so caught up in her own pain that she'd become the kind of selfish, cold person she despised? Maybe she'd been so intent on protecting herself that she'd completely missed God's gentle and tender ways in her life.

Her tired eyes burned with tears as she decided that no matter what the outcome, she had to find out the truth. She sniffed, blinked hard, knowing that she'd ask him tonight, just as soon as he returned from his chores.

Jeb nailed the last wooden shake shingle in place, descended the ladder and surveyed the small roof. His father's blatant neglect had almost taken a fatal toll on this place, but today Jeb had made a small dent in the repairs. He felt good about it, too—even if he lost the ranch, something just felt right about making this place as perfect as Lydia remembered.

After he'd finished his chores this morning and checked each of the cows getting close to calving, he'd headed out to the cabin and dove into the multiple repairs. Peering up at the sun's place in the blue expanse of sky, he knew it had to be close to two o'clock. There were still barn stalls that needed work in order to be ready for spring calves, beside all of his daily chores.

Spring had always been his favorite time of year. New life was emerging all around him, even when it seemed that his hope for steering clear of total failure was fading fast. Had Lydia not shown up three short days ago, the heavy weight of that reality might be near crushing. But her presence here had infused him with a fresh breath of hope.

Jeb strode inside the cabin and walked slowly around the place, pleased with the immense progress he'd made. When he neared the fireplace, one of the coarse granite flagstones beneath his foot teetered, scraping at the other stones around it. Hunkering down, he was about to pull it up to inspect further when a soon-to-be-mama cat came lumbering into the cabin, meowing.

"Hi there, girl," he said, scratching the feline under the chin as she nudged her face against Jeb's hand. He stroked her soft gray fur, taking the time to feel her taut sides and stomach. "You're getting close, aren't you?"

The cat peered up at Jeb, squeezing her eyes in that adoring way that always made Jeb smile. "You're sure friendly enough. Maybe you could have a little girl talk with Lydia—put in a good word for me," he said, standing.

When the pregnant mama did a circle eight around Jeb's legs, he smiled. "Are you looking for a place to have your kittens?"

The cat lumbered over to a corner where Jeb had stacked some rickety old crates. She glanced back at him, her eyes wide.

Jeb grabbed an old quilt he'd shaken out, turned one crate right side up and nested the quilt down inside so that she'd have a safe and warm place to have her kittens.

"The place is all yours," he said as the cat leaped into the crate and circled the area several times before she finally laid down.

Jeb smiled and left the newly repaired door ajar so the cat could come and go.

Pausing for a moment, he ran his hand over the space between the logs making up the cabin, where chinking had long since fallen away, and he thought about tonight's boxing match. He would give his challenger no openings—not even one. He had to come out fighting. Keep his mind and body totally focused until he felled his opponent.

He'd been fighting for the ranch, but something had changed in the past hours. Since Lydia had shown up, he'd grown increasingly aware of a huge rut he'd gotten mired in over the past years. He'd actually started to believe he was as much of a failure as his father had always said he was. And that maybe things would've been better had he not been born. Lydia might not have wanted to see him, but something deep in her crystal gaze begged otherwise. The caring way she looked at him had him longing to start living outside of what his father had always said of him.

The truth was. .he was fighting for himself now. And for the future he hoped to make with Lydia.

And this fight could not be more important. A win could mean the difference between walking away from this place with nothing but failure as his legacy and holding on to what he loved.

Lydia had waited all day long to talk with Jeb, but he hadn't shown his face even once at the main house. She'd taken it upon herself to mend curtains, pull weeds and do what she could around the place to help out, all the while with one eye trained on the path to home, watching for Jeb.

But he never came.

Now, by the dim lantern's light in her bedroom, she opened her father's tired leather saddlebag. She'd been so busy the past three days that she'd not even taken the time to go through its contents.

Holding the droopy flap open, she reached inside and pulled out a small framed photograph, the silver filigree nearly black with tarnish. As she peered at the sepia-toned image, a thick lump formed in her throat and her eyes burned.

She had been all of ten-years-old, sitting on the front porch, her thick pad of paper on her lap, long plaited hair trailing down her overly large shirt to touch her dungarees. Her black felt cowboy hat was perched at an angle on her head—just the way she liked it.

She remembered that day well. A traveling photographer, painfully thin and as rumpled as a shaggy-haired dog, had ridden onto the ranch, looking for business. Much to the photographer's chagrin, Lydia's daddy had said she didn't need to change into something fancy just for the picture—he'd wanted the photograph to be a *true depiction of his little girl,* he'd said.

She swallowed hard, missing him more in this moment than she had in months. He'd always been so good to let her be herself, not hemming her in as her aunt had done for five miserable years.

Gently fingering the image, Lydia agreed that there couldn't have been a truer depiction of *her.* Especially on that particular day.

She'd just returned home from the small cabin, where she'd written one of her many letters to Jeb. That letter, in particular, had been carefully penned with fanciful thoughts of a perfect life spent together. She'd drawn a picture of their wedding day, including every detail down to the small posy of daisies she carried. She'd even written her own little poem to him…a vow of sorts that she was sure would move him to tears one day.

The vivid memory filled her with a sense of loss. And longing. And sadness for what could've been. Had she been fighting an unstoppable force all these years?

She'd had every intention of getting her box of letters today, but she couldn't risk Jeb being there. Though it was dark now, she'd wait until the wee hours of the morning then she'd make her way out to the cabin because in a few short days she'd be living in town. She wouldn't have time to traipse back out here to look for them, and she couldn't risk Jeb finding her letters in the meantime.

Setting the photograph aside, she pulled out her daddy's Bible, its well-worn pages yellowed from age. She would never forget the nights he'd sit by the warm hearth fire and read to her. The stories had come alive for her then, and the truths had seemed so real when he'd put them in his own gentle everyday words. How could she have wandered so far from all that her daddy had taught her? Had her faith been sustainable only when her daddy was around to urge her toward the truth?

Sooner or later she'd have to take a good, hard look at what she believed and why. And on what her faith was based, because if her beliefs hinged on everything working out in her perfect little world, then she would get disheartened again and again—just as soon as life dished out a bitter portion, as it had five years ago.

A knowing chill coursed up her spine as thoughts she'd never had until now drifted, featherlight and yet weighted with profound meaning, into her mind. Had she thrown all her frustration and anger and sense of loss she'd experienced five years ago, *all*, onto Jeb? Had his rejection of her just been the breaking point for her faith?

She hugged her daddy's soft leather Bible against her chest, longing for the words she'd once found such hope in to somehow break through the stony wall she'd built around her heart.

She would do things differently...she had to.

A small but tangible wave of peace washed over her, and as she drew in a slow breath she set down the Bible. Reaching into the saddlebag again she pulled out a rectangular shoe-sized box. A paper-thin layer of caked dirt coated the locked box, filling in the small crack where the top and bottom met and around the tarnished brass corners.

"What is this?" she whispered, brushing it off. She couldn't recall ever seeing this box among her daddy's things.

She tried prying off the top, but it was locked securely. Lydia opened the saddlebag to look for a key when the sound of voices drifted through her opened bedroom window.

"Jeb, please. Not again." Sass's desperate plea made Lydia's heart sink.

"Sass, you know me. I'll be fine." His voice came from the barn.

"You'll get hurt again." Sass's voice broke, as though she was trying not to cry.

Lydia's heart clenched as she moved closer to the window, knowing she shouldn't be listening and yet unable to stop herself. She felt helpless to do anything, but compelled to do something to help.

"That's not going to happen," Jeb placated, just as he'd done two nights ago when he'd left at about this same time. "I'll watch my back. Don't you worry."

An eerie silence filled the night air. She didn't want to doubt Jeb's integrity. She wanted to cling to that peace she'd just experienced, believing that she'd misjudged God and life and Jeb. Lydia tried to dismiss what she'd heard, but it was useless.

"Lord knows I fret over you," Sass finally said, her words barely audible. "If I didn't have the good Lord to lean on, I'd be worrying my hands raw in my own grave."

"Let go of the reins, Sass. I have to go." The hint of irritation tainting Jeb's voice stole Lydia's next breath.

She clutched the windowsill, her blood near boiling. How could he disregard Sass like that after the years of love and service and nurturing the woman had provided for this family?

"Just listen to reason," Sass tried again. "This isn't the answer. You know it isn't."

Jeb sighed, loud enough that Lydia could hear. "It's the only card I have left to play."

Card…? Play…? Had Jeb been gambling? Is that why the ranch had been suffering so? Because Jeb had been putting the very land he said he loved in jeopardy?

Her stomach churned with instant anger. She'd thought that maybe she could trust him again. That maybe she'd been the one who'd been wrong. But the truth slashed with breakneck speed through her thin veil of hope.

She shoved her father's things back into the saddlebag. When she turned down the lamp to douse the flame she was determined, no matter what Jeb was doing, to climb right back up to a place of peace again—with or without him in the picture.

Chapter Seven

Lydia urged the gelding down the dark road, staying off to the side where the tree line met the roadway. She followed at a generous distance as he neared the edge of town. To what kind of shadows would his path lead?

Or was she judging him, yet again?

A distant wave of whoops and hollers drifted to her hearing, sending a chill snaking down her spine. As far as she was concerned, that kind of uproar at this time of night could birth *nothing* of value. She peered ahead, watching as Jeb neared a large barn near the town's edge—the very place where the loud ruckus seemed to be originating. The few windows spewed out yellow light into the night like futility's toxic breath. The large structure seemed as if to breathe with wild energy. Even from a good hundred yards away, she could see the distinct outline of scantily clad women, standing at the entrance to the barn like gaudy signs welcoming all sinners.

Lydia swallowed past a sick lump that had lodged in her throat, praying that Jeb wasn't prey to be caught in their mired web. The thought had no more crossed her mind when he diverted his stallion toward the barn and dismounted at the hitching post.

"No, Jeb…don't do that," she whispered, barely able to find her voice.

Lydia's heart sank clear down to her stomach. She reined her horse to an instant stop, blinking hard at the assaulting sense of betrayal.

Why should she feel betrayed? Jeb had made her no promises. In fact, he'd held his heart at a distance. She'd been the one who'd been foolish enough to believe that maybe she'd judged him wrong.

She watched as he strode to the barn, his long legs eating up the distance with clear and focused intent. When he reached the barn doorway, the two women closed in on him, like giant and dark spiders, clearly hungry for Jeb, their prime prey.

Disgust crawled along her spine. Shuddering, she wrenched her gaze from the repulsive scene. Every inch of her body ached with sadness and revulsion and anger, and all she wanted to do was to collect her things from the ranch and flee. Not more than an hour ago, she'd made a pledge to change her ways and to cling to peace, and already her vow was being tested.

Was peace worth the price?

She felt frozen right where she sat on her horse. Minutes ticked by as she willed herself not to turn around. Each passing second sent her soul tumbling into even greater turmoil. She could hardly breathe for the regret weighting her heart. Could hardly see for the anger narrowing her gaze.

Closing her eyes, she tried to collect herself, but until she got this weight off her chest, she doubted she'd ever take another long and easy breath again.

Maybe she needed to find her voice finally and let Jeb know *exactly* how she felt—and how she'd felt five years ago. Maybe then she could move on and embrace her future. Maybe then she could, for once and for all, rid her heart and soul of Jebediah Gentry.

She rode closer to the barn and dismounted at the hitching post. Her hands trembled uncontrollably as she secured the gelding, all the while rehearsing in her mind what she'd say to Jeb when she found him.

Would he be draped over a poker table? Would he have women hanging on him as though he was some coat tree?

Her stomach lurched at the thought as she neared the entrance. The raw and boisterous cheering coming from inside nearly drove her courage into the ground.

The same women who'd greeted Jeb were still standing there, their painted and narrowed gazes scanning her up one side and down another, as though she was a miniscule scrap of meat to throw into a den of hungry bears. Their brazen grins sent chills down her spine, and it was all she could do not to turn tail and run.

Unsolicited, a brief yet profound thought dropped into her mind like a lifeline sent down a deep dark hole. Was she judging them just as she'd judged Jeb? She didn't know what kind of lives they'd led that had brought them to this place.

For a moment, Lydia paused, longing for some kind of peace to fill her, but all she could seem to grasp hold of was her incessant need to have it out with Jeb.

With her fists balled, she strode right past them, gathered all the courage she could find in the corners of her soul and entered the barn. She squinted against the yellow light and smoky air to see a room full of men—and even some women—their focus set at the center of the barn.

When Lydia turned that direction, she felt her world give way.

Clad in just his britches and looking larger than life, Jeb stood in the center of a sawdust-covered, roped-off platform. His fists were raised. Head lowered. Every muscle was bunched and glistening in the lantern light. And he was fighting.

Jeb was *fighting* a meaty giant of a man.

What would possess him? In her idealistic mind, she could understand fighting for the honor of someone you loved. But *this*?

She couldn't tear her gaze away from him, watching as he

shifted back and forth across the floor. Lunging. Dodging. Bearing down on his opponent.

Though Jeb's cuts had opened and he was bleeding heavily, he was dominating the challenger. Jeb was almost toying with the contender as he'd jab and punch, wearing his opponent down as he'd work him into a corner then let him free again.

The opponent took a sudden shot at Jeb, his power-packed punch landing on Jeb's jaw, sending sweat droplets flying off into the smoke-filled air.

Lydia gasped. Slammed her eyes shut as she willed this horrible nightmare to stop.

The stale air hummed then surged with raw energy as she pried her eyes open and watched Jeb stand his ground. He gave his head a shake and bore down on the man as though his very life depended on it. Cocking his arm back, Jeb pummeled the contender once. Twice. Sending him stumbling back against the ropes and falling to the floor.

While Jeb shifted back and forth in front of the downed man, the crowd roared their sick approval.

"I've got fifty dollars on this fight!" one man howled.

"Do him in!" another screamed.

"Get 'im, Jeb. You're our man," another man yelled, the veins at his long thin neck bulging.

Something deep inside Lydia snapped as she heard a man in the ring counting, his sharp voice cutting through the frenzied roar. "One. Two. Three."

Jeb turned toward the crowd, his face looking far worse than before. He kept moving as though if he stopped he might not be able to move again.

"Four. Five. Six," the moderator shrieked as the whole place rumbled.

She couldn't stand to watch another minute of this. But her feet felt weighted to the packed dirt floor. She clenched her hands. Her head swirled with a thousand different emotions as Jeb heaved in a breath.

"Seven," the moderator called as Jeb peered out into the crowd, his shoulders slumped in fatigue. "Eight."

His opponent stumbled to standing. Swayed. Then locked his focus, as dark and sinister as a whole host of demons, on Jeb.

Jeb's head whipped in Lydia's direction as if he'd just caught sight of her. Under a furrowed, swollen and bloody brow, he peered at her through the smoke and haze.

"Lydia?" he called, her name lost in the howling snarl of spectators.

Just then the challenger lunged hard at Jeb. Growled. Cocked his fist back, but Jeb was unaware.

Lydia's heart came to a screeching halt. "Jeb! Watch out!"

Chapter Eight

Jeb flinched as his opponent's fist slammed into the side of his head.

Again.

And again.

And again.

He groaned. Struggled to fight back. Tried to get away, but he couldn't seem to move. Not even an inch.

"Jeb? Jeb...." The gentle voice seeped through the raging noise all around him. "It's all right, Jeb. Wake up."

Wake up? Had he been dreaming?

He willed his heavy eyes to open. Struggled to climb his way to consciousness. Pain assaulted every part of his body.

The lingering image of his thick and hungry opponent flashed in his mind. It'd been the fight of Jeb's life. And he'd been winning. But then a familiar glimmer of blue caught his attention off to his right. He'd turned. Spotted Lydia.

What was she doing there?

"Lydia...." He blinked, his swollen eyes throbbing as he struggled to focus.

"Thank God you're all right," she whispered, her soft breath drifting over him, coaxing him to wake.

Jeb struggled to drag himself out of his sluggish state. "What happened?"

"You were knocked out," she said, placing a cool cloth on his forehead, her touch, so soothing.

"Knocked out?" He formed the bitter words through swollen lips. His last chance at keeping the ranch had slipped right through his hands?

Failure's taunting voice was so close, trying to pummel him deeper and deeper. He had to climb above now or he'd never find his way out.

In some folks' eyes he'd failed. In his father's eyes, certainly. But Jeb had given *all* he'd had to give.

She grasped his hand, the feel of her quivering fingers nearly breaking his heart. "Jeb, I am so sorry. Had I not marched in there and distracted you, you probably wouldn't be lying here now."

He could *guarantee* he wouldn't be lying here now—he'd had his opponent worn down and the fight almost wrapped up—but he wasn't about to tell her that.

He loved Lydia and only wanted to make her happy. But would love be enough to carry them through a tough and uncertain future?

Jeb clenched his teeth and managed to roll over to his side, every muscle in his body screaming in pain as he shoved himself up to standing.

Grasping his arm, Lydia peered at him as though he'd just risen from the grave. "What do you think you're doing?"

"Getting up," he said, staggering a bit as he struggled to focus. "I have to get home."

Lydia held on tight. "You *are* home."

"What?" Peering around the room through swollen eyes, he spotted his small bureau of drawers, the pegs where he'd hang his clothes, and his worn boots flopped over in the corner. With a frustrated growl, he slid down on the edge of the bed again, trying to block out the hammering in his head.

Lydia sat next to him, her distress almost as palpable as the pain in his head. "The doctor helped me get you home. You don't remember anything?"

"Not a thing."

"Well, you were in and out of consciousness."

"Thank the good Lord you woke up!" Sass announced as she entered the room, her loud voice making his head pound even more. She set down a pitcher of water on the nightstand then peered at him, her eyes unusually red rimmed. "Jebediah Gentry, you *really* gave me a scare this time. Don't know what would've happened had this little lady not been there to pick up the pieces."

He flashed a grimace Sass's way. "That doesn't make me feel any better, Sass."

"This is all my fault." The sorrow filling Lydia's voice made Jeb want to wrap her up in a comforting hug.

"Certainly not, dear," Sass said.

"Don't blame yourself." Jeb reached for Lydia's hand and gave it a quick squeeze.

"Just look at you." Cupping his chin in her hand, Sass surveyed his face, and Jeb could tell by the way her eyes were still misted over that she'd been crying. "You poor thing."

He leaned away from her well-meaning attention, hoping to put her at ease. "I am not a poor thing. I chose to fight."

He just wanted to go about his day as though nothing had happened. And he'd do just that if only the room would quit spinning.

"Well, you'll be good enough to let me have my opinion, thank you," Sass quipped in that toe-to-toe attitude of hers.

"You always do," he grumbled.

"Now, you need to lay your head back down on that pillow and get some rest." Turning to the nightstand, Sass poured a glass of water.

"That's not going to happen. I've got chores that need tending." Jeb shoved off the bed and willed his legs to stay steady as Lydia stood beside him, her hand set gently to his back, as if she might have the chance of catching him if he fell.

"Take a sip and see if you can keep it down this time," Sass said, handing him a glass of water.

"What time is it, anyway?" He took a drink of the cool liquid.

"It's nine o'clock."

"In the *morning*?" he choked out, nearly splattering his housekeeper with a mouthful of water.

"Yes, in the morning." Sass perched her hands at her hips.

"Why did you let me sleep this long?" The moment he wiped a hand over his mouth, pain seared through the open cuts.

"We tried to rouse you, Jeb," Lydia offered.

"You need to stop worrying about the chores. Lydia, here, finished off the nightly ones and already did the morning chores."

"You did?" he asked, peering at her and feeling ashamed, pleased and grateful all in one. "You shouldn't have done that."

"It was the least I could do," she said, looking almost as fatigued as she had the day she'd shown up here.

"Jeb, all of this fighting is over," Sass announced, grasping his forearm. "You need to let go of this before you get yourself killed."

"I can't." Glancing downward, he noticed he was without a shirt and shoved his gaze to where it hung on a peg.

"There are some folks coming out to help today," Sass offered. "And if you were to ask me, I'd say it'd be wise of you to stay—"

"What are you talking about…*folks coming out here*?" he shot back retrieving his shirt. "Who? And *why*?"

"When the doctor helped get you home," Lydia began, taking the shirt from him and fishing for a sleeve that was inside out, "he asked if you would be able to take it easy for a few days. And I told him that *maybe* you might need a little help," she measured out, carefully helping him shrug into his shirt since it took him three tries to find the armholes. Longer yet to pull it over his head.

When her fingertips lightly grazed his chest, a quiver of undeniable awareness inched down his spine. "Listen...I appreciate the thoughtfulness and all, but I can see to things just fine on my own."

"I'm going to round up something for him to eat while he rests," Sass explained to Lydia as he tried to make his swollen fingers work enough to button his shirt.

When she breezed out of the room, Lydia took over buttoning his shirt. "Why were you fighting, Jeb? Is it because of the ranch?"

Jeb shuffled over to the corner to grab his boots, each step sending a shock wave of pain through his body. He set his back teeth and dragged in a deep breath. "Lydia, there are some things that I just won't talk about, and this is one of them." He sat down on the bed so that he could slide on his boots. "I have my reasons—or at least I *had* my reasons."

While he struggled at the simple task, Lydia hunkered down and assisted him. To say that his pride was pricked was a given, but even so, he breathed a sigh of relief for her kind consideration.

"Something is terribly wrong, Jeb." She leaned back on her haunches, her silky dark hair whispering over her forehead. "First you're working day and night, and then you're fighting—and for a crowd who seems to glory in the gore of it all."

"Oh, believe me...I'm *not* fighting for them."

"Well, then will you *please* tell me what is going on? *Please* let me help you?"

"There's nothing you can do." Once he tugged his pant legs over his boots, he stood again, his head and stomach churning with instant nausea. "Besides, this is my problem. Not yours."

"Jeb...."

"No!"

The wounded and frustrated way she looked at him just then plagued him with instant regret. Jeb had to wonder if his stubborn insistence to carry this burden alone was worth the price. Except for Sass, he'd let no one in on his dire situation. He'd handle things because he sure as shooting wasn't going to follow his father's awful reputation for complaining about what was wrong with the world, and those in it.

If folks only knew the half of what his father had really been like.

Jeb had often considered setting folks straight, but he just couldn't seem to bring himself to do so. He didn't necessarily want to sweep things under the rug, but somehow he knew the retribution he'd experience would be fleeting. He'd rather be known for what he'd made of himself than for what his father had done to him.

Had he made something of himself? Could a man with nothing more to show for himself than the shirt on his back be worth anything?

What he wouldn't give to have someone like Lydia stand by him when his faith in himself waned.

Glancing down at her, he couldn't help but long for her caring touch—it'd made him feel alive again. Her genuine concern had offered a lifeline of hope. And her very presence at the ranch had given him joy when he'd needed it most.

"That's just fine for you to say that you can't talk about things, isn't it?" Her mouth compressed to a grim line. "You can offer to be there for me if I need to talk, but you won't allow me to do the same for you?"

"Like I said—"

"I know…." Holding up her hands, she stepped away from him. "This is *your* battle to fight."

"It's nothing you need to worry about. Everything will be fine."

"*Really*? Everything will be fine?" she echoed, clutching her skirt and eying him with clear disdain. "It sure doesn't seem like everything is going to be *fine*. This ranch is falling apart, Jeb. And you're trying to hold the whole place together all alone, as far as I can tell. It's too much—you can't handle this alone."

Her words cut him to the core. He'd seen the disappointment in her expression when she'd arrived here. And yet, deep down he'd hoped that maybe she'd believe in him enough to see beyond what seemed glaringly apparent.

That he'd failed.

The notion wrapped his heart in life-sucking shame.

"Believe me…I know the ranch has seen its better days," he reasoned, trying not to fall prey to failure. "I take full responsibility for the condition it's in, too."

She hugged her arms to her chest, confusion and suspicion crimping her brow as she studied him. "It's not like you, Jeb, to let things go like that. At least not the Jeb I used to know. Have you really changed so much that you'd let this beautiful land and all the livestock you've worked so hard to raise, just fade away?"

"Is *that* what you think? That I'm *willingly* letting this place go?"

She swallowed hard, her slender throat convulsing. "What else am I to think? You're being evasive and all secretive."

After a long and painful moment of silence, he gave his head a shake and narrowed his harsh gaze on her. "Why do you think I started fixing up the little cabin, Lydia?" he challenged.

The stoic look on her face pricked both his heart and his pride.

"It was because of you," he continued, feeling the reins on his control slipping slowly through his hands. "I did that to please *you*. Because I could see how much the place meant to you and how sad you were when you saw what kind of condition it was in."

"I didn't ask you to do that for me, Jeb," she responded,

stubbornly. "I only wanted to get my father's things and leave this place, but you were the one who insisted I stay."

"You had nowhere to go. For all I know, you would've slept out in that little cabin."

She stared at him in that distant way of hers that made him feel strangely alone and completely in the dark as to what had changed so much over the past five years. She'd been at his side every waking moment years ago. But now… It was clear in the protected way she held herself that she didn't trust him or want him as a part of her life.

Sniffing, she lifted her chin a notch. "I'm not sorry that I followed you last night." Her gaze narrowed on him. "You might have been hurt terribly…or worse."

"I've managed just fine on my own—until last night, that is." All of a sudden he found himself irritated. Mostly by the fact that she seemed determined to uncover something amiss about him. "What did you think I was doing, anyway, Lydia?"

She threaded her fingers together at her waist. "I don't know."

"Well, you're suspicious about something." If he was guilty of anything, it was quietly taking his father's cruel treatment for so long—even after the man's death.

When the hint of moisture rimmed Lydia's gaze, Jeb felt instantly bad for his comment.

"Jeb…I was a distraction for you last night. And I want you to know that I am so sorry I caused you to lose the fight."

"It's over," he said, running the back of his hand over his weary, swollen eyes. "There's no use talking about it now."

When Lydia hugged her arms to her chest all Jeb could think about was pulling her into his embrace, holding her in his arms and never letting her go. Every last one of their fears would disappear and worries would melt away in each other's arms. He would breathe her in…Lydia. His delightful little shadow turned into a wonderfully confident young woman whose simple beauty rivaled nature's own.

"I have to know something, Jeb. So, please...*please* just answer one thing for me." Her voice sounded low and strained and so wary.

His hopes for ever having a relationship with her were slipping right through his hands. If he even had hope at all...

"What?"

Her gaze slid up to his forehead. "The scar on your forehead...did that happen the day I left five years ago?" she asked, her voice breaking with trepidation. "*Please*, answer me honestly."

He couldn't lie. But the prospect of guilting her didn't sit any better for him.

"It was a long time ago," he answered, carefully choosing his words and hoping they'd suffice. "You weren't at fault."

Chapter Nine

Lydia's heart plummeted hearing the truth and seeing it in his gaze.

Ever since she'd asked him about that particular scar the other night, she'd had this horrible feeling that there was more to the story than what he was letting on—just like everything else. Knowing that she'd distracted him to the point that he'd almost been killed, not once, but possibly *twice*, hung like a dank, heavy millstone around her neck.

What had she been thinking? On both occasions?

She'd been around green horses enough to know that you don't barge into a corral like some wild thing. And she certainly had enough sense about her to know better than to barge into a fighting match where she clearly didn't belong.

Hugging her arms to her chest, she avoided his shuttered gaze, recognizing that the desperate measures she'd taken had gotten her nothing but disgrace and pain—again. She was so much better off when she denied that integral part of her heart which felt things so deeply.

She couldn't stay here another night.

Still hugging her arms to her chest, she stood in the awkward silence, humiliation hanging over her like a dark cloud. And the unanswered questions nipping at her heels, challenging any savory thought she had about Jeb.

And yet his words…*that he'd fixed up the little cabin for her*, had filled her with the smallest amount of hope.

Just moments ago when he'd woken, she'd felt an overwhelming sense of relief that he seemed to be all right. She'd longed to tuck herself into his comforting embrace, even if it was just for a moment. Because now she knew she would never have him for a lifetime. The letters she'd written to him, the language transforming from a seven-year-old's simple statements of love to a young woman's heartfelt expressions, bent into her thoughts like a flower, wilting and fading to its certain death.

Her heart was beating nearly out of her chest as she braved a glance at Jeb, his face unrecognizable from the beating he'd received last night. He stood as stubborn and as proud as the mountains were rugged.

But the wounded look tucked into his swollen gaze—that might very well haunt her for the rest of her days.

"I'll be leaving," she said, finally. "Just as soon as I get my things and help with the chores." Turning, she started for the door.

"Lydia. Wait." He grasped her arm, his touch sending a warm rush clear through her.

Foolish hope nailed her feet to the floor. Her pulse slammed and swished through her ears. Her breath came hard and fast as she tried desperately to ignore her greatest wish.

"Don't go. Please."

For a moment she almost felt herself drifting toward him, as though some unseen force was drawing her to his arms. But the imprudence of giving in to that would only lead to more pain. For Jeb. And for her.

She moved out of his reach. "I can't stay, Jeb. Again…I'm sorry for any pain I've caused."

While she left the room it was all she could do to hold herself together. She'd run away—once. This time she'd walk away, knowing it was her best and only decision.

* * *

Lydia gathered her things and set them on the bed to pack. Throughout the day, she'd been lending a hand to those who'd shown up to help, but they'd all gone home now. And it was time for her to leave, too.

Jeb had been doing chores, though he'd kept his distance and that was just fine with Lydia.

It'd nearly broken her heart to see him struggling in spite of his obvious discomfort. He just couldn't hide the grimaces or the moments when he'd stop and close his eyes, breathing deep as though to ward off pain's battering force.

Wiping beads of perspiration from her brow and tender memories from her thoughts, she folded her nightdress and set it beside her father's saddle bag. She tried hard not to give in to the raw emotions bubbling to the surface. She couldn't allow herself to cry—not even when Sass had insisted she keep both of the beautiful handmade dresses along with the other items she'd let Lydia borrow.

Picking up the saddlebag, Lydia tipped it, letting the frame and Bible and locked box slide onto the bed.

A brass key tumbled out to land next to the Bible.

She'd figured her daddy had probably used it to tuck important papers away for safekeeping—just as she'd done with her letters to Jeb. Picking up the key, she slid it into the lock and gave it a half turn. With a click, the lid popped open as though the contents were bursting to get free.

A quiver of unexplainable anticipation inched down Lydia's spine as she lifted the lid. An envelope spilled over the edge as well as several monetary bills. As she peered into the box, the breath whooshed from her lungs.

Hundreds…maybe thousands of dollars had been stuffed into the box.

"Daddy…?" she whispered, shock clogging her throat. Her hands trembled. Her breath caught. "What is all of this?"

She lightly fingered the money, certain that she'd never seen so much in all of her days. Once her shock subsided enough to think straight, she opened the envelope and pulled out a letter, her daddy's familiar etching scrawled across the page.

Ready tears sprang to her eyes thinking about the little notes he used to leave for her, just to brighten her day. Setting her focus on the carefully penned date, her chest tightened realizing that he'd written the letter two days prior to his death.

My Dear Lydia,
April 20, 1888

You are probably wondering where all of this money came from. Over the years I have saved and invested, adding to the inheritance I received years ago from my father. I never spent much because it seemed that love was enough for our small family.

I know you will be wise and so I want you to have this. I've seen your heart, Lydia. The innocent and idealistic way you see the world is so much like your mama. The stubborn streak in you…that came from me. You feel things deeply, love deeply and you are as loyal as they come. Don't let life's sorrows and disappointments steal your joy.

Now, before I go, there are two things you must know.

Jebediah is an admirable young man who knows a thing or two about long-suffering. I've seen the way you look at him and I want you to know that I hold the utmost respect for him, which brings me to the second thing. There is a handful of money bound together at the bottom of this box that rightfully belongs to Jeb. I am counting on you to get it to him. Believe me when I say, he has earned it.

I love you, Lydia. Whatever you do from this point forward, please promise yourself that you will follow your heart. It's a beautiful one.
Love,
Your Dad

Lydia wiped at the tears streaming down her face. How could her father have known?

She stuffed the large sum of money back into the box, feeling more hope than she had in the last five long and lonely years. She shoved the box, Bible and photo into her daddy's saddlebag, knowing exactly what she needed to do.

Picking up her things, she raced downstairs, checking each room for Jeb, but he was nowhere to be found. When she found Sass in the kitchen, she came to a skidding halt at the doorway.

"Sass, where's Jeb?"

"You're not leaving are you, dear?" Sass peered sadly at the saddlebag.

"I am, but I need to give something to him," she said, confident in the fact that whatever happened with Jeb, she'd be all right. "It's important."

"Well, you better do it now." She draped the dishcloth in her hands over her shoulder. "Because we might not be here if you come back in a few days."

Lydia furrowed her brow, confused. "What do you mean?"

Sass heaved in a huge sigh and met Lydia's gaze. "I just might lose my job for this, but it seems I'm not going to have one anyway, so…"

"What is it, Sass?" she urged, grasping Sass's hand.

Lifting an apron corner, Sass dabbed at her eyes. "Jeb's losing this place."

"He's *what*?" Disbelief hollowed Lydia's stomach. She'd seen plenty of signs of disrepair and hardship, but she'd had no idea it was that bad.

"The bank is taking it over—but it's no fault of his," Sass added with a stiff upper lip. "That father of his left him with more than just a run-down ranch. He left him with a mountain of debt."

"How terrible for Jeb," she said on a ragged whisper. An overwhelming sense of urgency crowded in on Lydia. And right behind it, an overwhelming sense of peace. "Sass…thank you so much for telling me." She wrapped her arms around Sass. "Can you tell me where he is now?"

"I think you'll find him out in the little cabin."

Chapter Ten

Jeb lit the last of the three candles he'd brought with him, willing his heart to slow its rapid-fire pace. He glanced over at the crate where the mama cat lay, content as could be as she fed her six kittens.

"They're beauties," he said, adjusting the cloth where he'd nested Sass's delicious bread. He set a hand on the warm crock of her best stew, making sure it was still warm. Smoothed out the old lace tablecloth and nervously waited.

Would Lydia show up as he was sure she would?

Would she believe him?

Would his love be enough once she knew he had nothing to offer her much more than a crate?

After she'd walked out of his room this morning, he'd faced the hardest decision of his life. He had to let her know exactly how he felt about her. He could live with the disappointment of her walking away, but he would never be able to reconcile the regret of never having said anything.

On a deep breath, Jeb prayed that God would continue to soften his heart and that He'd soften Lydia's heart, too.

Just then delicate footsteps bounded up to the porch and came to an abrupt halt. Jeb grasped the back of the chair and faced the door.

When it creaked open and he saw Lydia standing there, her

father's saddlebag draped over her arm and her hesitant gaze meeting his, he thought his heart might just come right out of his chest.

"I'm glad you came," he said, swallowing hard.

Her wide-eyed gaze slid from him to the table, to the candles' yellow flame. "I'm sorry. I didn't mean to barge in. I was just—"

"This is for you." He motioned toward the glowing hearth and the finely set table.

She paused for a long moment, her attention drawn to the crate of mewling kittens. "Oh, that's so sweet," she whispered, setting down her saddlebag and heading straight for the kittens. "Thank you, Jeb."

"You're welcome to the kittens, but I was meaning this," he said, gesturing to the table.

The clear shock in her gaze as she stopped, hovering over the crate of kittens, pierced his heart. "For me?"

Nodding, Jeb stepped forward and held out his hand to her, praying she'd take it. Forever.

"It's beautiful. Just beautiful," she breathed, placing her trembling hand in his.

"Lydia…I have to say something," he began, his heart skipping several beats.

"No, I need to say something." Pulling her hand from his, she backed up a step. "Please."

"Go ahead," Jeb uttered, bracing for rejection and praying for a miracle.

"Jeb Gentry," she began, her lower lip quivering ever so slightly as her crystal blue gaze filled with unshed tears. She tucked her hands under her chin. "I love you. I have *always* loved you. I don't want to leave, but if you can't find a place for me in your heart, just say the word and I will walk out of here and *never* bother you again."

His heart stuttered to a halt. "You *really* feel this way?"

She gave a vigorous nod. "Yes. Oh, yes. I have forever."

"*Forever?*"

"Well...since I was probably six-years-old." The most endearing pink blush colored her fair cheeks.

He moved a step closer, his breath hitching at the vulnerable way she peered at him. "Why didn't you say something?"

"I did, Jeb." She pressed a hand to her mouth, her misty gaze almost breaking his heart. "That day I ran out to the corral I said all that and more."

His brow furrowed in disbelief. "You *did*?"

Lydia gave several adamant nods. "You mean you didn't know?"

He recalled that scene, but could remember nothing of the sort. "I must've been so focused on calming the stallion that I didn't even hear you."

"So, you didn't *intentionally* ignore me?" A single tear slid down her face.

"Never." He reached for one of her hands and held it in his. "I saw you though, Lydia. And I'll tell you this...I'd never seen a more beautiful sight than I did that day. You'd always been my young shadow." Jeb trailed his fingertips down her cheek, cherishing this moment and the feel of her satiny skin against his. "And then all of a sudden, you were this beautiful—" his breath caught "—*beautiful* woman. I didn't even know what to do with the thoughts stampeding through my mind."

"But you told me to go away." When another tear trailed down her cheek, Jeb wiped it away. "You said that I was a distraction."

Jeb pulled up her hand up to his mouth and pressed the lightest kiss there. "You were a distraction all right...a *beautiful* distraction."

"But what about last night?" Sweet as can be, she tugged her hand from his and set it featherlight against his face. Her gaze traveled over every cut and bruise and scar. "I distracted you and got you knocked out."

"Awww...darlin', don t worry about that," he said, grasping her hand and tugging her closer to him. So close that he could almost feel the heat of her body. "I'll heal. And besides you were so much better to look at than that roughed-up fella I was fighting."

When guilt darkened her beautiful gaze, he tugged her closer.

"Lydia, there's been a lot that's happened over the past years—things that'll take some time to tell you about, but if you aren't doing anything for the rest of your life," he braved, searching her gaze for any kind of hesitation, "how would you feel about spending it with me? I don't have a thing to offer you but my love. But I can guarantee you that I will love you completely."

"You *really* feel this way?" she choked out, tears spilling down her cheeks now.

"With all my heart. I've felt this way from the moment I saw you as something other than my young shadow."

"But I loved being your young shadow."

When her brow furrowed, Jeb wrapped his arms around her and pulled her into his embrace. She felt so right in his arms, as though their union was meant to be.

"Believe me when I say…I want you to be more—*far* more than just my shadow. I want you to be my bride," he uttered, breathing in the faintest scent of lilies as she melted in his arms. "Lydia Townsend, will you marry me?"

She sniffed. "On one condition," she said, peering up at him. "But you have to promise me you will accept it first."

Jeb grinned, figuring that no matter what the future held, he'd be hard-pressed to deny her anything. "This sounds vaguely familiar."

Lydia reached up and held his face between her hands. "If I marry you, then all that I have is yours."

"That's not a problem. I already love all of you, Lydia," he said, smoothing her hair from her face and placing the softest kiss to her forehead.

"No, Jeb...I mean *all* that I have." Ducking out of his arms, she crossed to the saddlebag by the door and pulled out a wooden box. When she opened the box and spilled out money—hundreds and hundreds of dollars on the floor—the breath whooshed from Jeb's lungs.

She picked up a bound stack and held it out to him. "There's a note on it for you. It should help explain."

He blinked hard, staring at the large stack of money in her hand, shocked. Completely shocked.

"Do you want me to read it to you?" she asked when he couldn't seem to do much more than stare at the stack of bills.

He nodded, the lump in his throat making it nearly impossible to talk.

Lydia's face shone as bright as the sun as she pulled the note from where it'd been bound with the money. "Dear Jeb," she began, glancing up at him, her eyes glistening.

"You're a fine young man with a natural bent toward this land—it's in you and I know you'll make it better than I ever could. Believe me when I say, I wish I could've done more to help situations with your father.

"You have a good and honest heart, Jeb. This money is what you would've earned from all of those cattle drives your father never paid you for. I want you to have it.

"One more thing. Take good care of my little girl.

"Fondly,

"Hank."

When she held the money out to him, he swallowed hard, barely able to breathe as the extent of things hit him square in the chest. His father had never paid him a cent. He'd made big promises at the front end of cattle drives, but would always end up gambling away Jeb's earnings.

"I can't take this," he said, his throat all raw. But even as the words crossed his lips he felt unease in his heart, as though he was stubbornly refusing something that might very well be the lifeline he'd been praying for.

"He said you earned it." She turned over his hand and placed the stack in his palm. "He wanted you to have it."

"But—"

"And I want you to have this," she said, bending down and gathering together the pile of money she'd dumped out and stuffed it back into the box.

He shook his head, adamant. "Lydia, I can't—"

"Well, this treasure and me," she said, standing and folding her arms at her chest, "we come together. You agreed that if you marry me, *all* that I have is yours."

"I just didn't know that—"

"Jeb Gentry, I love you. And yes, I would love to be your bride."

"I do," Jeb said, his deep rich voice echoing in Lydia's soul like some ancient call to oneness.

From the trees came a bird's happy spring melody…as beautiful as the brilliant green leaves budding on the branches. The sun shone bright and warm and the air smelled of new life.

Lydia stood at the steps of the cabin, where Jeb had added new floorboards to the porch and a brand new window with glass panes as clear as the finest crystal. But as beautiful as everything was, she couldn't take her eyes off Jeb.

Despite the bruising still marring his face from his last and final fight two weeks ago, he looked utterly handsome in his simple dark brown britches, cream-colored shirt and his matching vest that hugged his thick chest. The wholly intense and warmly loving look in his eyes sent her stomach to fluttering uncontrollably.

This day…the day she'd dreamed of for most of her life, was far better than she'd ever imagined. Far better than the pictures she'd drawn or the letters she'd written.

"And do you, Lydia Townsend," the kindly preacher said, gently drawing her attention, "take Jebediah Gentry to be your lawfully wedded husband?"

"I do." Glancing up at the preacher who stood on the porch steps, she leaned toward him and whispered, "Do you mind if I give Jeb something?"

"A kiss?" he said, grinning while the small gathering of folks chuckled.

A warm blush colored Lydia's cheeks as she peered at Jeb and saw the sweet passion darkening his gaze. "Well, that, too. But I have something…" Shifting her small posy of spring flowers to one hard, she reached into the side pocket Sass had sewn in her beautiful off-white wedding dress and tugged out a stack of letters, bound by a blue ribbon, the color of the sky. "These are for you, Jeb. They're letters I've written to you from the time I was a young girl," she confessed, her throat clogged with emotion. "They're silly, really, but I want you to have them."

Jeb's earnest expression lent her confidence. "I'm sure they're not silly, Lydia." Taking the letters from her, he peered down at them as though he'd just been given the most priceless gift.

"This one, in particular, you have to read," she said tapping the very top one.

"Right now?"

She nodded, swallowing nervously.

He slid the letter out of the stack, gently opened it and read.

Watching his expression, she pictured every single word and read right along with him.

My Dearest Jeb,

I have waited for you all my life, but I have to be patient and wait for the perfect time to marry you. I may be young, but Daddy always says that, "when you know something's true, you just know." I have known we were meant to be together from that first time you picked a wild daisy over by the corral and gave it to me. I was almost seven then and now I'm ten.

I love you, Jeb. I will always love you.
You are my ideal husband.
Love,
Lydia

Tears pooled in Jeb's dark brown eyes as he set his gaze on her. She gently tugged the letter from him and handed the stack to the preacher.

"Oh, Jeb…I mean every word of that and more," she whispered, sure she'd died and gone to heaven for the absolute bliss she felt.

Jeb raised his hands, quivering and warm, to her face. He peered down at her with the most intense and loving gaze Lydia could imagine.

"I love you, Lydia," he said, his voice barely audible as he cupped the back of her head and slowly lowered his head to hers.

The moment his lips touched hers in a sweetly passionate kiss, her sheer bliss spun to even greater heights. A thousand tiny quivers shot from her head to her toes and back again. She could barely breathe. Could barely hear the wedding-goers clapping, over the beating of her heart for Jeb.

She leaned away enough to meet his dark and distinctly masculine gaze. She was satisfied. Healed. And confident in his love.

"You are my ideal husband."

* * * * *

Dear Reader,

Thank you so much for reading Jeb and Lydia's story. It is my hope that you saw a little of yourself in the characters. Certainly, the desire for love is inherent in us all.

When my daughter was young, I delighted in watching her dream about her happily-ever-after. I've kept her endearing letters and adorable drawings, loving the innocence penned with washable markers. Just recently the two of us were looking through those keepsakes, thoroughly enjoying the sweet way she had portrayed what was in her heart, and reflecting on the years in between.

When life's trials come, we might believe we were foolish to hope. Was it wrong to dream? Not at all. It is essential to our growth and sense of purpose. Dream, but know that the road from innocent drawings to the altar (or wherever the destination may be) can be strewn with hurdles, walls and deep pits. But it is in journeying that we often find grace, forgiveness and God's abiding love that will carry us through hardship.

So, dream, hope and live life knowing that you are God's favorite! And that nothing can separate you from His love.

With sincere affection,
Pamela Nissen

Questions for Discussion

1. When Lydia sees Jeb for the first time after five years, the same feelings of shame and humiliation come flooding back. Have you experienced a similar situation? If so, how did you handle it?

2. In the face of financial hardship, Jeb resorts to desperate measures to make ends meet. Have you faced a similar situation? If so, what kind of feedback did you get from those around you?

3. Lydia's father provided hope and faith and guidance in Jeb's life. Do you have someone like that in your life?

4. Jeb's father's legacy weighs heavy, and yet Jeb refuses to let others help carry the burden. Have you ever carried a burden alone? How did you feel?

5. Lydia begins to wonder if she has judged Jeb wrongly. Have you ever judged someone only to find you were wrong? How did you handle the situation?

6. Faced with insurmountable odds, Jeb begins to believe the words his father spoke over him for so many years… that he is a failure. Have you ever found yourself agreeing with that kind of lifeless lie? If so, what was your eye-opening moment?

7. Disillusioned by life's tragic circumstances, Lydia nails all of her hurt on Jeb. Do you remember a time when you reacted in the same way? How did you find healing?

8. Jeb's pride nearly stands in the way of the answer he has prayed for. Have you experienced a similar situation? If so, how did you respond?

9. Just as soon as Lydia finds a measure of peace, that peace is threatened. Have you ever felt like you were tested right after having a change of heart? How did you handle the situation?

10. Jeb realizes that he's in a fight for his life every bit as much as for the ranch. Do you remember a time when the situation around you mirrored what was happening in your heart? Explain.

INSPIRATIONAL

Love Inspired. celebrating 15 YEARS
HISTORICAL

COMING NEXT MONTH
AVAILABLE MAY 8, 2012

MISTAKEN BRIDE
Irish Brides
Renee Ryan

HOMEFRONT HERO
Allie Pleiter

THE HOMESTEADER'S SWEETHEART
Lacy Williams

THE MARSHAL'S PROMISE
Rhonda Gibson

REQUEST YOUR FREE BOOKS!

2 FREE INSPIRATIONAL NOVELS
PLUS 2
FREE
MYSTERY GIFTS

Love Inspired.
HISTORICAL
INSPIRATIONAL HISTORICAL ROMANCE

LIH1B

When Brooke McKaslin returns to Montana on family business, she has no intention of forming any new relationships, especially with a man like Liam Knightly. But things don't always go according to plan....

Here's a sneak peek at MONTANA HOMECOMING by Jillian Hart.

"What's your story?" Brooke asked.

"Which story do you want to know?"

"Why adding a dog to your life has been your biggest commitment to date."

"How many relationships do you know that have stood the test of time?" Oscar rushed up to him, panting hard, his prize clamped between his teeth. Liam scrubbed the dog's head.

"Ooh, tough question." She wrestled with that one herself. "My parents are divorced. My father has divorced twice. The twins' mother has been in and out of marriages."

"My parents are divorced, too. Although they both live in Washington, D.C."

"The lawyers?"

"Both workaholics. Both are Type A."

"Things you inherited?"

"Mostly." He tugged his keys from his pocket, the parking lot nearer now. "Maybe I inherited the bad marriage gene."

"I know the feeling."

"That's why you're still single?"

"One reason." The truth sat on the tip of her tongue, ready to be told. What was she doing? She swallowed hard, holding back the words. What was it about Liam that made her guards weaken? She'd nearly opened up to him. She shook her head. No way did she know him enough to trust him. "It's my opinion men cause destruction and ruin wherever they go."

"Funny, that's my opinion about women." His slow grin made her heart skip a beat.

Good thing her heart wasn't in charge. She was. And she wasn't going to let his stunning smile weaken her defenses any further. Time to shore them up. She hiked her chin and steeled her spine.

"I know that's not fair." Liam winked. "But that's how it feels."

So hard to ignore that wink. She let it bounce off her, unaffected. She'd gotten as close to him as she was going to. Best to remember she worked for him, she was leaving as soon as the trial was over and the last thing she wanted was a man to complicate things. She had a life again. No way was she going to mess that up.

You'll love the rest of MONTANA HOMECOMING, from one of your favorite authors, Jillian Hart, available May 2012 from Love Inspired®.